Entwined Publishing books by L.M. Somerton

The Augur

SEEING BLOOD

L.M. SOMERTON

ENTWINED PUBLISHING

Seeing Blood
ISBN # 978-1-80250-622-8
©Copyright L.M. Somerton 2025
Cover Art by Kelly Martin ©Copyright December 2025
Interior text design by Entwined Publishing
Published by Eternal, an Entwined Publishing imprint

Published in 2025 by Entwined Publishing, United Kingdom.

Entwined Publishing is a division of Totally Entwined Group Limited.

SEEING BLOOD

Dedication

Our differences make the world a more
interesting place to be.

Chapter One

"Why is it that Sunday afternoons always come around way too fast?" Bryn Ashton sat cross-legged on the floor of his bedroom, leaning back against the bed. "It's not fair." He shoved the last chunk of his candy bar into his mouth.

"Are you talking to yourself or me?" Gunnar Ericson, Bryn's lupine partner in the Gene Control and Research investigation team, loomed in the doorway.

Bryn balled up his candy wrapper then tossed it at the trash can. He missed. Gunnar snorted his amusement. Bryn glared at him. "Hey! Gimme a break. It's not easy aiming from down here, and I guess I was making a general statement of discontent."

"You couldn't hit a full-sized dumpster from three feet away and how many times in the last four months have we had a Sunday off?"

"Twice."

"Exactly, so be grateful that Warden was feeling generous and gave us today."

Bryn didn't want to think about their enigmatic, workaholic boss. "We could be doing something a lot more interesting. In your bed. Naked." Bryn eyed his partner's broad shoulders and long hair. His cock stirred. "I think we've mastered the art of kissing. Isn't it time we got to second base?"

"All in good time. As I keep telling you, a bit of anticipation doesn't hurt."

"That's a matter of opinion. You know I touch you all the time, right?" Bryn's augur abilities worked through touch and, from the start, Gunnar had never avoided it.

"Sure."

"So I know what your future intent is."

"Yeah."

"Gunnar!"

Gunnar chuckled. "Okay. Full disclosure. I'm not trying to tease you."

Bryn huffed. "Sure you're not."

"I don't want our first time to be here at headquarters. I can't wait to get my hands on you, but not here, where we work. It needs to be special."

"Oh my…you're a closet romantic!" Bryn scrambled to his feet.

"What's wrong with that?"

"Nothing." Bryn closed the gap between him and Gunnar. "It's sweet." He walked into Gunnar's arms.

"I am *not* sweet!"

Bryn tilted his head. "It's not a bad thing, even for a big bad wolf." He parted his lips. Gunnar took the hint and they were engaged in a satisfying kiss when his cell sounded. The ringtone was the theme from *Jaws*. Bryn rested his forehead against Gunnar's chest. "You have got to be kidding me. Warden."

"That man never takes a day off," Gunnar muttered, fishing his cell out of his pocket. "Ericson." He listened for a few seconds then the call ended. "In a shocking new development, we're wanted in the conference room."

"Well fuck. You gonna give me any more of a clue?" Bryn asked.

"He said, and I quote, 'get your asses downstairs now'. I don't know any more than you do."

Bryn sighed. "Let me grab my boots."

Five minutes later he was stomping down the stairs after Gunnar. He hadn't bothered with gloves or dark glasses because everyone in the building was used to his glowing eyes and knew better than to touch him. When they got to the conference room, Warden was waiting. Their admin assistant, Emmett Salisbury, hustled toward them from the direction of the staff entrance at the back of the building.

"Hey guys, what's up?" He shrugged off his yellow raincoat to reveal a red sweater vest and white shirt paired with blue jeans.

Bryn shrugged. "No idea but I think we're about to find out. No bow tie?"

"I was in a rush. I had plans to go out for tacos with Talbot." Talbot Dunne was Emmett's roommate and worked on the GCR's tech team.

"Bummer. Gunnar and I had plans too." Bryn grinned. Emmett blushed.

Bryn didn't know if their boss had another name to add to Warden, but he'd never dared ask. Warden sat at the head of the table dressed in an immaculate black suit, white shirt and subdued gray tie. He glanced at Bryn and frowned.

"Mr. Ashton, why do you always dress like an attendee at a goth rock concert?"

Bryn glanced down at his ripped black jeans and My Chemical Romance T-shirt. "Not sure I'd call this band goth rockers, sir...more like...uh, never mind." He sat his ass down before he got himself in more trouble. Warden's piercing stare was enough to curb even his tongue.

"Thank you for coming in, Emmett," Warden said in a much softer tone, bestowing Emmett with the trace of a smile. Emmett blushed even more then ducked his head. He pulled a notepad and pen from his satchel.

"No problem at all, sir."

"What's going on, boss?" Gunnar took the seat next to Bryn.

"Yeah, tell us, Warden. I had a fun evening in planned for my God-given, long-overdue day off." Bryn cast a sly look in Gunnar's direction.

"You need to readjust your priorities, young man. There are training courses for that," Warden replied.

"Why does that sound like a threat?"

"Because it is. Now shut up and listen." Warden's laser glare could have drilled a hole in sheet metal. "You'll all be aware that some gene-affected individuals spend time at The Facility undergoing a range of tests and personal development, mostly if they have chosen a career path in law enforcement or the military."

Bryn pressed his lips together in a tight line to stop yet another sarcastic remark. His own stay at The Facility had been lengthy, unpleasant and not exactly voluntary. *Would be so justified.*

"In the last six months I've been receiving disturbing reports that some of these individuals have been experiencing varied levels of psychosis. In the first instance, our scientists were concerned that this might be an effect of a new gene mutation but tests showed that was not the case. Blood samples, however, did reveal the presence of a narcotic. A new synthetic drug that we haven't come across before."

"Sounds nasty," Gunnar commented.

"Indeed. None of the people concerned were habitual drug takers so we weren't, and still aren't, sure how this got into their systems, but the effects can be catastrophic. Enhanced abilities specific to both lupines and sanguines were found and, to start with, it appears that this is the only development but, after time, other traits begin to manifest."

Gunnar frowned. "Such as?"

"Paranoia, blood lust, increasing aggression and eventually hemorrhaging in the brain leading to death."

Emmett glanced up from his note taking, white-faced. "Who would do that to people?"

"Someone with no morals and zero compunction about using people for his own ends." Warden stood and clasped his hands behind his back. "Someone like Salvatore Russo."

"Wonderful," Bryn said. "The Hammer. Our favorite mob boss. Had to be him, didn't it. Only worse option would have been our neighborhood psycho pen pal, Dr. Templeton."

"Thank you for that observation, Bryn."

"How do you know it's him?" Gunnar asked.

"A better contribution, Detective. We know because last night, Boston PD raided what they thought was a meth lab. What they found was a production facility for this synthetic drug that the people they rounded up were calling Thanacrine. Several of those arrested have confirmed links with Russo."

"In Greek mythology, Thanatos was the personification of death," Emmett contributed. "He was a minor figure, often referred to but rarely appearing in person. That could be the root of the name."

"I thought Thanos was a Marvel character," Bryn said.

"Thanos was a warlord from Titan, whose objective was to bring stability to the universe by wiping out half of all life at every level no matter what it took...so he's a possible inspiration too," Emmett conceded.

"Thank you, Emmett," Warden said.

"So production has been stopped?" Gunnar asked.

"No. This was one small place. Russo isn't stupid. It's better to spread the risk across multiple facilities than concentrate efforts in a single location. Less of a financial hit if one place gets raided. There will be more."

"And he'll have another one up and running to replace this one before we can blink," Gunnar said. "So what's our interest?"

"Boston PD is handing the investigation over to us. We are better placed to make the connections between the people who've been affected, and it falls within our remit. They'll continue to support when manpower is needed."

"That's a big case to take on."

"Which is why I've drafted in an additional resource to assist. Someone with first-hand knowledge of what's been happening." Warden avoided meeting Bryn's curious gaze.

Bryn leaned forward in his seat. "Tell me you fucking didn't...Warden..."

"Am I missing something?" Emmett asked.

"I really hope not," Bryn replied.

"This case demands the best we can offer." Warden stared at the door and, without raising his voice said,

"You can come in now." He rifled through a manila folder with the kind of forced casualness that set off every one of Bryn's finely tuned warning signals. Bryn braced for impact.

Giles Delacourt made his entrance. The sanguine moved with the kind of fluid grace that made catwalk models look clumsy. He was all long limbs and perfect posture in a charcoal suit that probably cost more than Bryn's monthly salary. His dark hair, shot through with elegant streaks of silver at the temples, was swept back from high cheekbones. He looked like he'd stepped out of a Renaissance painting, all aristocratic features and knowing eyes, with the kind of face that made people forget to breathe. The bright lighting should have made him look washed out. Instead, it seemed to create its own shadows around him, highlighting the sharp line of his jaw and the subtle curve of his mouth that always suggested he knew something Bryn didn't. Bryn's stomach knotted.

Warden actually stood up when Giles entered, like he was greeting nobility. Bryn remained exactly where he was. He'd learned the hard way that beauty could be the deadliest weapon in Giles Delacourt's arsenal. Gunnar was also on his feet, a warning growl rumbling in his throat. Bryn reached for his hand and tugged him back into his chair.

"Mr. Delacourt," Warden said, extending his hand. "Thank you for coming."

Giles took it with the kind of old-world courtesy that went out of style before the Industrial Revolution. "The pleasure is mine, Warden." His British accent was a smooth blend of old money and older privilege that made everything sound like poetry. Or a threat.

With Giles, it's usually both. Bryn's head throbbed. Separation hadn't dulled his memory of how that voice could make the most brutal lessons sound reasonable, even necessary. The way Giles could make breaking someone seem like an act of kindness.

Gunnar was bristling, his eyes dark with fury. Bryn was grateful, and though watching Gunnar rip Delacourt's head off would have been satisfying, violence wouldn't help the investigation. *I'm not even twenty-two, I shouldn't be expected to have achieved this level of restraint.*

Warden gestured for Giles to take a seat and resumed his own. Giles settled into one of the free chairs. His eyes, a shade of brown so dark they almost looked black, found Bryn's across the table. "Hello, dear boy. You're looking well."

Bryn had forgotten how much weight Giles could put into simple words, how he could make a casual greeting feel like fingers trailing down his spine. He didn't respond and gritted his teeth.

"Mr. Delacourt has been kind enough to offer his expertise on the Thanacrine case," Warden said.

"How generous of him," Bryn commented.

Giles' lips curved. "Now, Bryn, there's no need for hostility. We're all on the same side here."

"Are we?" The words came out sharper than Bryn intended. The air in the room had that peculiar heaviness it always got around Giles, like the atmospheric pressure before a thunderstorm.

"Bryn," Warden said, his tone carrying a clear warning. "Mr. Delacourt has provided valuable intelligence about the effects of Thanacrine and has been conducting some investigations already. His knowledge could be crucial to locating more production facilities. He has agreed to assist us in a consulting capacity. He'll be working directly with you and Detective Ericson."

"That's not going to…" Bryn started, but Warden cut him off.

"This isn't a request. Whatever personal history exists between you and Mr. Delacourt is irrelevant to the current situation."

And you know all about that history. Bryn felt Giles' satisfaction like a physical thing, a cool current in the air. He gripped the arms of his chair until his fingers ached. He couldn't look at Gunnar.

"The latest batch is even more potent," Giles said. "The effects are devastating."

Don't fucking guilt trip me, you bastard.

Warden cleared his throat. "Allow me to introduce Detective Gunnar Ericson, Giles," he announced, gesturing at Gunnar, who offered a curt nod, his expression conveying his displeasure. "Gunnar is Bryn's partner."

"Protective. Interesting."

"And this is Emmett, our talented admin support."

Emmett glanced up from his laptop, his eyes wide behind his glasses. He blinked, and gave a shy, almost apologetic smile. "Uh, hi."

"Well then." Giles gave a lazy smile. "I'd say we're going to make quite the team. The dynamics will be *very* interesting."

The conference room felt smaller with each passing second. Bryn forced himself to take steady breaths, fighting the urge to bolt from his chair. He could feel Gunnar's concerned gaze but couldn't bring himself to meet it. Not with Giles sitting there, radiating that infuriating calm. Bryn didn't want to give away how close he and Gunnar really were.

"Perhaps we should begin with what we know about the distribution network," Warden suggested, though his tone implied more of an order.

"I've managed to trace the probable routes of several shipments moving through the northeast corridor," Giles said.

"And you didn't think to share this information sooner?" Bryn couldn't keep the edge from his voice.

Giles' smile didn't waver. "Information gathering takes time, dear boy, even with the resources of The Facility to hand. Especially when one wishes to avoid detection. Mr. Russo's organization is...shall we say, particularly paranoid about new faces these days."

"I wonder why," Bryn muttered.

"Something to do with a recent court case, I understand," Delacourt said. "You'll have to tell me all about it."

Gunnar cut in before Bryn could say anything else. "Let's stick with this case, shall we? What's the delivery method?" he asked, his tone professional but cool. "If they're targeting gene-affected individuals specifically, they must have a way to ensure the drug reaches the right people."

"Ah, that's where it gets interesting." Giles pulled a small leather notebook from his jacket pocket. "They're using legitimate medical supply chains. Several private clinics that cater to our kind have been compromised. The drug is being administered through routine blood work and standard treatments. As you know, all sanguines and lupines are tested once a year as part of an ongoing national study. A trace of Thanacrine on the needle of a blood draw syringe is enough."

Emmett scribbled on his pad. "I can cross-reference clinic locations with reported cases when I have my laptop," he offered, not so shy with a challenge to work on.

"Good thinking." Warden nodded. "We need to identify any patterns in the targeting."

"There's more," Giles continued. "The clinics aren't random. They're all connected to a healthcare management company called Helix Solutions. On paper, it's a legitimate business. But dig deeper..." He slid a USB drive across the table to Emmett.

Bryn watched the drive move across the polished surface, his mind racing. "Helix Solutions. Why does that sound familiar?"

"Because"—Giles' eyes gleamed with something that might have been approval—"they received a rather substantial investment from one of Russo's shell companies six months ago. Something that was mentioned in the trial of Russo's accountant."

"Right before the first cases started showing up," Gunnar added, frowning.

"Indeed." Giles leaned back in his chair. "The question is, how deep does the infiltration go? How many medical professionals are knowingly involved, and how many are being used?"

"We need to get someone on the inside," Warden said, but Gunnar was already shaking his head.

"No way. It's too risky."

"Not necessarily." Giles' voice had that silken quality that always preceded his worst suggestions. "They're looking for gene-affected subjects. The drug doesn't touch anyone that isn't. We could send someone in for routine testing, or get someone employed at a clinic who's completely normal." He eyed Emmett.

"We need to think about the specifics," Warden said, breaking the tension. "Emmett, head up to your office and start running those clinic locations. Gunnar, I want you to pull everything we have on Helix Solutions. Talk to your contacts at Boston PD. And Bryn..." He paused, meeting Bryn's eyes with unexpected empathy. "I need you to work with Mr. Delacourt on identifying potential entry points. If anyone goes in, it'll need to be you because you'll have to read the staff somehow."

Bryn wanted to argue, but the weight of what they were dealing with settled over him. People were dying. His personal history with Giles didn't change that fact.

"Fine," he said, pushing back from the table. *Nothing about this is fine.* "But Gunnar takes the lead on planning."

"Of course," Giles agreed. "Shall we relocate or continue working here?"

"The conference room is needed for some after-hours maintenance," Warden said.

Gunnar shoved his chair back. "Our office is too small for all of us, but Emmett will need his equipment. We can use the table in our apartment. More space for mapping everything out."

"Very well," Giles acknowledged. "Lead the way, Detective Ericson."

As they filed out of the conference room, Bryn couldn't shake the feeling that they were walking into something potentially fatal. *Why does my life have to be so fucking complicated?* "This was supposed to be my day off," he complained, not expecting sympathy from anyone.

Chapter Two

Bryn and Gunnar's small apartment on the top floor of GCR HQ wasn't designed for strategic planning sessions but with only one conference room in the building, it was the best option available. The table, usually home to a potted plant, Gunnar's keys and various charging leads, was now covered with maps showing clinic locations that Emmett had printed out. Giles stood by the window, silhouetted against the light. He hadn't asked any questions about Bryn and Gunnar's living situation but Bryn knew he'd be taking in every detail. He tried to avoid looking in Giles' direction while Emmett, now happily working on his laptop, applied some order to their information.

"There are twenty-three clinics in the northeast corridor alone," Emmett said, adjusting his glasses as he tapped away at his keyboard. "All acquired by Helix Solutions within the last eighteen months."

"And how many reported cases of lupines or sanguines affected by the drug have there been so far?" Gunnar asked, marking locations with a red Sharpie.

"Thirty-seven confirmed, but…there are probably more. Some of the symptoms could be mistaken for standard drug reactions or mental health issues, especially in the earlier stages."

Bryn fidgeted, annoyed that his sanctuary had been violated by Giles' presence.

"You're thinking too loudly, dear boy," Giles commented without turning from the window. "How about you share with the class?"

"How exactly did you get involved in this? Because last I checked, you were supposed to be in London on an extended break."

Giles turned, the fading sunlight casting half his face in shadow. "Ah, you've been keeping tabs on me. How touching."

"Answer the fucking question."

"One of my former students was affected by the drug. Not that I knew what it was at the time." Something flickered across Giles' face, too quick for Bryn to read. "The effects were…particularly unpleasant. I made inquiries."

"And decided to investigate without telling anyone," Bryn said.

"I informed the appropriate parties when I had something concrete to report." Giles moved away from the window. "Emmett, could you pull up the mortality rates for the affected individuals?"

Emmett typed rapidly. "Um, of the thirty-seven cases you've identified, twenty-two resulted in death. Average time from estimated first exposure to death is forty-eight days."

"Jesus," Gunnar muttered. "That's fast."

"Indeed." Giles leaned over the table, studying the map. "And the progression of symptoms has accelerated in more recent cases. I assume because the drug is being altered. Refined. I suspect Russo is seeking a way of creating the perfect soldiers for his private army. This is all about power and money. Predictable and so tedious."

Bryn scowled. "So what's your brilliant plan? Send me in as what, exactly? A patient?"

"Actually" — Giles straightened — "I was thinking more along the lines of me going in as a potential investor. Helix Solutions is looking for new capital."

"What about their security?" Emmett interrupted, either oblivious to the tension or deliberately trying to break it. "Their systems have to be sophisticated if they're working with gene-affected individuals."

"I'm sure they are," Giles agreed. "But I don't intend to do anything that means avoiding security. People and their fallibilities are the key to this plan and that's where you come in, my dear Emmett. Your research skills and connections could be very useful."

Emmett blushed at the attention. "I mean, I could probably... Wait, how do you know anything about me?"

"Mr. Delacourt has apparently done his homework on all of us," Gunnar said, not sounding pleased about it. "Haven't you?"

"Knowledge is power, Detective Ericson. Something I'm sure you understand, and I like to know who I'm working with." Giles moved to examine one of the clinic locations more closely. "This one. The Burlington. It's their newest acquisition, still being renovated. Lots of new hires. That's our best point of entry."

"You know a lot about this place..." Bryn started, but a sharp knock at the apartment door cut him off. Bryn went to open it and one of the staff from the building's employee restaurant nodded at him. She was holding two bags of takeout.

"This arrived for you guys. Warden asked me to bring it up."

"We didn't order anything," Gunnar said.

"No." Giles smiled. "I did. I thought we might be here a while, and I remembered how cranky Bryn gets when he's hungry."

Bryn mumbled something under his breath but took the bags. "Thanks, Madge." He pulled the door closed.

"Shall we discuss strategy over dinner?" Giles said. "I ordered extra dumplings. You still like those, don't you, Bryn?"

Bryn set the bag down harder than necessary. "Stop it."

"Stop what?"

"This…this thing you're doing. Acting like you know me. Like nothing's changed. Like you didn't…" He cut himself off, aware of their audience.

"Perhaps," Gunnar interjected, "we should focus on the plan. The Burlington clinic. What are you proposing?" He gave Bryn's shoulder a squeeze.

Giles looked away from Bryn. "A two-pronged approach. I make contact as a potential investor while Emmett researches their employees. We'll need a few days to establish credentials that will hold up to scrutiny, but…"

"Three days," Emmett said suddenly. Everyone turned to look at him. He ducked his head but continued. "Helix is having an open day for potential investors on Thursday. I found a reference in the *Wall Street Journal*."

"Excellent," Giles praised. "That should work nicely. It gives us enough time to prepare. Clear a space." He began unpacking the food containers. "Let's eat while we plan? Cold Chinese food is not nearly so appetizing."

"The investor angle could work," Gunnar said, "but, like you say, we'll need a rock solid background story. Bryn goes nowhere near that place without it."

They ate in silence for a while, straight from the cartons. When they were done, Emmett cleared away and, at Giles' polite request, scurried into the kitchen to make tea for him and coffee for everyone else.

"There's a private equity firm specializing in medical technology. They've been making strategic acquisitions all along the eastern seaboard. That could be an option," Giles said.

"A shell company?" Gunnar asked.

"Perfectly legitimate, I assure you. Though their ownership structure is…deliberately complex."

"And you know this because…"

"I have a stake in the organization. The documentation will pass any level of due diligence."

"And you have expertise in medical technology. But what about Bryn? What's his reason for being there?"

"He'll be my personal assistant."

"No fucking way!" The words burst out before Bryn could stop them.

"Think about it. It makes sense that a high-powered investor would travel with an aide," Giles said. "Oh, Emmett, you are a delight." He took the tea Emmett offered him.

Bryn's temper was a hair's breadth shy of boiling point. Playing the part of Giles' assistant would mean being his subordinate and acting accordingly, something that Giles would love and Bryn would detest. *And the smug bastard knows it.*

"We need to discuss the risks," Gunnar said. "All of them. Bryn's not doing this if I'm not happy he'll be safe and Warden will support me on that."

"No way am I doing it anyway," Bryn stated.

"Of course." Giles' tone shifted, becoming more businesslike as he ignored Bryn's comment and responded to Gunnar. "The security at these clinics is substantial. Armed guards, surveillance, and most concerning, blood scanners at every entrance."

"Blood scanners?" Emmett asked as he finished handing out coffee.

"A new technology, developed specifically for detecting gene-enhanced individuals. A single drop is all it takes." Giles leaned forward. "Clever, isn't it?"

"And once again for the room…you happen to know this because…?" Bryn let the question hang.

"Because I helped design the scanners. The analysis element, anyway."

"Of course you did. So I guess you have a way of getting us past them."

"What I understand," Gunnar said in a voice that was dangerously quiet, "is that you're asking my partner to walk into a potentially lethal situation without full disclosure. That's not happening."

"Your concern is admirable, Detective. But perhaps we should let Bryn speak for himself?"

"Perhaps you should both stop talking about me like I'm not fucking here. I need some space." Bryn headed for his bedroom, closing the door behind him with measured violence. He took a deep breath then sat on the edge of the bed, head in his hands.

The door opened, and Bryn tensed, but it was Gunnar who came to sit beside him.

"You okay?" Gunnar asked.

"Define okay." Bryn tried for a smile but couldn't quite manage it. "Sorry about…him."

"Don't be. Knowing what he put you through, I'd really like to detach parts of his anatomy. Don't think

Warden would appreciate that, though. I've sent Emmett home and told Giles to go for now."

"Thanks. His voice, his mannerisms, even his fucking cologne all bring back memories of things I've tried hard to forget, you know?"

"All I know is that Warden must have felt there was no other option than to bring him in. I don't like being put in this position."

"Me either."

"It took all my limited willpower not to choose bloodshed when he came into the conference room," Gunnar added.

"I hate that he can still get to me like this. One look, one word, and I'm right back there...at The Facility."

Gunnar turned and gripped the nape of Bryn's neck. "You're not there. You're here, with me." He traced paths along Bryn's cheekbones with his thumbs. "And I won't let him hurt you again."

The fierce protectiveness made Bryn's chest tighten. "I know."

"Do you?" Gunnar squeezed a little. "Because I mean it."

Bryn swiveled to straddle Gunnar's thighs then leaned toward him. Gunnar took the hint and responded with a fierce kiss, sliding one hand into Bryn's hair while gripping his waist with the other, pulling him closer. Bryn slipped a hand under Gunnar's shirt, mapping the warm skin of his back, feeling the muscles shift as Gunnar deepened the kiss. When Gunnar licked a trail down Bryn's neck with his tongue, Bryn tilted his head to give him better access.

"Mine," Gunnar growled against his throat, and the possessiveness in his voice sent shivers down Bryn's spine. "No one else gets to touch you like this."

"Yours," Bryn agreed, breathless, pulling Gunnar up for another searing kiss. He tangled his fingers in Gunnar's long hair. Time disappeared as they traded kisses that moved from desperate to more tender, hands exploring every inch they could reach while still dressed. When they pulled apart, they were both breathing hard.

"Stay with me tonight?" Bryn asked. "Just...stay. Hold me. Nothing more."

Gunnar pressed a gentle kiss to his lips. "If that's what you want."

Bryn stripped to shorts and a T-shirt while Gunnar used the bathroom then they swapped before sliding beneath the comforter. Though it was the first time they'd shared a bed it wasn't awkward, and Bryn was exhausted enough not to mind that nothing physical was going to happen.

They lay together in the darkness, Bryn resting his head on Gunnar's chest, listening to his steady heartbeat. But sleep wouldn't come.

"So many dead," he said. "And those are the ones we know about."

"We don't have to do this. We can find another way. Focus on the production facilities rather than method of distribution."

"But if Russo really is building some kind of pumped-up mob army..." Bryn let the thought hang. "What happens when he perfects this Thanacrine? We *do* have to do this." Bryn pressed closer, drawing comfort from Gunnar's warmth. "But we do it our way. We can't let Giles call the shots."

"We have three days to go through every detail of this plan. Every contingency. Every exit strategy. And if anything feels off..."

"We pull it," Bryn finished. He focused on Gunnar's heartbeat, steady and strong, and tried not to think about what tomorrow would bring.

Chapter Three

Bryn awoke before his alarm, Gunnar's arm still draped protectively across his chest. It was tempting to take a hold of Gunnar's wrist and take a peek at his future intent, something that often resulted in Bryn becoming both hard and needy. He didn't do it, because even though Gunnar never minded Bryn poking around in his head, doing it while he was unconscious seemed wrong. Instead, Bryn stayed still, memorizing the warmth and weight of Gunnar's well-muscled arm. Then there was a knock at the apartment door. Emmett had a key and always let himself in. Warden usually called Gunnar on his cell rather than ascending four flights of stairs, which left the least palatable option.

"Fuck," Bryn muttered, extracting himself from Gunnar's hold. He checked the time. "It is way too early to be dealing with this. Gunnar, wake up, I think Giles is here."

"He's too fucking early," Gunnar mumbled.

"Tell me about it, but I think he's at the door."

"Let him wait."

"He'll quit being polite and break through it if I don't go out there." Bryn scrambled out of bed then yanked on his jeans. "You need to be in your own room. I don't want him knowing about us."

"Goddammit. If I didn't already have enough reason to hate him." Gunnar, clad only in black briefs and T-shirt, hauled himself out of bed. "I was warm and having a very...stimulating dream about you. Gonna take a shower. A cold one."

Bryn hooked his tongue back into his mouth then went to answer the door.

"Giles. You're early."

Giles, immaculate as usual in a navy pinstriped suit, white shirt and cravat, gave a pained sigh. "That's a matter of opinion. I only dragged myself up here to tell you that we are back in the conference room today. We need more space and Warden wants to join us. He's had better kit set up for Emmett and rescheduled other meetings that were booked in there."

"Probably wants to make sure we don't kill each other," Bryn said.

"Aren't you all sunshine and flowers before your coffee? Where's Detective Ericson?"

"Dunno. He often runs at this uncivilized time of day."

"Hmm. You still can't lie worth a damn. No matter. Try to be quicker than the average sloth."

Giles turned on his heel, leaving Bryn scowling at his back. "There is not enough coffee in the city to give me the will to deal with him." He shut the door. "Shower. Coffee. Food. Giles fucking Delacourt can wait."

Within half an hour, he and Gunnar were fit to face the world. Giles had already commandeered the conference table, spreading documents across the available space. Warden sat at the head of the table, his expression unreadable.

"Ah, you're here," Giles said without looking up. "I trust you both slept well?"

Bryn ignored both the stated question and the implied one. "What's all this?"

"Your new life, dear boy." Giles slid a thick folder across the table. "For the next three days, you're Bryan Reid-Cobb, my indispensable executive assistant. Yale educated, ruthlessly efficient, and devoted to the success of my business."

Emmett hurried in. "Sorry I'm late! But I found something about their hiring patterns that you need to see." He headed for his computer set up next to Warden.

"Hold that thought, Emmett. First," Warden said, "let's be clear about the timeline. The investor event is Thursday morning. That gives us three days to transform Bryn into a convincing executive assistant and ensure our cover story will hold up to scrutiny."

"Which is why," Giles said, "Bryn and I have an appointment later this morning with Boston's finest tailor. It's not Saville Row, but needs must. I can't have my assistant looking like he shops at…thrift stores."

Bryn gritted his teeth. "There's nothing wrong with thrift stores and I'm not your dress-up doll."

"No, you're a professional about to infiltrate a highly secured facility where the slightest mistake could get you killed." Giles' voice had a steel edge. "So you'll wear what I tell you to wear and learn what I tell you to learn. Unless you'd prefer to explain to the next victim's family why we failed?"

Bryn put a restraining hand on Gunnar's arm. "He's doing it deliberately. Ignore him."

"Tone it down, Delacourt, or you and I are gonna have a problem." Gunnar gave a warning growl.

"How sweet. Shall we continue?"

Bryn shrugged. "Get on with it."

Giles smoothed his cravat. "After the tailor, we'll need to address that hair."

"What's wrong with my hair?" Bryn's hand went to his head.

"Nothing that a proper stylist can't fix." Giles' smile didn't reach his eyes. "Bryan Reid-Cobb wouldn't be caught dead with that mess."

"You're enjoying this way too much." Gunnar gave Warden an accusing glance as if to say 'this is all your fault'.

"On the contrary, Detective Ericson. I'm simply ensuring our success." Giles turned to Warden. "Speaking of which, have you made any progress on the security protocols?"

Warden nodded toward Emmett, who pulled up a series of diagrams on the screen at the end of the room. "Their system is state of the art, but the IT geeks have identified several potential weak points. The investor event will give you the best chance to get close enough to exploit them."

"Show me," Bryn said, grateful for the change in topic. He studied the building schematics on the screen while trying to ignore how Giles' presence made his skin crawl.

"The main security hub is here" — Emmett pointed — "but there's a secondary system that operates independently. That's where it gets interesting."

"And complicated," Warden added. "One wrong move and—"

"And I end up dead," Bryn finished. "Yeah, I got that part." He felt Gunnar tense beside him and wished, not for the first time, that they could reach for each other openly. But that would give Giles too much ammunition, and they couldn't afford any distractions. Not with so much at stake.

"Once you're in, it shouldn't be difficult to get reads through introductory handshakes," Warden said.

"Maybe," Bryn acceded, "but truth reading won't be likely if I can't retain contact."

"Anything you can learn will be more than we have now."

"Well then," Giles said, "shall we begin your transformation, *Bryan*? The tailor awaits."

Withholding a sigh, Bryn followed Giles out of the conference room for what promised to be hours of humiliation. He cast a glance at Gunnar who seemed suitably sympathetic. *He never complains about my clothes. I think he likes me in ripped jeans...*

"Oh, and Bryn?" Giles paused before they left the building. "Do try to look less like you're heading to your execution. Executive assistants generally display a bit more enthusiasm for their work."

"You should be thankful I'm going along with this at all. It's not in my job description," Bryn said, pulling on his gloves. *Three days. I just have to survive three days of this.* He shoved his dark glasses on. *At least now he can't look me in the eye.*

Warden had assigned them a driver and it didn't take long to get to the tailor's shop, which was tucked away in a corner of downtown. Their driver stayed with the vehicle, right outside the door. Inside, the premises smelled of wool, leather, and money. Lots of money.

Bryn scowled while Giles greeted the owner like a long-lost friend.

"Paolo, it's been too long. I do so appreciate you giving us this time when you're in such demand."

"Giles, my old friend. It's my pleasure. Is that Richard Anderson's work you're wearing?"

"It is. You always did have the best eye."

"For the best work. Very nice. But to business. What have you brought me?"

"A challenge." Giles stood aside to give Paolo a better view of Bryn.

"Oh my…" Paolo ushered Bryn onto a low wooden platform. "Arms up. Like scarecrow."

"I know, but he has potential. I'm training him to be a top-class executive assistant but he needs to look the part. Ignore the gloves and glasses…he has issues. Bryn, this is Paolo Vittorio. Do what he says."

Bryn stood there while Paolo circled him with the predatory focus of a shark that had discovered a nice plump seal.

"No, no, no." The elderly Italian tugged at Bryn's sleeve. "Everything wrong. Shoulders—disaster. Waist—catastrophe. You let him dress himself?" This last part was directed at Giles, who sat in a nearby leather armchair looking far too amused.

"Sadly, yes. But that's why we're here, isn't it? You have three days to make him presentable for an important meeting I'm attending."

Paolo made a choking sound. "Three days? Impossible! This needs three weeks minimum. Maybe three months." He poked Bryn's ribs with a measuring tape. "Stop slouching!"

"I'm not…"

"Slouching!" Mr. Vittorio insisted. "And tension here, here, and here." He jabbed various parts of Bryn's anatomy with alarming accuracy. "Bodies must be relaxed for proper fit. You are like statue. Very bad statue. Not Italian."

"Perhaps," Giles suggested, "we could see the Welsh wool options while Bryan tries to become less…statuesque?"

"The blue-black superfine? Yes, yes." Paolo shuffled away, still chattering away in Italian about impossible timelines and American barbarians.

"Having fun?" Bryn asked once the tailor was out of earshot.

"Immensely. Though, I must say, you're taking all the joy out of it with that expression. Try to think happy thoughts."

"I'm thinking about all the ways to make death by measuring tape look accidental."

"Ah, there's that creative spirit."

The next hour was a blur of fabric swatches, increasingly intimate measurements, and Paolo Vittorio's running commentary on everything from Bryn's posture to his choice of socks. "Criminal! In my shop, wearing these…these…abominations! Inhale," Paolo commanded for the fifteenth time, wrapping his measuring tape around Bryn's chest.

"I *am* inhaling."

"No, no. From diaphragm. Like opera singer. Like this— *HHHNNNN!*"

"I am *not* making that noise."

"Make noise or measurements wrong. Wrong measurements, bad suit. Bad suit…" Mr. Vittorio crossed himself. "Catastrophe."

From his armchair, Giles snickered. Bryn shot him a look that promised future vengeance.

"Now, arms up. Higher! You are man, not penguin!"

"Is this really necess—?"

"Necessary? Like air! Like water! Like proper sleeve length!" Mr. Vittorio's tape snapped against Bryn's biceps.

"Ow!"

"Too much gym. Muscles make fabric angry."

"Muscles make fabric angry," Bryn repeated. "I don't even go to the gym. I'm allergic."

"*Si!* Fabric must flow, must drape. Your muscles…" Mr. Vittorio made angry gestures at Bryn's arms. "They fight fabric. Very disrespectful."

"Now, try on. Gentle! Fabric feels fear."

Bryn caught Giles' eye in the mirror. "I will make you pay for this."

"Dear boy, the bill for these suits already ensures that." Giles smiled his shark smile. "Though, I must say, Paolo's artistic temperament is worth every penny."

Bryn was clad in sections of fabric and pins.

"Arms up again! And now…" Mr. Vittorio stepped back, head tilted. "Walk!"

"Walk where?"

"Anywhere! Everywhere! Must see how you move. You walk like angry bear. Must walk like…like…"

"Like you have somewhere important to be and someone's life depends on you getting there," Giles supplied. "Which, incidentally…"

Bryn paced the length of the shop, trying to channel how he imagined an executive assistant would walk. Mr. Vittorio made sounds of deepening distress.

"No, no! Too much shoulder! Too much…" He waved his hands expressively. "Too much prison yard!"

"I've never been to prison," Bryn protested.

"Then why walk like planning escape, eh?"

The fabric was removed and handed to Paolo's assistant. The next forty-five minutes involved Bryn learning to walk, sit, and even stand— "Like civilized person, not cage fighter." By the end, his patience was hanging by a fraying silk thread.

"Three days. You can collect," Paolo said. "You can always come back for small alterations later." He shook his head, presumably at the state of the world in general. "Be gone. We need to work."

Giles ushered Bryn outside and, once on the pavement, Bryn took several deep breaths. "I'm starting to think this whole mission is an excuse for you to annoy the hell out of me."

"Not at all. Though I must admit, watching you try not to commit violence while being measured for your waistcoat was a delightful bonus. Now, we can discuss proper sock selection over lunch back at HQ."

Bryn's response was remarkably close to Mr. Vittorio's loudly expressed opinion of polyester blends.

When they got back to headquarters, Emmett was deep in his research hole. "It's not just the patient deaths," he said, surrounded by empty coffee cups. "Staff members have been disappearing too. Always from specific departments. Research, security, medical records."

"Cleaning house?" Gunnar suggested.

"Or recruiting," Giles suggested.

Bryn sighed. "Someone give me some good news."

"Lunch is on the way," Emmett contributed.

"There'd better be donuts or I'm withdrawing my labor."

"I ordered your favorite," Emmett said, looking up from his screen. "And I got extra because of...well, everything. We also have meatball subs because that's what Gunnar requested. Turkey on rye with salad for Giles and Warden."

"I hope you knew better than to get me salad?" Bryn said.

"Of course, but… I think I might be onto something interesting that's unrelated to our food order. I noticed the external security cameras at the Burlington clinic tend to glitch every day at exactly three-fourteen in the morning. Probably a coincidence, though." He paused. "Probably."

"Your optimism is both adorable and terrifying. Please tell me those donuts are coming with a side of hazard pay."

"No hazard pay," Emmett said cheerfully. "But I did get you an extra-large coffee."

"Well everything is fine and dandy then."

Gunnar chuckled. "Someone had a tough morning getting fancy. Let's get him sugared up. Today is going to be a long haul."

Chapter Four

Tuesday morning brought what Giles called 'cover story boot camp'. Hour after hour of drilling on financial terminology, corporate protocols, and the painful detail of being an executive assistant.

"No, no, no," Giles sighed after their third practice run. "You're still reacting to everything I say. Bryan wouldn't bristle at my requests. He's chosen this role, excels at it."

"Maybe because *Bryan* doesn't have the misfortune to know the real you," Bryn snapped.

"And who might that be? The person currently watching you butcher the pronunciation of 'quarterly earnings forecast' for the fifth time?" Giles pinched the bridge of his nose. "Can you not say it without sounding like you're ordering at a drive-through?"

Bryn slumped in his chair. "Well, excuse me for not majoring in Corporate Buzzword Studies at Harvard Business School."

"That's exactly the attitude I'm talking about." Giles began pacing. "Though I must admit, your creative interpretation of EBITDA as 'eating burritos in the dark again' was…memorable. I do hope that's not a reflection of how you spend your evenings."

"It's not my fault the finance world runs on alphabet soup," Bryn complained. "And there's nothing wrong with drive-through food, it minimizes people interaction."

"Perhaps we need to rebuild this cover identity from scratch so you can use words of one syllable." Giles' oozed sarcasm.

"Fuck off." Bryn straightened. "Shall I fetch your artisanal water, sir? I hear it was hand-harvested from Antarctic glaciers by free-range penguins."

"Better," Giles said, straight-faced. "But perhaps dial back the sarcasm by about eighty percent. We're aiming for devoted assistant, not passive-aggressive barista."

Gunnar, who had just come back into the room, snorted and Bryn glared at him.

"What? That was kinda funny."

"You're supposed to be on my side," Bryn protested.

"I'm on the side of whatever keeps you alive."

"Good man." Giles grinned, which made everything triply annoying.

"I hate my life."

"You'd hate being dead more," said Gunnar, stealing Bryn's coffee cup and draining the last dregs. "Disgusting. Like being back at the precinct."

"Right. That's it." Bryn pushed his chair back. "I'm going to go heist Gunnar's Harley and ride it off a cliff. It'll be less painful than whatever this is."

"Touch my baby and you won't be sitting comfortably for a week," Gunnar said.

Emmett chose that moment to return. His eyes widened and his cheeks pinked. "How's it going?" he asked, surveying the scene...Bryn with his head now on the table, Giles looking exasperated, and Gunnar examining the empty coffee pot with palpable disappointment.

"Oh, just peachy," Bryn mumbled into the tabletop. "I've learned sixteen ways to say 'yes sir' without sounding sarcastic, how to spell 'paradigm' without autocorrect, and that Giles is Satan in an Armani suit. Actually, I already knew that last one."

"I'm wearing Brooks Brothers today, thank you very much," Giles corrected as if Bryn should know such an obvious fact, straightening his pristine cuffs then adjusting his gold cufflinks.

Emmett set down his laptop. "Maybe we need a different approach. Bryn, what would make this easier for you?"

"A lobotomy? Time machine? Different genetic makeup?"

"I was thinking more along the lines of incentives," Emmett said.

Gunnar perked up. "Like those dog trainers who use treats?"

"I will end you in your sleep," Bryn hissed.

"Look, I get it," Giles interrupted. "You hate my guts and this isn't your world, but we need you to blend in long enough to figure out what Salvatore Russo is up to and why."

Bryn finally lifted his head. "Fine. But I need more coffee. And something that doesn't involve corporate speak for at least the next hour."

"Deal," said Giles, glancing at his watch. "How about we work on the non-verbal cues? Like how *not* to look as though you want to murder your boss when he asks you to reschedule a meeting."

"Can't promise miracles," Bryn replied.

Warden strolled in. "Any progress?"

"Define progress," Giles replied. "We've moved from complete disaster to impending catastrophe, so…we're heading in some kind of direction."

"I understood the term EBITDA," Bryn offered. "Even if my definition was…creative."

"He's getting there," Gunnar translated, already heading toward the door. "I'm making a coffee run. Anyone else?"

The chorus of "God, yes" was unanimous. "And bring me my incentive," Bryn yelled after him. "I need treats."

As Gunnar left, Bryn sighed but picked up his flash cards. "Let's try once more. At least with this cover, when someone tries to kill me, I'll be able to politely schedule their assassination attempt between your lunch meeting and the quarterly review. Perhaps I should send a memo to Dr. Templeton."

"Who?" Giles asked.

"No one," Warden interjected.

Probably shouldn't have mentioned that name. I don't think Giles will be impressed that my biggest fan is a serial killer.

"Dr. *Everard* Templeton," Giles mused, his eyes narrowing. "A gentleman with some very antisocial proclivities, if memory serves."

That got Bryn's attention. "You know him?"

"Not personally, but I make it my business to know about everyone who might want to kill my associates,"

Giles replied. "Professional courtesy. Your hand in interrogations and court cases has inevitable consequences."

Warden shot Giles an inscrutable look. "Perhaps we should get back to our current problem."

"Indeed. I've planned something different," Giles said. "Instead of memorizing corporate jargon, let's focus on your observational skills."

"Finally, something I'm good at," Bryn declared.

"Debatable," Giles murmured.

"The investor reception will have around fifty guests. Your job isn't to impress them with financial acumen, it's to watch, listen, and blend in."

"Like a Swiss cheese plant with ears," Bryn suggested.

"A plant that can fetch coffee and take notes," Giles corrected.

Warden sighed. "We need to practice some scenarios. What happens when someone asks you about Giles' latest acquisition?"

Bryn straightened and adopted a distant expression. "I'm afraid Mr. Delacourt's calendar is quite full, but I'd be happy to schedule some time for you to discuss that with him next week." He paused. "How was that?"

Giles looked surprised. "Not terrible."

"I can do deflection," Bryn said. "It's the pretending-to-care-about-profit-margins part I struggle with."

Gunnar returned, balancing a cardboard tray of coffee cups and a white bakery bag. "Incentives have arrived," he announced, setting the bag in front of Bryn. "Courtesy of the staff restaurant."

Bryn peered inside. "Chocolate croissants? You're forgiven for the dog trainer comment."

"I have a call pending with a business associate in Miami," Giles said. "A real one that I've not been able to reschedule. Bryn can sit in, take notes, observe."

"This feels like punishment," Bryn grumbled, reaching for a croissant.

"Consider it immersion therapy," Giles said. "You'll need to recognize normal behaviors to spot abnormal ones at the reception."

Fifteen minutes later, Bryn found himself in Giles' makeshift 'office' — the end of the conference table — surrounded by Emmett's three computer monitors. Emmett, Warden and Gunnar had made their escapes muttering various excuses, to Bryn's disgust. Now he watched Giles transform before his eyes. Gone was the sarcastic pain in the ass Bryn had been sparring with all morning. In his place sat a focused executive, rapidly scanning financial reports.

"Take this down," Giles said without looking up. "We need clarification on the Houston proposal, specifically regarding the distribution channels mentioned in section four."

Bryn scribbled on his pad, oddly fascinated by this other version of Giles.

"Also, I want detailed information on why the San Diego factory numbers are fifteen percent below projections. Don't let them blame it on supply chain issues again."

"Where did you learn to do this?" Bryn asked.

Giles glanced up. "Do what?"

"This…" Bryn gestured vaguely at the setup. "The corporate shark thing. It's like watching someone put on a mask, but from the inside out."

The corner of Giles' mouth twitched. "Power has its own particular thrill. You might be surprised. Working at The Facility is...pleasurable, but once my most interesting subject was taken away from me... Well, I enjoy the finer things in life, which necessitates other income streams."

The video conference chime interrupted them, and Giles brushed non-existent lint from his shoulder. "Watch and learn. Try not to look homicidal when the CFO starts talking."

"No promises," Bryn whispered. For the next forty-five minutes, he observed in reluctant admiration as Giles navigated complex negotiations, switching effortlessly between authoritative demands for information and subtle flattery. When the call ended, he leaned back in his chair with a satisfied expression.

"I'm disturbed by how good you are at this," Bryn admitted. "It's making me question whether you've been living a double life all along. I thought your main interests were science and psychology."

"Your view of me to date has been somewhat limited by your circumstances," Giles said. "What did you notice about the dynamics?"

Bryn tapped his pen against his notepad. "The older guy on the left, Reynolds? He's the real decision-maker even though he barely spoke. Everyone else in the room with him checked his reaction before answering."

Giles nodded, looking impressed. "Good. Nothing happens without his say so. What else?"

"The finance guy was lying about the production delays. His explanation changed slightly each time you circled back to it."

"Absolutely. That's exactly the kind of observation you'll need at the investor reception so we can target who you touch. People betray themselves in small ways."

"Like how you touch your cufflinks when you're about to say something particularly cutthroat?" Bryn offered.

"I do not."

"Three times during that call, including right before you eviscerated their proposal."

"Interesting theory," Giles said, moving his hands away from his sleeves. "Perhaps you're more observant than I gave you credit for."

"I'm full of surprises," Bryn replied. "Though I'm still not calling you 'sir' without thinking bad thoughts."

"Baby steps," Giles sighed. "Let's get the others back in here and show them you survived a whole hour alone with me without attempting corporate manslaughter."

"The day is still young."

The day in question drifted on and later that afternoon Emmett's deep dive into employee records at Helix revealed patterns that made no sense. There were staff with perfect qualifications but no digital footprint prior to five years ago and security personnel with sketchy backgrounds.

"I think Russo could be building something," Gunnar said. "An organization within the organization. He wants his drug in as many gene-affected people as possible and for that he needs collaborators."

"Like a corporate Russian doll?" Emmett asked, studying the screens. "Only instead of cute wooden figures, it's filled with ghosts. You could be right. Look at this. Saskia Arnold, hired last year as head of R&D. Two PhDs, publications in all the right journals, recommendations from top institutions. But dig deeper…" He pulled up another window. "Her entire academic career is a masterwork of digital fabrication. The papers exist, but the methodologies are vague. Her co-authors are either dead, retired, or unreachable. It's perfect. Too perfect."

"How many others?" Gunnar asked.

"I haven't gotten through everyone yet, but at least fifteen so far across various sites, all in key positions."

Gunnar frowned. "They're hiding in plain sight. They may even be doing other genuine work but meantime, they're finding subjects to experiment on."

"Do you think they all know what they're doing?" Emmett asked. "I mean, are we looking at willing participants?" He shoved his glasses up his nose for the umpteenth time.

"I'd guess they are," Gunnar responded.

"And if Russo can do this, create people, histories, entire lives out of thin air—what else can he do?" Bryn contributed.

"We know he has a very long reach," Gunnar said. "Money talks and he has plenty."

"So does fear. I have the IT guys working on hacking more secure servers at the clinics but it might take a while," Warden said.

Bryn nodded. "Okay, so even if I manage to pull off a decent impersonation of a corporate high-flyer, how are we going to deal with the blood scanners at this place? I won't get past the door if they work out I'm gene-affected, especially if they can't place me as lupine or sanguine."

"Ah." For the first time, Giles looked uncomfortable. "There may be a slight vulnerability in the detection protocols. Something I left in as a back door. One that involves…some physical discomfort."

"Color me shocked." Bryn said. "You think you could enlighten us?"

Giles pulled a small metal case from his jacket pocket. Inside, nestled in black foam, was a row of clear capsules filled with a pale lilac liquid. Each was the size of a large vitamin tablet. "The scanners work by analyzing specific markers in your blood," he explained, picking one up. "But they can be fooled if those markers are temporarily altered. This" — he held the capsule up to the light—"will modify your blood chemistry for approximately six hours."

"And the significant physical discomfort part?" Bryn asked, eyeing it with suspicion.

"Let's just say the modification process isn't gentle. Side effects can include fever, nausea, and what some test subjects described as feeling like their veins were running with bee venom."

Emmett let out a low whistle. "That's specific. I got stung on my arm once and it really hurt."

"The good news is the side effects only last about twenty minutes," Giles added, as if that made it better. "The bad news is those twenty minutes will feel like twenty hours. You'll need to take the drug at least thirty minutes before attempting to pass through any scanners, so timing will be crucial."

Bryn glared at Giles. "So to be clear. Your solution to getting past the scanners is to poison me?"

"Temporarily modify your blood chemistry," Giles corrected. "Poison is such an ugly word."

"So is sociopath, but here we are." Bryn picked up one of the capsules, holding it like it might bite him. "What about you, you're sanguine? You'll have to pass the scanners too."

"What I am is not a secret. You are."

"And you're absolutely sure this works?"

"I tested it myself," Giles said. "Multiple times."

Bryn stared at the innocuous object between his fingers. "So not only do I have to pretend to be your lapdog, but I also need to voluntarily swallow something that will make me feel less than happy while maintaining a working brain cell or two." He put the capsule back in the case.

"Now you're catching on," Giles replied, snapping the case shut.

Bryn took a long gulp of coffee. "What about my eyes? I won't need my gloves but won't wearing dark glasses seem a bit odd?"

"If anyone asks, we'll say you have impaired vision. No one will challenge that. We have approximately eighteen hours before we need to be in position. That gives us enough time to review the building schematics, finalize the extraction protocol, and yes, Bryn, go through those flash cards one more time."

Bryn groaned but didn't argue. The stakes were becoming higher by the minute. This wasn't only about infiltrating a suspect organization, it was about uncovering whatever Salvatore Russo, aka The Hammer, was building with his ghost employees, fabricated histories and evil drug. *And stopping him.*

Chapter Five

Wednesday dawned clear and cold. In the sanctuary of Bryn's bedroom, Bryn and Gunnar lay snug beneath the comforter. They'd shared a bed three nights running, nights of skin-to-skin contact and coziness but nothing more. Bryn couldn't contemplate the idea of going back to separate rooms because that would be surrendering something precious he'd waited too long for.

Gunnar, ever disciplined, got up early to run. He slipped from beneath the covers with practiced stealth, but Bryn wasn't truly asleep. Through half-lidded eyes, he watched Gunnar move about the room, admiring his impressive physique as he dressed in the dim light.

"You're not as sneaky as you think," Bryn mumbled.

Gunnar paused, halfway through pulling on a thermal running top. "I was trying to let you sleep."

"And miss the show? Not a chance." Bryn propped himself up on one elbow. "Though I'd rather you were getting back into bed than leaving it."

Gunnar chuckled. "Five miles now means I can justify pancakes later. With you." He leaned down and pressed a kiss to Bryn's forehead. "Stay warm."

After the soft click of the door, Bryn rolled into Gunnar's warm spot, breathing in his lingering scent. He hugged Gunnar's pillow, a poor substitute for the real thing, but comforting nonetheless then dozed, waiting for Gunnar's return.

Forty-five minutes later, he heard it...the heavy tread of running shoes in the hallway, the rush of the shower starting up. Only then did he drag himself out of bed to answer the siren call of coffee.

Breakfast was quiet. Gunnar, flushed from his run and shower, hummed while he cooked pancakes and prepped fruit. Bryn enjoyed the lack of noise and unnecessary chat. Gunnar seemed to understand his need for head space before what was going to be a stressful, Giles-infested day.

"Are you worried about the investor event?" Gunnar asked, sliding a plate of blueberry pancakes across to Bryn.

Bryn nodded, pouring a sizeable puddle of maple syrup. "A lot could go wrong."

"You've prepped and I know you. You might tease Giles that you're useless at this, but I know better."

"Maybe, but if I'm being observant, won't they be too? What if someone spots that I'm reading them?"

"You've been in tough spots. We have an extraction plan and much as I'd like to strangle Giles with one of his own fancy silk cravats, don't forget what you told me about him. His sanguine qualities are strong. He won't let anything happen to you — you're too valuable to him."

"As a fucking experiment."

"Yeah, but a rare one."

"I guess it's one time when being a freak might be a benefit rather than a disadvantage."

Gunnar refilled Bryn's coffee mug. "Drink this. You're gonna need it and if you call yourself that again, I will spank your bare ass until you cry."

"Might not be the worst thing in the world…oops, did I say that out loud?"

Gunnar shook his head. "Fuck's sake. Get yourself downstairs before Giles comes calling."

The dress rehearsal for the investor's meeting took place in Warden's office and felt like the world's most twisted job interview. Giles played potential investors while Bryn navigated complex questions about market strategy and return on investment.

"Better," Giles admitted. "Though your disdain still shows when you call me 'sir.'"

"The maybe I should call you Giles."

"No. Mr. Delacourt will suffice, though."

"Why no false name for you?"

"Because my name is in my company records and they will likely have done due diligence on their guests. I'm not difficult to find, nor is my picture. My involvement in development of the blood scanners is also public knowledge. Any trace of you was wiped from the virtual world when you were identified as an augur and the tech team here has protocols in place to ensure you never reappear."

"Fair enough." *Never wanted a career as an Instagram influencer anyway.*

"Warden is sending someone to collect your new clothes and I've arranged for a stylist to come in to do something about that mop of yours. She should be here shortly. This afternoon you'll take one of the capsules so you know what the side effects feel like then tonight, you and I will check into a downtown hotel appropriate for a visiting investor."

They walked back to the conference room where Gunnar had been dealing with members of the GCR's security team, setting up surveillance points for the following day and at the hotel that night.

"Where are we staying?" Bryn asked.

"The Four Seasons. I had Emmett book the presidential suite. Anything less would be suspicious for someone of my caliber," Giles replied. "It's in Back Bay, with views over the Public Garden. The kind of place where they change your sheets if you so much as wrinkle them."

Before Bryn could comment, a petite woman with electric blue hair burst into the room, dragging a rolling case behind her.

"Darling Giles! I am here! The security guard who let me in was very handsome, no?"

"Hello, Marie, my angel. We'll make space for you to set up at the end of the table. Do you need your customer to get his head wet?"

I'd quite like to hold your head down in a bucket of cold water, Giles. For about ten minutes. Bryn gave the lady a fake smile.

"No, no. Not necessary. Is this him?" She approached Bryn. "I'm Marie, and I'm here to save your hair from the tragedy that has befallen it. *Mon dieu*, who's been cutting this? A gardener with a lawnmower?"

"I do it myself," Bryn admitted.

Marie clutched at her chest. "You wound me!" She opened her case then spread a plastic sheet on the floor before positioning a chair on it. She then whipped out a black cape with flourish. "Sit. We have much work to do."

For the next hour, Marie fussed and clucked and occasionally gasped in horror as she transformed Bryn's hair with liberal use of a water spray bottle, scissors and brushes. Gunnar, who had finished his security planning, watched with barely concealed amusement.

"No, no, *no!*" Marie exclaimed, making everyone jump. "You cannot keep running your fingers through it. You are to be an executive assistant, yes? Executive assistants do not fidget! They glide! They float! They certainly do not mess up my precision cutting by treating their hair so!" Marie spun him around to face the small mirror she'd placed on the conference table. She'd somehow managed to make Bryn look both professional and stylish. "Now, product! You must use product! This is not optional!"

She proceeded to demonstrate proper hair product application with the intensity of someone defusing a bomb, while Gunnar shook with suppressed laughter in the corner.

"I don't see what's so funny," Bryn muttered.

"You look like you're expecting that gel to explode," Gunnar managed between chuckles.

Emmett glanced up from his laptop. "Given your track record, that's not entirely outside the realm of possibility."

Warden, who had been observing from the doorway, cleared his throat. "Marie has worked a small miracle."

"Hey!" Bryn protested. "I looked fine."

Warden took the diplomatic path and didn't respond.

"Thank you for your services, Marie. I believe we're finished here," Giles said.

Marie packed up her supplies, but not before fixing Bryn with a stern look. "If I see you again and this is ruined, we will have words. Many words. Most of them French. And you" — she gestured at Gunnar — "I would very much like to get my hands on your…hair. Giles has my number."

After she left, Bryn turned to the others. "Is it too late to shoot our way in instead?"

"Yes," came the unanimous response.

"I hate all of you."

"You look great," Emmett said. "The style suits you."

Bryn couldn't be mad with Emmett. He huffed. "Fine. Shall we get the next bit over with? Though I'm not sure what's worse, the haircut or taking the capsule." It was worrying that Giles didn't respond.

"We should do this in the bathroom," Giles said, opening the case containing the capsules. They glowed lilac under the lights. "Trust me, you'll want to be near the facilities."

"And you're sure this won't kill me?"

"Not even close," Giles replied. "Though you might wish it would for about twenty minutes."

Gunnar moved closer to Bryn. "I'll stay with you."

Bryn took the drug from Giles. "So I just…swallow it?"

"Obviously. And then we wait. It should only take five minutes to begin working."

Bryn took a deep breath then swallowed the capsule before he could think too hard about it. It went down easily, tasteless and smooth. "Now what?"

"Now we wait," Giles said, checking his watch. "And when it starts…try to remember that it will end."

The first five minutes were anticlimactic. Bryn and Gunnar retreated to Bryn's ensuite bathroom in their apartment where Bryn sat on the closed toilet lid, while Gunnar leaned against the wall beside him.

Then Bryn felt it, a slight warmth in his stomach that quickly turned into a burning sensation. "Oh," he said, "that's…unpleasant."

The burning spread, racing through his veins like liquid fire. His hands began to shake, and sweat broke out across his forehead. "Okay, that's not nice."

"Beginning of phase one." Giles stuck his head around the door. "Initial systemic response."

"Fuck your phases, and fuck you, Giles," Bryn gasped as the burning intensified. It felt like his blood was trying to claw its way out of his body. His vision blurred, the bathroom light too harsh. Gunnar squeezed his shoulder.

"Oh fuck," Bryn managed through clenched teeth. The pain was getting worse, radiating from his core to his extremities. His fingers and toes tingled like they were being stabbed with thousands of tiny needles. "Oh fuck, the bee venom thing makes sense now."

He doubled over, fighting the urge to be sick. Gunnar moved his hand to the back of Bryn's neck, cool against his burning skin. The touch helped, giving him something to focus on besides the inferno raging through his body. The contact didn't instigate a read because Bryn's focus was very much elsewhere.

"Phase two," Giles announced, his voice seeming to come from very far away. "Peak reaction."

Bryn wanted to tell Giles exactly where he could stick his phases, but he couldn't form words anymore.

The pain had become all-consuming. He slid off the toilet seat and Gunnar caught him. He lowered him to the cool tile floor.

"Is this normal?" Gunnar's voice was tight.

"Completely," Giles assured him. "Though his reaction seems more intense than average. Probably due to his augur physiology."

"You might have mentioned that possibility beforehand," Gunnar said.

"Would it have changed anything?"

Bryn pressed his face against the tile floor, desperate for any relief. Time lost all meaning—it could have been minutes or hours that he lay there, trembling and sweating, while his blood burned and his muscles spasmed.

Then, gradually, the pain faded to manageable discomfort. His vision cleared, the light no longer feeling like daggers in his eyes.

"Phase three," Giles said. "Resolution."

"If you don't stop with the phases," Bryn croaked, "I'm going to throw up on your fucking Italian shoes."

"He's feeling better," Giles observed. "Return of verbal hostility indicates recovery."

Gunnar helped Bryn sit up. The room spun for a moment before settling. "That," Bryn said, "wasn't a fun time."

"But educational," Giles added. "Now you know what to expect tomorrow."

"Yeah, now I can look forward to it with informed dread instead of ignorant dread. Much better." Bryn accepted the glass of water Gunnar offered, taking small sips. "Please tell me it won't be worse the second time."

"It won't be worse," Giles said. "But it won't be better, either. The body doesn't build up tolerance to this particular process."

"Fantastic." He let Gunnar help him to his feet. "And I have to do this, then immediately go act normal?"

"Do you ever act normal? You'll have about thirty minutes between taking it and our arrival to recover."

"At least Marie isn't here to see what this did to her masterpiece." Bryn peered into the mirror. His hair was a disaster, plastered to his head with sweat.

"You should rest," Giles said. "Take a shower. We'll head to the hotel in an hour. You'll want to be fully recovered before we check in."

Bryn nodded, too drained to argue. "Next time you create a back door in a security system, maybe consider one that doesn't feel like dying?"

"I'll add it to my list of design improvements," Giles replied. "Right after 'make it impossible to detect' and 'don't get caught in the first place'."

Chapter Six

Bryn walked two steps behind Giles' left shoulder as they approached the front desk of the Four Seasons. *If I were a dog, I'd be walking to heel. Fuck my life.* His new clothes were constricting enough to be a suit of armor and the lingering effects from the capsule made his collar way too tight. *Or maybe it's because I can't remember the last time I wore a tie. Damn strangulation device.*

"Good evening and welcome to the Four Seasons." The receptionist gave a professional smile. "How may I assist you?"

"Delacourt," Giles said, his entire demeanor that of a man who expected the world to bend to his wishes. "I believe you have the presidential suite reserved."

"Of course, Mr. Delacourt." She tapped her keyboard. "And will Mr. Reid-Cobb be joining you this evening?"

"That's me," Bryn said, keeping his tone polite but distant, suggesting he dealt with such matters a hundred times a month. "Mr. Delacourt's executive assistant."

The receptionist's smile never wavered. "My apologies. I have you both right here."

Giles stepped away as if any future engagement with menial tasks was beneath him. Bryn dealt with the rigmarole of identification checks, getting a credit card on file and listening to the spiel about the facilities, which got on his last nerve but he managed to smile through it. It wasn't the receptionist's fault that his life sucked.

"And would you like assistance with your luggage?"

"That won't be necessary," Bryn answered. "I can manage."

"Of course, sir. Here are your key cards. You should take the elevator to your right which requires the card for access to the upper floors. Please don't hesitate to contact us if you need anything at all."

"Thank you." Bryn pocketed both cards then picked up their bags.

In the elevator, Giles maintained his aloof expression until the doors closed. "Not bad."

"I loathe Bryan already," Bryn said, fighting the urge to loosen his tie. The capsule's aftereffects were making everything feel too warm. Being in a confined space with Giles was not where Bryn wanted to be.

Giles grinned. "Learn to love him."

"I hate you so much right now."

"I know."

The presidential suite's foyer opened into a vast living area with floor-to-ceiling windows showcasing Boston's glittering skyline. Everything was cream and gold and understated luxury. Bryn went to check the two bedrooms.

"Very nice. Master bedroom is on the left so I left your bag in there," he reported. "Emmett arranged a sweep for surveillance devices."

"Yes, Gunnar's team also did a thorough check this afternoon. Try to get some rest. Tomorrow will be…"

"Challenging?"

"That's one word for it." Giles glanced at his watch. "You should order dinner in an hour. I'd suggest a shower and change before then."

Bryn nodded, heading toward his room. He paused at the door. "What do you want to eat?"

"Beef tenderloin, rare, with roasted vegetables and a 2015 Bordeaux." Giles smiled. "Which you would know if you'd memorized the brief on my dining preferences in the file."

"There was a brief on your dining preferences?"

"Page seventeen. After the section on my preferred meeting protocols but before the notes on my travel requirements."

Bryn stared at him. "You're not joking, are you?"

"Bryan would know these things," Giles said. The comment was calm but barbed all the same.

"Bryan needs to get a fucking life," Bryn muttered, disappearing into his room.

He heard Giles call after him, "Page twenty-three. My thoughts on work-life balance and appropriate leisure activities for executive assistants."

Bryn closed his door a tad too hard. He needed to decompress for a while so he lay back on the ridiculously comfortable bed, dealt with the room service order then made a much more welcome call.

"Everything okay?" Gunnar answered so fast he had to have been holding his cell.

"Fine. Just weird. This whole thing is weird." Bryn stared at the ceiling. "Did you know there's a TV that comes up out of a cabinet at the foot of the bed? Like something from a spy movie."

"Is Giles still breathing?"

"He is, but it's only been two hours." Bryn smiled at the protective edge in Gunnar's voice. "He's actually being…well, still Giles, but almost helpful. In an annoying way, of course."

"I don't like you being alone with him."

"I know. I don't like it either but he needs this to work as much as we do." Bryn rolled onto his side. "Besides, I'm pretty sure I could take him in a fight now. Assuming that capsule doesn't eradicate dirty fighting skills."

"How are you feeling?"

"Better. Still warm. Everything's a bit…sharp. But nothing like before." He paused. "Thanks for staying with me through that, by the way."

"Always."

"I miss our bed. This one's too big and too fancy and doesn't have you in it."

"It's only for one night."

"Assuming we don't all get killed tomorrow."

"That's not funny."

"Sorry." Bryn sighed. "I should go. I need to shower then room service is coming. Apparently 'Bryan' gets up at an ungodly hour to review the day's schedule and check the international markets."

"Of course he does." Gunnar's voice softened. "Call me if you need anything. I'm only four floors down. Try not to murder Giles before morning, but if you do I'll help hide the body and give you an alibi."

"No promises," Bryn said, but he was chuckling as he hung up.

* * * *

Bryn slouched into the suite's dining area at six-thirty, yawning until his jaw cracked. He had on his oldest ripped jeans and a ratty T-shirt. Giles was already there, immaculate in a charcoal suit and deep red silk tie, reading something on a tablet while sipping coffee.

"You look terrible," Giles said.

"Thanks. That's exactly what an executive assistant needs to hear before a critical meeting." Bryn slumped into a chair, eyeing the elaborate breakfast spread on the table. "Did you order everything on the menu?"

"I like to have options."

Bryn reached for the coffee pot, only to have Giles slide it away.

"You need to learn how to pour coffee."

Bryn stared at him. "It's six-thirty in the morning. There cannot possibly be a wrong way to pour coffee and if you don't let me have that pot, violence will occur."

"There are at least seven wrong ways, and you were about to demonstrate four of them." Giles set aside his tablet. "Watch."

What followed was possibly the most pretentious coffee-pouring demonstration in human history. Bryn watched in sleep-deprived disbelief as Giles explained the proper angle, the correct distance from cup to pot, the optimal pouring speed, and something about respecting the coffee's natural flow that Bryn was pretty sure he'd made up.

"There," Giles finished. "Now you try."

Bryn picked up the pot and splashed the coffee into his cup without following any of Giles' instructions.

"You're doing that on purpose."

"Am I? That doesn't sound like something *Bryan* would do."

"Bryan also wouldn't look like he got into a fight with his pillow and lost."

"My pillow," Bryn said with dignity, "was actively hostile. I think it was stuffed with the hopes and dreams of other executive assistants who didn't meet your standards."

A ghost of a smile crossed Giles' face. "Your hair is a disaster."

"I will deal with my hair when I have a shower. After food and coffee." Bryn grabbed a muffin. "I have priorities."

"Hmm." Giles pushed a small silver case across the table. "You'll need to take another capsule in about two hours."

"I hate you."

"So you keep saying. Bryan would never say that to his boss. Not within earshot, anyway."

"He probably has a dart board with your face on it in his very expensive apartment. Or maybe a voodoo doll to stick pins in."

"Page thirty-one," Giles said, returning to his tablet. "Bryan has family money. He lives in a penthouse in Manhattan. No dart boards."

Bryn dropped his head onto the table. "I'm going to need a lot more coffee."

"Pour it properly this time."

"I'm adding 'proper coffee pouring' to the list of things I'm going to make you regret teaching me."

"That's more like it," Giles said with what could have been approval. "Your threats should be subtle and coffee-related."

"My life sucks." Bryn poured another cup.

"While we're alone, I've been meaning to ask… How have your abilities been developing?"

Bryn tensed. "You mean since you spent three years trying to break them? Or me? It was hard to tell which."

"Both, perhaps. But it worked, didn't it? You're a stable, functioning adult, well quasi-adult, and you're still alive."

Bryn went quiet for a moment, remembering the endless training sessions, the pain, the humiliation. Giles' teeth in his vein. "Not sure stable is accurate," he said. "But I suppose it worked. When I touch someone, I can switch easily from memory to intent to truth. I don't get overwhelmed. Still get headaches, though."

"And the physical contact? You've learned to manage that better?"

"You mean can I handle being in crowds without having a mental breakdown? Mostly. The gloves help." Bryn reached for a piece of toast. "Accidental contact isn't so easy to control."

"Show me," Giles said, extending his hand across the table. "Take a look at my strongest memory."

Bryn stared at him. "Seriously?"

"Consider it a final test before today's performance."

With a sigh, Bryn reached out and grabbed Giles' wrist. He closed his eyes. "Fuck, Giles…your strongest memory is of tasting my blood for the first time." He pulled his hand away.

"Very good."

"You knew what I'd see, didn't you?"

"There were several possibilities. All from your training."

"You know," Bryn said, reaching for the coffee pot again, "one of these days, you're going to have to acknowledge that you actually give a damn about what happens to me. Beyond how I taste."

"Page forty-two," Giles replied. "Professional relationships and maintaining appropriate boundaries."

"I hate that I don't know if you're making these page numbers up anymore. Also, pretty sure there's nothing in that manual about proper sanguine-augur etiquette."

"We will always have a unique relationship, you and I. There's no getting away from that."

"Unique is one way of putting it," Bryn replied. "Most people would call it profoundly dysfunctional."

"Would you have preferred a different trainer? One who coddled you with platitudes instead of preparing you for what's out there?"

"I'd prefer one who didn't look at me like I'm both a weapon and a snack."

"At least I recognize your value in both capacities," Giles said with the ghost of a smile. "Most would only see the weapon."

Bryn stared at him. "How comforting."

Chapter Seven

The investor event was everything Bryn had expected and dreaded — sterile corridors, forced smiles, and enough corporate doublespeak to drown in. Giles moved through it all with practiced ease, all crisp confidence and strategic handshakes. After an insomnia-curing presentation, they were now on a tour in small groups. Bryn trailed behind Giles, notebook in hand, playing the dutiful assistant while surreptitiously watching clinic staff. He was hating every second and hoped it didn't show on his face.

"And here's our advanced neurological mapping department," Dr. Elise Howard, the company's medical director, announced, gesturing to a lab filled with equipment that to Bryn, looked like it belonged on a space station.

"Fascinating," Giles responded, seeming impressed. "Bryan, make a note to schedule a follow-up discussion with Dr. Howard's team. This is an area of specific interest for me."

"Of course, Mr. Delacourt," Bryn replied. He dodged contact with an older businessman, hyper aware that he wasn't wearing his gloves. He was still fragile from taking Giles' second purple capsule and didn't want to exhaust himself further with accidental readings. *That damned pill may have gotten me past the scanners but I'm never taking one of them again. Not even if Warden offers me an entire weekend off.*

Dr. Howard was fawning over Giles. "We're excited about the therapeutic applications. Our early trials show remarkable promise."

When she turned to offer her hand to Bryn, he hesitated for a fraction of a second before accepting it. The moment their skin made contact, glimpses of her future intent flashed into his mind. *Changing access codes. Altering data on a spreadsheet. Fear and greed.* Bryn maintained his neutral expression through sheer force of will as Dr. Howard released his hand and turned back to Giles. He clenched his fist, digging his nails into his palm. The slight pain helped.

"Mr. Delacourt, if you'll follow me, our CFO is eager to discuss the projected returns," Howard said, leading them back toward the conference room wing.

Bryn gave Giles a brief nod to let him know he'd managed a read.

"I hope your notes are thorough, Bryan."

"Yes, Mr. Delacourt." *I hope your hair falls out and you develop a severe gastrointestinal issue in a crowded elevator.* Bryn gave him a fake deferential smile. Giles smiled right back, his eyes knowing. *Why does he also seem to know what I'm thinking?*

Back in a meeting room, the CFO, Harrison Fuller, silver-haired with a predator's eyes, rose to greet them.

"Mr. Delacourt, delighted you could join us today," Fuller said. "Your reputation precedes you."

Bryn fought down a snigger. *I'll bet it does.* But then Fuller clasped his hand, almost taking him by surprise. Bryn zeroed in on intent and saw him shredding documents then putting a flashy Rolex around his wrist. He had an important meeting coming up and he was picturing Salvatore Russo. *Fuck, he's going to meet with The Hammer.* Bryn released the handshake as soon as propriety allowed. A small mallet began banging the inside of his skull and he was glad that his presence was immediately ignored. Fuller's attention was all on Giles and Bryn was happy to be invisible.

"Coffee, ladies and gentlemen?" offered a young server who had been circling the room and the small clusters of people gathering after their tours.

"Black for Mr. Delacourt," Bryn responded. "Nothing for me, thank you." He didn't need caffeine exacerbating his growing headache. He wasn't one of the fortunate people that caffeine helped. He took the offered cup then handed it to Giles. As the conversation progressed into financial projections, Bryn made a show of taking detailed notes while documenting which executives seemed least comfortable and who avoided eye contact. A staffer approached to distribute presentation folders and when she handed Bryn a copy, their fingers brushed.

Packing suitcases. Planning a trip. Leaving after dark. She's scared.

Bryn blinked, clearing his vision. When he glanced at her, the staffer was watching him with an odd expression but she soon moved away. Giles had his coffee so Bryn went to fetch himself a glass of water from a carafe on a side table. He reached for the bottle at the same time as a huge man in a dark suit and tie. He had an earpiece in one ear.

"Sorry," Bryn murmured as their hands collided. It was a brief contact but what he saw spooked him more than anything else he'd seen so far. He jerked back, splashing water onto the carpet.

"Careful there," the man said. "Ty Brunt, head of security."

"Hi and uh, my apologies," Bryn replied. "My fault. I'm so clumsy."

"Not a problem, it's only water." Brunt's tone implied any further misadventures would be rewarded by a life-limiting experience. He radiated hostility and barely contained violence.

Bryn caught Giles' eye and returned to his side. Brunt was watching him and he felt like a bug under a microscope. "Sir, could you excuse me for a moment? I need to use the restroom." Giles gave him a dismissive nod and Bryn left the room for the reception area where the staffer with the folders was hovering. Bryn gave her what he hoped was an encouraging smile.

"Tough crowd, huh?"

"Uh, yeah... You're not really Delacourt's assistant, are you?" she asked, her voice low.

"I've been with Mr. Delacourt for almost four years now." *Stretching the truth but not really a lie.*

"Then why did you look at the quarterly report upside down for ten minutes without noticing?" she challenged. "And why do you keep searching everyone's faces like you're memorizing them?"

"Miss, I'm not sure..."

"They're planning something terrible," she interrupted, whispering. "In the sub-basement labs here and at other sites. Gene-affected test subjects who haven't signed proper consent forms. Drugs that don't have government clearance. Falsified data." She glanced around. "I've been gathering evidence, but they're watching me."

Bryn made a split-second decision. *If she made me, who else did?* "If you have something to show me, now would be the time."

"I'm Mira." She pulled a USB from her pocket. "Tell me I'm not wrong about you."

"You're not. I thought I was doing a better job of staying under the radar." Bryn took the drive.

"On there are two sets of clinical trial results. The real ones show severe neurological side effects in sixty percent of participants. The published ones that they're planning to submit show only three percent. There's also a list on there of drug manufacturing sites. Uncontrolled, unlicensed ones."

"You're taking a huge risk giving me this."

"You're taking a huge risk too. People are dying," Mira said. "My brother is lupine. I don't want him to be next."

"I need to get back," Bryn said. "I've been gone too long. You're planning to run. Do it."

Mira's eyes widened. "How did you…"

"Call in sick tomorrow and don't come back."

She gave a brief nod. "Where can I find you?"

"The GCR." Telling her was a calculated risk but Bryn wanted to give her a lifeline. *She might need it.* "Now point me at the bathroom because I think we're being watched." He was aware that Ty Brunt was looming in the conference room doorway but didn't think he'd arrived there early enough to see Mira pass him the USB. He waited to make sure no one followed her as she walked away then spent a few minutes in the men's room before returning to Giles' side in the conference room. He caught Brunt watching him and avoided eye contact. *Being the subject of that man's attention is not comfortable. We need to get out of here. How can I get Giles to stop talking?* He leaned in close to Giles, his voice a low murmur, "We need to go. Now."

Giles wound up his conversation as if nothing had happened. "Quite fascinating projections," he said to Harrison Fuller. "I'll be in touch but for now, I have another engagement to get to. Bryan, is the car waiting?"

"Yes, Mr. Delacourt." Bryn noticed Ty Brunt move to position himself closer to the conference room's exit. As they moved toward the door, Bryn tried to keep his posture relaxed, notebook tucked under his arm. The USB drive was deep in his inner jacket pocket but to him it was broadcasting a tornado warning.

"Mr. Delacourt," Fuller called out as they reached the threshold. "A moment?"

Giles turned, his smile perfect. "Of course."

By the time Fuller released them, after some irrelevant, suck-up pleasantries, Bryn was sweating.

"Keep walking," Giles murmured.

Three more steps. The sunlight beyond the lobby doors was blinding after the conference room's subtle lighting. Bryn blinked despite his dark glasses. Outside the clinic, several expensive cars were lined up. Gunnar was leaning against their ride, his eyes locked on the clinic's entrance. His jacket was open, his holster visible. Bryn caught his gaze. A slight nod. Nothing more. They were feet from the car when Bryn heard a radio crackle behind them. He glanced back to see Ty Brunt speaking into a walkie talkie and had to resist the urge to run to Gunnar.

Gunnar opened the rear passenger door of the car like a professional chauffeur. Bryn slid across the seat and Giles followed, pulling the door shut. Gunnar got behind the wheel.

"Drive," Giles ordered.

Gunnar shot him a look in the rear view but didn't ask questions. He pulled away and merged into traffic without hesitation. "I'm guessing you got something," he said.

"Several reads from different people, and this." Bryn pulled out the USB drive.

Giles took it, turning it over in his palm. "This was an unexpected bonus."

"I'm worried about the woman who gave it to me."

"She must have been desperate for help to take the risk of trusting you."

"She worked out 'Bryan' was faking it. Her intent was to run. I told her she should." Bryn exhaled, rubbing his temples. His headache had settled into something dull and persistent. "Mira, that was her name, is scared and she's right to be."

Gunnar cut a sharp left, taking a less direct route back to their hotel. "We've picked up a tail," he said.

Bryn twisted to look through the rear windshield. "Where?"

"Black sedan, two cars back."

"The security guy was suspicious of me. It must be him."

"Lose them," Giles said. "We won't be that difficult to trace to the hotel but let's make them work for it. We'll go back there anyway. Everything should seem legitimate."

Gunnar smirked and stepped on the gas. Traffic blurred past as he weaved through afternoon congestion. Bryn gripped the door handle as they narrowly missed clipping the side mirror of a delivery truck. The black sedan kept up.

Bryn swore under his breath. "Persistent."

"Not for long," Gunnar muttered. He took a hard right down a side street, then another, slipping into an abandoned lot sprouting random greenery from its cracked asphalt. The sedan didn't appear and he waited a full minute before reversing out and returning to the main road. "Not my first rodeo."

"What now?" Bryn asked.

"Back to the hotel as planned," Giles said. "We left the clinic because I had another engagement to get to and that's what's going to happen. In our suite. As soon as we let Warden know we're back, he'll come over and we can review everything together."

Bryn closed his eyes and attempted to relax in his seat while Gunnar drove back to the hotel, taking a circuitous route. Bryn's headache was painful and he needed to scavenge the room service menu as soon as possible. He opened his eyes again only when Gunnar pulled into the underground parking lot of their hotel, coasting into a spot near the elevator. He shut off the engine and turned in his seat, looking at Bryn.

"You're wiped. How bad *are* you feeling?"

Bryn swallowed, forcing himself to straighten. "I'll manage. I just need food and water."

Gunnar gave him a look that said he wasn't buying it. "Let's get to the room. If what's on that drive is as bad as I think it could be, we're about to have a lot more problems."

Bryn sighed, slumping against the headrest. "Fantastic."

Gunnar opened the car door and stepped out first, scanning the garage before giving the all-clear. Giles went after him, slipping back into his businessman persona. Bryn took a beat longer before following. The lingering images from his reads filled his head and made him nauseous.

They rode the elevator to their floor in silence and when they reached their suite, Gunnar went in first to check it was secure. Once in the room, Bryn sank onto the couch, pressing his palms to his eyes. Giles got onto his cell, presumably giving a head's up to Warden.

Bryn groaned, rubbing his eyes. "Before I pass out, are you ordering food, or are we embracing a slow descent into starvation?"

Gunnar grinned. "You're trusting me with the room service menu?"

"Yes, because starving to death is not my preferred option and I don't think I can focus on the print."

"What do you want?"

"Food. I don't know. Anything that's bad for me."

"Just order something before I regret all my recent life choices," Giles said. "I take my steak very rare. I'm going to freshen up while we wait for Warden." He sauntered across to the master bedroom.

Bryn waited until Giles was safely out of earshot before slumping back against the couch with a dramatic sigh. "I don't like him."

Gunnar snorted. "Really? I'd never have known."

"No, no. I extra dislike him. He's got that" — Bryn gestured vaguely — "thing. The smug, 'I'm better than you' thing. It's not just our past."

"I get it. I do. But we need him."

"I'd rather chew glass than admit that."

"Then chew fast, because room service is on its way."

When the knock finally came, Bryn was on his feet before Gunnar could react, yanking the door open to grab the laden tray from the bewildered hotel employee. He thumped the tray onto the low table then explored before digging in like he hadn't had a decent meal in a week.

Gunnar watched as Bryn inhaled a burger in record time. "You realize chewing is a thing, right?"

Bryn pointed a fry at him. "Leave me alone."

"The food isn't going anywhere."

Bryn grunted, already halfway through a second burger. "You'd better start eating yours before I get to it. Nice choices, by the way."

Gunnar sighed, shaking his head. "Burgers, fries and cheesecake is not revolutionary." He grabbed a plate. "But always hits the spot."

Food made Bryn's headache recede to a manageable throb, which was good because Giles returned to eat. Bryn eyed his steak, barely seared, sitting in a puddle of blood. "Is that still mooing?"

Giles gave him a toothy grin. "I've tasted better."

"I hate you."

"I know. Delicious, isn't it?"

Warden's arrival, with Emmett in tow, was the only thing that stopped the conversation descending into all-out war. Gunnar gathered up plates then shoved the tray out into the corridor. They all sat around the lounge area and Bryn raided the mini-fridge for drinks as they were on Warden's dime.

"You're pale," Warden commented.

"Yeah, getting my freak on does that." Bryn scowled.

"Do you want to spank him, or should I?" Giles addressed his comment to Gunnar. "Or perhaps we should take it in turns?"

"He fucking needs it. I've told you before about calling yourself a freak," Gunnar said, his tone low and growly.

"As have I," Giles contributed.

"Something we agree on."

"God help me," Bryn grumbled. "Emmett, how about some support?"

"They're right, Bryn. You aren't a freak." Emmett's eyes glistened. "I don't like it when you put yourself down."

"Sorry." Bryn couldn't stand upsetting Emmett.

Emmett gave him a shy smile.

"Still like my plan better," Gunnar said.

"Shall we get on?" Warden suggested, except it wasn't a suggestion. Bryn got his thoughts in order while Giles went through his observations of the investor meeting and set the scene with some of the key personnel. Then he handed the floor to Bryn.

"So," Gunnar said, dropping into a chair opposite him. "What exactly did you see?"

Bryn blinked. "Doctor Howard is intending to change some access codes, not sure what to, and she's planning to alter data. Fear and greed were all over her. She's scared of getting caught, but she wants whatever she's being promised."

"And Fuller?"

Bryn shook his head. "He's going to personally destroy some documents. But that's not what stuck with me. He's meeting with Salvatore Russo and from the way he was admiring his Rolex, I'm guessing he's already on the payroll."

Gunnar stiffened. "That's the evidence we need that Russo's definitely behind all this. Not a surprise, I know, but confirmation."

"Yeah," Bryn agreed. "There was no sense of fear from Fuller either."

Giles tapped his fingers on his knee. "What about the security guy?"

Bryn hesitated. "Ty Brunt. He's not just head of security, he's part of whatever's happening. When I brushed against him, I saw..." He swallowed, the image still sharp in his mind. "I saw blood. Too much blood. Unconscious men on gurneys, probably test subjects. Bodies soaked in blood. And a furnace. I'll leave you to work out his intent."

The room fell into silence. It was Giles who spoke. "And the young woman who gave you the USB, Mira?"

"She intends to run because she knows what happens to people who ask the wrong questions. If she's right, they're experimenting on gene-affected subjects without consent, covering up serious neurological damage, and falsifying data." Bryn leaned back against the couch. "This is more than unethical. It's a goddamn slaughterhouse."

"So to summarize," Warden said, "the clinics are dirty with several staff involved up to their necks. The USB is evidence and I'll get our IT people to check it out in a secure environment in case of viruses. What else?"

"We were followed from the clinic," Gunnar said. "I lost them, but it's only a matter of time before they track us down. They'll have security video of the event too. Russo will recognize Bryn if he gets to see it."

Warden nodded. "The three of you can stay put for the night. Bryn needs to recover, and I need time to assess our next move. Emmett and I will head back to base. Keep your doors locked. If they're onto us, they might test the waters."

Gunnar nodded. "The security team is watching all entrances."

"A direct order to do nothing," Bryn said. "I might actually enjoy this."

Gunnar snorted. "Get some sleep while you can. This shit show is only going to get worse."

"Thanks for that. Just what I needed to sweeten my dreams. You want to check under my bed for monsters?"

"Sleep, menace."

Bryn made sure he wiggled his butt a little extra as he sloped off to his room.

Chapter Eight

Bryn awoke to the sound of his phone vibrating against the nightstand. He squinted at the screen. *Four-thirty. Fuck.* The caller ID flashed *Gunnar.*

"Yeah?" Bryn's throat was dry, making his voice rough.

"Get dressed. We've got to go."

"What? Wait, why are you calling me? Aren't you here?" Gunnar had said he'd spend the night on the couch in the suite's sitting area and Bryn had slept better because of it.

"I'm on my way back up there from a briefing with the security team."

"Did something happen?"

"No. It was a quiet night. I was letting them know what's going down. They'll be going back to HQ. We're taking one of their armored vehicles and I have a vest for you."

"Okay…" Bryn shook off his grogginess. "So what *is* going on? Where are we going and do I get breakfast first?"

"The IT guys got into the USB. There's another Thanacrine manufacturing site in the city and Boston PD's going to raid it. Warden got us an invite to the party."

"Oh goody." Bryn's exhaustion from the day before was an unwelcome companion. His head still throbbed a bit, a lingering effect from so many fast reads, but this wasn't something he could sit out. "Mira's information paid off faster than I expected. I hope she's okay."

"Yeah, me too. I'm here. You decent?"

"Does it matter?"

The bedroom door opened and Gunnar appeared, grinning. "Nope. Nice shorts."

Bryn tossed his cell onto the bed. "Perv." He fished in his bag for clean clothes, happy not to have to wear a suit.

"We need to get to some industrial area in the south of the city. It's the third location on the drive."

Bryn pulled on jeans and a long-sleeved black tee. "How many are there in total?"

"Twelve."

"Jesus!"

"Yeah. Not great."

"What's the plan?"

"Cops are going in at six-thirty. Warden wants us there to identify and question anyone who might be connected to the clinic."

"Okay. What about Mira? Any word?"

"Warden had her apartment checked out and she's gone. Smart woman."

"Good. I don't want her ending up as collateral damage."

"Emmett will sort the hotel check-out and I've asked one of the security guys to find us some breakfast."

"So long as it comes with coffee." Bryn grabbed his boots then followed Gunnar into the lounge area. Giles stepped out of his adjoining room, already dressed in another new suit. He eyed Bryn with unconcealed amusement.

"I assume our morning plans have changed?" Giles asked. "Do you own any jeans *without* holes in them?"

"No." Bryn hoped the unsaid 'fuck off' was loud and clear.

"PD's hitting a site linked to the clinic," Gunnar said.

Giles nodded. "Then don't let's keep them waiting."

Bryn knelt to lace his boots, his fingers working automatically while his mind raced. *Twelve manufacturing sites. This has gone way beyond experimental medicine and into mass production.* "You think we'll find anything?" Bryn asked, glancing up at Gunnar.

"If The Hammer's involved, they'll have cleared out already." Gunnar checked his weapon before sliding it into his holster. "He's bound to have his claws into some dirty cops but we might catch some stragglers."

"Or evidence they couldn't move in time," Giles added, adjusting his cufflinks. "Even the most meticulous operations leave traces."

Bryn remembered what he'd seen in Ty Brunt's mind. The unconscious, or maybe dead, men on gurneys, the blood, the furnace. His stomach churned. "I'm still not completely back to normal," he admitted. "Those reads at the clinic took more out of me than usual. They were close together and it was a pressured situation."

"Then we'll control what you have to do," Gunnar said, frowning.

Giles nodded. "We have other resources and methods of extracting information."

Bryn eyed him. "You'd enjoy that, wouldn't you?" Giles remained inscrutable but Bryn detected a glint in his eye.

"Speaking of resources," Gunnar interrupted, tossing a bulletproof vest at Bryn. "Put this on."

Bryn caught it. "Are we expecting trouble?"

"Always where Russo's involved." Gunnar handed another vest to Giles, who accepted it with a slight nod. "And after what you saw in Brunt's mind…"

"Point taken." Bryn slipped the vest on over his shirt, adjusting the straps.

"The armored vehicle's downstairs," Gunnar continued, checking his phone. "Boston PD sent the coordinates. We've got forty minutes to get there for a briefing before the raid starts."

"Let's hope traffic's light."

In the pre-dawn, the hallway was deserted as they made their way to the elevator. When the doors slid open to the underground parking garage, a black SUV with tinted windows waited near the exit, engine running.

"Huh, I was expecting something more…chunky," Bryn said.

"The glass and body shell are armored," Gunnar said. "Were you picturing a tank?"

Two members of the GCR's security team stood beside the vehicle, nodding in recognition as they approached.

"All quiet still, sir," one reported to Gunnar. "No suspicious activity."

"Good. We'll take it from here."

Gunnar slid into the driver's seat, Bryn taking shotgun while Giles settled in the back.

"Food?" Bryn asked hopefully as they pulled out of the garage.

Gunnar pointed to a paper bag on the console between them. "Breakfast sandwiches, from the smell. And there's coffee in the cup holders."

"You're a saint." Bryn grabbed the coffee first, the cup's warmth seeping into his cold fingers.

"Security guys always know where to get their hands on decent food and coffee. It's on the qualification requirements for the job."

"I appreciate their expertise."

As they navigated through empty streets, the city still mostly asleep, Bryn couldn't shake a growing sense of unease. Whatever they found at this site would change things. The evidence on Mira's drive, combined with his reads at the clinic, painted a picture of corruption and cruelty that went deeper than they'd imagined.

"You're quiet," Gunnar observed, glancing over.

Bryn took another sip of coffee. "Just thinking."

"About?"

"About what Russo's planning."

"We'll find out one way or another," Giles said from the back seat.

Bryn delved in the bag of food. "You want anything?" he asked Giles.

"Coffee is fine for me."

"Gunnar?"

"I ate already."

Bryn grabbed a still-warm sandwich. "Oh, yum."

"Heathen."

"Can it, Giles. A sausage patty, egg and cheese…food of the gods, and these hash browns are gourmet."

Gunnar's cell rang and he answered through the car's speaker system. "Ericson here."

"It's Warden. There's been a development." Warden's calm, controlled voice filled the vehicle. "Boston PD did a preliminary reconnaissance. The site is active. They've detected thermal signatures indicating at least two dozen people inside."

"At this hour?" Bryn leaned forward. "That's not normal shift work."

"Exactly."

"We're fifteen minutes out," Gunnar replied.

"Make it ten," Warden ordered. "I don't think this can wait until six-thirty."

The call ended and Gunnar accelerated.

"So much for a leisurely breakfast," Bryn muttered, stuffing half a sandwich into his mouth.

"Eat fast," Gunnar advised. "I've got a feeling we're going to need all the energy we can get."

The industrial district loomed ahead, a patchwork of warehouses and manufacturing plants.

"There—" Gunnar pointed. "Northeast corner."

Bryn swallowed the last of his sandwich, crumpling the wrapper. "Doesn't look like much." It was a nondescript concrete building with security lights illuminating its perimeter.

"That's the point," Giles remarked from the backseat. "Anonymity is essential for operations like this."

Police vehicles were gathered a block away, positioned out of the line of sight of any cameras to avoid detection. Gunnar pulled alongside them then cut the engine.

"Showtime," he said. "Ike Reynolds is in charge of the op. I know him. Good man."

Captain Reynolds met them as they exited the SUV, his expression grim. He shook Gunnar's hand before acknowledging Bryn and Giles with a curt nod.

"Glad you made it," Reynolds said. "Things have gotten weird. Thermal imaging initially showed twenty-seven distinct heat signatures inside. Most concentrated in what appears to be the main production floor, with a few scattered in what we believe are office spaces."

"Movement patterns?" Gunnar asked.

"That's the strange part. They aren't moving. We thought maybe the heat was from machines at first, but the signatures are definitely human. We also detected unusual power consumption. Whatever they're doing in there, its drawing serious electricity."

"What's the entry plan?" Giles asked.

Reynolds led them to the hood of his car where a schematic was spread out. "The building has four access points — main entrance here, loading dock on the east side, fire exit on the west, and what appears to be a staff entrance in the back." He jabbed his finger at each location. "We'll hit all four simultaneously."

"Any intel on armed personnel?" Gunnar asked.

"Can't confirm, but we're proceeding as if they're hostile."

"Russo doesn't hire rent-a-cops," Gunnar pointed out. "If there's security, they'll be professional. Ex-military, most likely."

Reynolds eyed him. "My people know what they're walking into."

Bryn studied the schematic, visualizing the layout. "Any basement levels?"

"None that we can detect, but the building plans filed with the city are twenty years old. Plenty of time for unauthorized modifications."

"Where do you want us positioned?" Gunnar asked.

"Stay with me in the primary strike team," Reynolds replied. "I need your eyes on whatever we find in there."

A tactical officer approached, radio in hand. "Sir, perimeter teams are in position. SWAT is ready on your mark."

Reynolds checked his watch. "We move in five. Get your people in position."

As the officer hurried away, Reynolds turned back to them. "Last chance to back out. Once this starts, it's going to move fast."

"We're in," Gunnar confirmed without hesitation.

"Good."

They followed Reynolds to the tactical van where his team was making final preparations. Officers in black body armor checked weapons and communications equipment, expressions grim.

"You sure about this?" Bryn asked Giles as they hung back from the others. "This isn't exactly your kind of operation."

"My kind of operation?" Giles gave a feral grin as he removed his jacket and tie. "I've been in the GCR since you were in diapers." He rolled up his sleeves and pocketed his gold cufflinks.

"Yeah, but not doing this." Bryn gestured to the SWAT team checking their weapons.

"There's a lot about me you don't know."

Bryn didn't have a chance to respond as Gunnar approached with three radio earpieces.

"Channel three," he said, handing them out. "Keep radio discipline. Short, clear communications only."

Bryn inserted the earpiece, wincing as static crackled through it. "No fancy heroics, right?" he said to Gunnar. "We're here to identify and question, not lead the charge, and I have a vested interest in all your bits staying intact. Giles — not so bothered."

"Stay close and follow my lead."

Reynolds gathered his team for final instructions. "Remember, we're looking for both evidence and potential victims. Anyone not in obvious security or staff clothing is to be treated as a possible hostage, but also a potential threat until proven otherwise. Clear the rooms, secure any evidence, and watch for booby traps or self-destruct mechanisms."

The mention of self-destruct made Bryn's stomach tighten. "They'd do that? With their own people inside?"

"Wouldn't be the first time," Reynolds replied, sounding grim. "These operations value secrecy above human life."

The radio crackled. "All teams in position, Captain."

Reynolds tapped his ear piece. "Copy that. On my mark." He checked his watch one final time. "Three…two…one… Execute!"

The tactical teams moved simultaneously on all four entrances. The main breach team surged forward, their battering ram making short work of the front door.

"Police! Down on the ground!" Shouts echoed through the building as they rushed inside.

Bryn followed Gunnar, heart pounding. The reception area was empty, the front desk and visitor chairs abandoned. The tactical team split up, clearing side offices before moving toward the main production floor. It was the smell that hit Bryn first. Antiseptic overlaid with something chemical that he couldn't place. The fluorescent lighting was harsh, revealing a sprawling open space filled with laboratory benches and equipment. And people. Dozens of them, just as the thermal imaging had indicated, but not the way Bryn had expected.

"Jesus Christ," Gunnar exclaimed. Workers in white lab coats littered the floor, apparently unconscious.

"Police! Hands where we can see them!" Reynolds shouted, but not one person moved.

Bryn approached the nearest figure, a young woman. Her eyes were open but blank and unblinking. "Hey," he said, waving his hand in front of her face. No reaction. "I think she's dead."

Around the room, officers were finding the same thing. Nearly two dozen people lay dead.

Gunnar came across to Bryn, his expression dark. "Don't touch anything. A medical team will be here soon."

"Captain!" A shout from the far side of the floor drew their attention. "You'd better come see this!"

They hurried toward the voice, passing through a set of heavy double doors into what appeared to be a more specialized area. The room was colder and full of medical equipment. Curtained cubicles lined one wall. Three of them were occupied.

"Gene-affected," Bryn observed. The man in the first chamber had visible lupine features, the other two were pale enough to be sanguines. All three were connected to complex monitoring equipment and were either unconscious or sedated.

"Test subjects, I guess," Gunnar sounded disgusted.

Reynolds turned to a nearby officer. "Get a medical team in here now. And find someone who can safely disconnect these people."

"Sir," another officer called from a computer terminal, "you might want to look at this."

The screen showed a countdown timer. 03:42… 03:41… 03:40…

"Shit!" Reynolds grabbed his radio. "All units, we have a potential self-destruct sequence. Begin evacuation procedures right now. We have three minutes.

"We need to find the server room," Giles said. "That's where the central data will be stored."

"We don't have time!" Reynolds argued.

"We make time," Gunnar countered. "Or this whole operation will be for nothing."

Bryn spotted an unmarked door. "There, that might be it." He pointed.

"Go," Reynolds ordered. "You have three minutes. Not a second more."

Gunnar, Bryn and Giles rushed toward the door and found it locked with an electronic keypad.

"Can you just, you know, rip it off?" Bryn asked Gunnar.

"I have a better idea. Stand back." Gunnar grabbed a nearby chair then swung it into the lock with lupine-powered force. The lock smashed, shattered plastic fragments flew everywhere and the door clicked open.

Inside, rack-mounted servers hummed, blinking lights reflecting off the walls. "This is it!" Giles moved to the main terminal. "Explains the power usage."

"Can you stop the countdown?" Bryn asked.

Giles typed rapidly. "Unlikely. But I can do this." He pulled a device from his pocket. "This is a specialized data drive. I can download everything before it's destroyed."

"How long?" Gunnar snapped.

"Two minutes, maybe less."

From the server room door, Bryn watched as the evacuation continued, precious seconds ticking away. The three gene-affected individuals from the chambers had been disconnected from their equipment and were being carried out on stretchers.

Bryn's earpiece buzzed. "Sixty seconds!" Reynolds' voice warned. "Everyone out now!"

"Gunnar?"

"Almost done. Go!"

"Like hell," Bryn retorted.

Giles was still working, the data transfer in progress.

"We need to get out," Gunnar insisted.

"Thirty more seconds," Giles replied without looking up.

The terminal beeped. "Transfer complete." Giles yanked the drive free, tucking it into an inner pocket. "Now we run."

Bryn was already moving and they sprinted for the exit, the countdown in Bryn's ear. The main production floor was already empty, the bodies gone. They shot through the broken front door as a series of muffled thumps sounded from inside the building.

"Get down!" Gunnar shouted, tackling Bryn to the pavement. But the expected explosion never came. Instead, the lights inside the facility went dark, and smoke began pouring from vents in the roof.

"Not bombs," Giles observed as they stood. "Data destruction. They're frying the electronics and hard drives."

"Everyone accounted for?" Reynolds demanded, moving through the gathered officers.

"All clear," one of officers reported. "But we have bodies laid out along the sidewalk."

Bryn watched the smoke rising from the building. "They knew we were coming."

"They did," Gunnar agreed.

"Those people were left there to die."

"Seems so. Russo is brutal."

More emergency vehicles began arriving, ambulances and additional police units.

"What now?" Bryn asked.

"Now," Giles said, patting his pocket where the data drive rested, "we find out what they were up to."

Forensic teams in hazmat suits approached the building and staff from the ME's office were already at work, moving methodically between the bodies laid out on the sidewalk. Bryn watched as paramedics tended to the three gene-affected individuals they'd rescued. The lupine was growling as an EMT tried to insert an IV. Gunnar walked across to them. "Careful," Gunnar warned. "We don't know what they've been doing to him."

"You're a wolf?" the patient asked.

"Yeah," Gunnar grinned. "Gunnar Ericson, GCR. How are you doing?"

"I feel like hammered crap. Went into a clinic for the mandatory blood draw and that's the last I remember. Where the fuck am I?"

"It's a long story. Let the medics get you sorted first, okay? They're the good guys."

"Okay. Name's Orwell Armitage, by the way. I think I saw you at the Wolf Run."

"Yeah? Cool. We'll be in touch, Orwell. Get yourself sorted first, okay?"

"Yeah. Not feeling so hot."

Gunnar rejoined Bryn and Giles. Captain Reynolds came over, not looking happy. "Initial opinion is that all the lab workers were poisoned. Some kind of cyanide derivative that activated through the ventilation system. Happened recently enough that they were still warm enough to show up on the scans. The room where the others were was on a different system, so it was targeted action."

"Mass suicide?" Bryn asked, incredulous.

"Or murder," Giles replied. "Ruthless."

Bryn shivered at the trace of admiration in Giles' tone. *That man's psyche is all kinds of wrong.*

Chapter Nine

A black SUV pulled up to the perimeter of the cordoned-off area, and a woman in a tailored pants suit stepped out. She flashed her credentials to the officers manning the barricade and, having been waved through, walked toward their group.

"Captain Reynolds," she said, her tone crisp and authoritative. "I'm Special Agent Mercer, Federal Task Force. This is now a federal case. Give me a quick update."

Reynolds bristled. "With all due respect, Agent...Mercer, this is still an active crime scene under city jurisdiction."

"Not anymore." She handed him a document. "Presidential directive. All matters concerning illegal gene modification fall under our purview."

Gunnar stepped forward. "We've got nearly two dozen dead, Agent. This isn't just about gene mods. And as GCR operatives, I believe *we* have jurisdiction."

Mercer's eyes were cold. "And we have reason to believe this facility is connected to a network of illegal enhancement operations. The implications go far beyond local concerns." Her gaze shifted to Giles. "Did you recover any data?"

Gunnar moved to position himself between Giles and the federal agent. Bryn leaned toward him. "Something doesn't feel right," he whispered.

"Agreed," Gunnar replied. "The timing is too convenient. And I've never heard of a task force overriding GCR authority."

"Something you'd like to share, Detective?" Mercer glared.

Giles cleared his throat. "Perhaps we should keep things cordial." He held out his hand. "Giles Delacourt."

"Gunnar Ericson." Gunnar shook hands too, which left an opening for Bryn.

"Bryn Ashton. You said you were from a federal task force?"

The agent couldn't avoid the handshakes or the question. "That's right. Now about the data..."

"She's lying," Bryn announced. "I only had time for a truth read."

"*You're* the augur?" There was a sneer in the fake agent's voice.

"Nice to meet you too," Bryn retorted. "Whoever you are."

"So where *are* you from?" Captain Reynolds asked, pulling his gun. "Or do I need to arrest you?"

"That's above your pay grade, Captain."

"We'll continue this conversation at the precinct. Standard protocols still require GCR to file initial findings on gene-related crimes. If you come up with a satisfactory explanation for your presence, I'm sure the intelligence will be shared."

Mercer's lips thinned into a tight smile. She pulled out a cell. "One call is all that's needed."

Gunnar didn't wait for further discussion. He nodded to Giles and they headed toward their car.

"We need to move fast," Giles said once they were inside the vehicle. "There's something very wrong here."

"Where do you think she's from?"

Gunnar's brow creased. "She might be official. If she is, the question is, what department? If she isn't, that's a whole other ball game. Reynolds will keep her tied up for a while so let's go find out what was worth killing two dozen people to keep secret."

As they pulled away from the scene, Bryn glanced in the rearview mirror. He didn't envy Captain Reynold's position.

Once they were back at HQ, Bryn's sense of relief was strong. The morning could have gone so much worse than it did and he was still pissed at both Gunnar and Giles for putting themselves at risk. He stomped upstairs to the apartment while Giles went to check in with the geek squad and Gunnar headed to Warden's office. Bryn got himself a glass of milk then dug two Twinkies out of the cupboard. He didn't sit but lounged against the kitchen counter, mulling over the events of the morning. It wasn't easy to stay mad at Gunnar when not so long ago Bryn had put himself in danger at the hands of a serial killer.

So not the same. He yawned. *Maybe I should take a nap.* His cell buzzed with an incoming message. *Or maybe not.* A quick glance had him swallowing the last bite of his Twinkie. Warden didn't like to be kept waiting so he made his way to Warden's office and found the others waiting for him.

"Finished brooding?" Giles asked.

"Fuck off. You could have gotten my partner killed today, Giles."

Giles gave an infuriating shrug. "That's the job."

There were too many witnesses in the room to stab him with Warden's paper knife or bash him over the head with a stapler. Giles smirked like he knew what Bryn was thinking and Gunnar moved between them.

Warden tapped his pen on the edge of his desk. "Thanks to your excellent work at the investor event yesterday, we have data backing up our suspicions that this is about more than a mafia turf war. Russo has deep pockets but his resources aren't infinite. I'm certain there's other funding behind this and after today's encounter with *Agent* Mercer, if that was even her name, I have concerns that there's something going on at a government level."

Giles nodded. "There have always been factions that don't approve of the approach to management of the gene-affected. It's one more flavor of prejudice."

"And if you can't eliminate a problem, you turn it to your advantage," Gunnar said. "Lupines are already stronger, faster and have sharper senses. Sanguines heal fast, some" — he eyed Giles — "move even faster than lupines. With those abilities enhanced further, both would make excellent cannon fodder in any frontline action."

"So what's The Hammer getting out of this?" Bryn asked. "There has to be something in it for him if he's doing the dirty work, manufacturing the drug then pumping it into unsuspecting victims."

"I agree," Warden said. "But that remains a mystery for now. Next, Bryn should read the victims recovered from today's raid. One of the sanguines has since died, he never regained consciousness, but that leaves us with two potential sources of information."

"Where are they?" Gunnar asked.

"West Roxbury VA Medical Center," Warden responded. "Emmett will make the arrangements for you to visit later this afternoon. I want you and Giles to accompany Bryn in case either of the victims needs reassurance. They'll respond better to those who are gene-affected in the same way as they are."

Fabulous. More time with my least favorite person. Bryn glared at everyone. "Someone bring snacks or we're gonna have a problem."

After such an early start, and an adrenaline-fueled morning, all Bryn wanted to do was vegetate on his beanbag and eat junk food. Neither was an option. Emmett had commandeered the conference room so they relocated and Bryn was stuck while Gunnar and Giles strategized about lines of questioning. Warden had stayed in his office and, as no one was asking Bryn for input, he had time to think. That was a mistake. "Who's the person at the top of The Hammer's list of people he'd most like to kill?" he blurted out.

"What?" Gunnar stared at him.

"Think about it. We were talking about his motivation for doing all of this. I get that a few super-soldiers might be of use to him in his line of work, but he could have gotten them keeping his drug business small scale. So what would be more valuable to him?" Bryn didn't want to give voice to the answer.

"Oh fuck." Gunnar growled, the sound deep in his throat.

"Yeah, that about sums it up," Bryn muttered.

"What are you two going on about?" Giles asked.

Gunnar shook his head. "Jesus, Giles, for a genius scientist type you sure are slow on the uptake. The answer to both of those questions is the same. Bryn."

Light dawned in Giles' eyes. "Fuck."

"After bringing down The Hammer's accountant, Bryn has to be top of his hit list. Russo already had a chance to kill him and didn't take it," Gunnar said. "That can only mean he sees more value in keeping him alive. If Bryn could be compelled to work for him, Russo would be assured of loyalty in his organization."

"Not only that, he'd be able to extract information from his enemies and rivals," Giles contributed.

"So what are the odds that Russo has been promised Bryn as his prize for orchestrating this shit show?"

"And they've both found a clue," Bryn said, under his breath.

"Don't act like a brat," Gunnar said.

"Damn lupine hearing. Anyway, I think I'm entitled to act up, don't you?"

"No," Gunnar and Giles replied in unison.

"You two ganging up on me is getting real old."

"Suck it up, buttercup."

"Really, Gunnar?"

Gunnar patted Bryn's hand, letting his touch linger. Bryn's face heated like he'd entered a sauna. Giles smirked at him but didn't say anything.

I need a cold shower. Fuck me, Gunnar is one kinky wolf. He wasn't going to get the image of Gunnar indulging in some ass play while Bryn was tied to the bed out of his mind for some time. *If that's his intent, I really hope he acts on it.*

"So nice to see such a...close...working relationship has developed between you two," Giles said.

"You wouldn't know a good relationship if it smacked you in the face," Bryn grumbled. "Though, in the name of science, I'm willing to test that theory out."

Giles chuckled. "Maybe not. But it sure is entertaining watching you dance around each other. When are you going to take him properly in hand, Detective?"

"When I'm good and ready," Gunnar grumbled. "Not that it's any of your goddamn business."

Giles shrugged. "Does Warden know about you two?"

"More than we do," Gunnar said.

Bryn wasn't sure what that meant but he needed the subject changed and fast. "I'm hungry." That seemed to be a safe topic and Gunnar loved food.

"I'll bet you are." Giles didn't as much as blink as he spoke.

"Let's find Emmett then hunt down some food," Bryn said, getting desperate.

Gunnar took pity on him. "We can do that. I'll make grilled cheese. I also spotted apple pie in the apartment fridge."

Giles gestured them away. "Go. I'm not hungry."

Don't recall asking him to join us or for his permission. Bryn scowled but couldn't stay mad for long when Gunnar's grilled cheese was on offer.

* * * *

Three hours later they were signing in at the hospital. Gunnar had driven a roundabout route, constantly checking for a tail. He didn't spot anyone and relaxed once they'd entered the secure premises. The three of them were escorted to a room with two beds where Orwell Armitage, the lupine, and the sanguine, whose name was Trent Gordon, were being looked after.

The room was a study in institutional sterility. The off-white walls were broken by a single window covered by gray vertical blinds. The metal-framed beds had smooth covers with neat corners. There wasn't too much in the way of medical paraphernalia, which Bryn took as a good sign. A rolling table extended across each bed for meals and to one side of each sat a single squat metal chair. The air carried the distinct scent of disinfectant and Gunnar kept wrinkling his nose. Privacy curtains were drawn back to the wall.

The sanguine occupied the bed furthest from the door. His skin, which would have been naturally pale, now had a translucent quality with blue veins mapped beneath the surface. His eyes were ringed by circles so dark they seemed bruised. His breathing was shallow and he exuded weariness. Giles walked across to talk to him, indicating that the others should talk to Orwell first.

The lupine was sitting up, his big frame hunched and his cheeks flushed. When Bryn got closer he could make out a yellow tinge to the bloodshot whites of Orwell's eyes. Orwell raised a hand in greeting to Gunnar.

"You look terrible," Gunnar said.

Bryn winced but apparently it was the right thing to say because Orwell snorted with laughter.

"Say it like it is, Detective."

"Call me Gunnar, and this is my partner Bryn."

"The augur. The doc told me you were coming. You want to take a peek in my head, huh?"

"We think it might help us track down whoever is responsible for what happened to you, and others."

"I don't remember anything beyond arriving at the clinic."

"That's okay. If your subconscious has buried something, Bryn will still be able to see it."

"Wow. Okay. If it helps. Are you gonna do vamp boy as well? He's been real sick."

"If he's okay with it. Our colleague over there is a vamp too."

"It helps you know, having someone around who knows…"

Gunnar nodded. "Bryn is very good at this. You won't feel a thing and I'll be the one asking a few questions, okay?"

"Sure. Let's go."

Bryn took the metal chair and gave what he hoped was a reassuring smile. "The wrist works best," he said as he grasped Orwell's arm. "I'm going to look at your most powerful memory first, okay?"

"Yeah, tell me what you're seeing."

"Okay." Bryn closed his eyes and the images came instantly. "I'm seeing blood, a pool of it on the floor of the room. I think it's a lab. It's not your blood. You feel… Confused… Horrified, but you can't move however hard you try. There's a needle in the back of your hand taped in place. You can feel it. You're watching two orderlies drag a body away. They're smearing blood across the white floor. It's a stark contrast. The body, a vamp I'd guess, has blood coming from his eyes and mouth, his ears, and from beneath him. The scrubs he's wearing are stained dark…"

It took effort not to yank his hand away. Bryn opened his eyes to a concerned expression on Gunnar's face. He gave a quick nod to show he was okay even as a slow throb started up behind his eyes. Orwell seemed shell shocked.

"That's all news to me. What the fuck is going on at that place?"

"Did you overhear any conversations?" Gunnar asked.

"Not that I recall."

"Truth," Bryn confirmed.

"Did you get names of any other patients?"

"No. Fuck, I'm useless, aren't I?"

"Of course not," Gunnar said. "You're the victim here."

"What did they put in me?"

"It's a drug called Thanacrine. It enhances gene abilities," Gunnar said. "But so far, it's failed. Subjects have developed severe psychosis and become extremely violent."

"I didn't get that way, though. At least, I don't think I did."

"Truth," Bryn said. "The drug is being refined. It's possible you were given a new derivative."

"Lucky me."

Gunnar frowned. "Was there any particular reason you went to the clinic you did?"

"I got an invitation by email with a specific appointment. It seemed legit because I was due my annual blood draw, though thinking about it, previously I've had a reminder to make a date with the clinic of my choice. Guess I assumed the process had changed."

Bryn gave a brief nod to indicate Orwell was telling the truth as he saw it.

"You still have the email?"

"I don't think my cell or clothes made it out of the clinic. Could be anywhere. But if I log onto a computer, it should still be there on the server."

"We'll arrange for that to happen so you can forward it to GCR's tech people," Gunnar said. "Might be useful. Thanks, Orwell. Bryn needs to take a look at your vamp friend now but if anything comes back to you that you think might be relevant, you contact the GCR and ask for me, okay?"

"Sure. Think I need a nap. All I seem to do is sleep."

His eyes were already closing so Bryn and Gunnar moved to the next bed.

The man huddled beneath his covers watched them approach. His eyes, pupils dilated, tracked Bryn's every movement. Giles vacated the chair.

"I'm going to track down some blood for him. He's hungry, and I don't mean he has the munchies. Cookies and milk isn't going to cover this."

"I can't believe it sounds appealing," Trent said. "I've never craved blood before."

"The effects of the drug should wear off in time," Giles said. "If you can avoid sinking your teeth into our augur in the meantime, that would be nice." He grinned and the vamp bared his teeth in response.

"No promises."

Gunnar growled.

"Oh, and the wolfy one has no sense of humor."

"Not helping, Giles." Bryn took a seat. "Giles told you about what I'm going to do?"

"Yeah. You're a bit of a rarity."

"I don't recommend it. You consent?"

"These people need stopping, so yes. Do your worst."

Bryn grasped Trent's wrist. "Gunnar, you want to start?"

"How about you tell us what you recall first, Mr. Gordon?" Gunnar said.

"Call me Trent. Mr. Gordon is my pops. Not much. I had an invite to attend the clinic for the annual blood draw. I was due so it seemed fine."

"Your invite came by email?"

"Yes."

"Carry on."

"The only difference to previous dates was that the nurse used a vein in the back of my hand instead of my arm. I remember a scratch as the needle went in, then nothing until I came round in that place you found us. The hunger for blood was all-consuming but I was strapped down. I fought the restraints and broke them — I was much stronger than usual. I think it took three of them to get me on the floor. Then there was a jab in my thigh. It must have been a sedative because everything kind of faded. Next thing I knew you guys arrived and there were tubes coming out of my body. Couldn't decide if I was dead or alive."

"I'm sorry you went through that," Gunnar said. "Bryn is going to take a look at your memories now. It's not that we don't believe you, Bryn knows you're being truthful, but there might be something in there that your brain is protecting you from."

"Go ahead."

Bryn concentrated. What he saw was filmed by a blood red haze. Trent's strongest memory was of Orwell being strapped to a bed, of men in scrubs leaning over him. Bryn picked up a combination of lust and hunger before the memory went dark.

He gave the sanguine a brief smile. "Your strongest memory is of Orwell being brought into the room we found you in. I think you wanted to eat him. In more ways than one." He grinned.

The sanguine scowled. "You're fucking dangerous, aren't you?"

Bryn laughed. "Sorry. I can't filter what I see and I can't lie about it. It is what it is."

"And I think we're done here." Gunnar nudged Bryn's chair with his foot just as Giles returned with a blood bag and a nurse.

"Talk to him," Bryn whispered to Trent. "You never know, and wolves are hot."

Gunnar pulled him away. "You know I can hear you, right?"

"Can you? Wow, who knew?" Bryn pulled his gloves on and pushed his dark glasses up his nose.

"Will you two stop acting like a married couple?" Giles snapped. "Almost everyone in this room has enhanced hearing."

"Oops. My bad." Bryn's face heated but he put his lack of caution down to his now pounding head and an urgent need to sleep. "Time to go."

Chapter Ten

Bryn slumped in the passenger seat of the armored car, his head against the window. The pounding behind his eyes had intensified, and the brightness of the afternoon sun wasn't helping. Despite the warmth of the vehicle, a chill seeped through his body.

"You okay?" Gunnar asked, glancing over as he navigated through traffic.

"Peachy. The usual post-read hangover." He adjusted his dark glasses, pressing them against the bridge of his nose. "It'd be nice if I'd had an actual drink to warrant it. Do you think any of that was useful?"

Gunnar shrugged. "Neither of them told us much we didn't already know. The email invitations might lead somewhere. That's a change in procedure worth looking into."

"And the hunger from our sanguine friend was...intense." Bryn shuddered. "Whatever they pumped into him definitely enhanced his natural vamp instincts."

From the back seat, Giles leaned forward. "The blood bag seemed to help stabilize him. His pupils were already returning to normal when we left."

"Lucky Orwell," Bryn murmured with a smirk.

Gunnar shot him a look. "You're incorrigible."

"Just trying to spread joy and romance wherever I go."

"I'm sure Orwell will appreciate your matchmaking efforts," Giles said.

Bryn winced as they hit a pothole. "Can we stop somewhere? I need food and painkillers, not necessarily in that order."

Gunnar nodded. "There's a diner up ahead. We can grab something to go."

Twenty minutes later, armed with hot chocolate, loaded hotdogs and fries, they were back on the road to GCR headquarters. Bryn had swallowed two pills from Gunnar's ever-present supply and was now picking at his food, his appetite dulled by pain. He forced himself to eat anyway, knowing that his body needed it.

"You should rest when we get back," Gunnar said, his tone leaving no room for argument.

"Yes, mom," Bryn replied, though the prospect of his beanbag or bed was growing more appealing by the minute.

"Eat your dog."

"I...never mind." Bryn concentrated on his food. Gunnar's care was kind of cool.

When they arrived at GCR HQ, Emmett met them in the hall, tablet in hand. "Warden wants a debrief," he informed them. "Conference room in fifteen."

Bryn groaned. "Can't you tell him I'm dying?"

"I could," Emmett replied with a slight smile, "but you know he'd tell you to walk it off and get back to work."

"Fine," Bryn sighed. "But I'm bringing coffee. Gunnar got me hot chocolate on the way here and I'm already having caffeine withdrawal symptoms."

"Already arranged." Emmett's efficiency was impressive. "Oh, and there's mail for you, Bryn." He handed over an envelope.

Bryn stared at the envelope. The precise, artistic handwriting was instantly recognizable. His stomach roiled.

Gunnar caught the change in his expression. "What is it?"

"Dr. Templeton," Bryn said, holding up the envelope. "Seems my pen pal misses me."

Something flickered across Gunnar's face — too quick to identify, but enough to make Bryn pause. "What?" he asked.

"Nothing," Gunnar replied, too quickly. "Where did it come from?"

"Emmett just gave it to me."

"It was in Warden's mail when I collected it this morning. I put it to one side because it was addressed to Bryn. I should have thought…"

"Not your fault, Emmett. Things around here have been hectic," Gunnar said.

"I still should have realized. I've seen one of those envelopes before, after all." Emmett nibbled on his lower lip. "I'm so dumb."

"You're as far from dumb as it's possible to get. Like as far away as Pluto, or as far away as I'd like Giles to be. No, wait. That'd be in another galaxy at least." Bryn gave him a quick hug. "I'll open it during the debrief.

Warden will want to know what our friendly neighborhood psycho has to say."

The conference room was cool and quiet, a minor relief for the hammering in Bryn's head. Warden sat at the head of the table, his expression as unreadable as ever. Giles had positioned himself by the window, leaning against the sill, arms crossed. Emmett busied himself setting up the coffees for everyone.

Bryn slid into a chair and reached for the mug Emmett offered him. "Thanks, Emmett."

"We were discussing the mysterious federal agent," Warden said. "Agent Mercer, if that's even her name."

"She's not in any federal database I can access," Emmett added. "Not under that name."

"The question is, who is she really working for?" Warden said. "That's our primary concern. If there's a government faction involved in this Thanacrine operation, we need to identify it."

"Or she could be one of Russo's people," Giles suggested. "A convincing federal agent would have clearance to remove evidence before we could analyze it."

Bryn half-listened to the conversation, his attention drawn to the envelope folded in his jeans pocket. He pulled it out and placed it on the table.

"We might have a more immediate problem," he said, interrupting whatever Warden had been saying. "I got another letter from Everard Templeton."

The room fell silent. Warden scowled.

"When?"

"Just now. Emmett gave it to me when we arrived."

"Open it," Warden instructed. "We know there won't be any trace evidence."

Bryn slid his finger under the flap and tore it open. Inside was a single sheet of ivory paper, covered front and back with Templeton's elegant script. Bryn took a breath and began to read aloud.

"My dear Bryn,

I trust this letter finds you well, though I suspect 'well' might be a relative term in your line of work. I've been following your recent activities with interest, as much as one can from afar. The Walmart situation was fascinating. I'm glad you survived the encounter. And Thanacrine – a drug that enhances gene expression? What wonderful potential for chaos.

I've been reflecting on our last encounter, particularly that moment when you were in my mind. Such an intimate connection we shared. I wonder if you still think of it, as I do.

I'm curious. Do you have nightmares about me? I imagine what you saw in my head left quite an impression. Does Detective Ericson comfort you when you wake up screaming? Your relationship with him is…intriguing. The wolf protecting his mate. How primal.

Speaking of wolves, I've been studying some fascinating research on lupine gene expression. Did you know there are theories about dormant genetic triggers that could exponentially increase already enhanced abilities? I wonder if your friend Mr. Russo is aware of these studies. His pharmaceutical endeavors sound rather aligned with such research.

I do hope you're being careful, Bryn. There are so many predators in the world, and not all of them wear their nature as openly as I do, or as your detective does with his charming canine attributes.

Until next time, Everard

P.S. Give my regards to Detective Ericson. I trust he's shared my previous correspondence."

Bryn glanced up from the letter, which he was crumpling in his fist. Warden's expression was thunderous, Giles looked thoughtful, and Emmett was already making notes on his tablet.

"Previous correspondence? What's he talking about, Gunnar?" Bryn asked.

Gunnar shifted in his seat. "There was another letter a while back."

"And you didn't see fit to share?" Bryn's tone could have frozen fire. "What the hell, Gunnar?"

It was Warden who spoke. "You'd just come out of dealing with the Walmart killer, Drake Romano. I made a judgment call."

"A judgment call?" Bryn could feel his temper rising. "It wasn't your call to make!"

"I disagree," Warden said.

"Where's this letter now?"

"In my desk drawer."

"Get it. Now." Bryn was at boiling point. He felt sick.

After a nod from Warden, Emmett left the room. The tension in his wake was palpable.

"The doctor appears to have sources of information he shouldn't," Giles observed, breaking the silence. "The specifics about the Thanacrine drug and its effects are particularly concerning."

"And how does he know about Russo's interest in Bryn?" Gunnar added.

Bryn's headache was intensifying by the second. "That's what I'd like to know."

Emmett returned a moment later, envelope in hand. "Here," he said, placing it on the table.

Warden opened the envelope and extracted another single sheet of paper. He pushed it across to Bryn. "It's a lot more succinct."

"*I haven't forgotten you. See you soon, Everard.*" Bryn swallowed.

"It was mailed from Dallas, Texas."

Bryn examined the envelope from the latest letter. "This one was sent from Tulsa, Oklahoma." He stared at the two envelopes side by side, his vision tunneling until they were all he could see. The room around him faded away, the others' voices becoming distant and muffled as if underwater. The pounding in his head kept time with his heartbeat. "And you all decided I was too fragile to handle it?" He looked around the table, taking in each face. "A committee decision on my mental health, was it?"

"It wasn't like that," Gunnar started.

"Really? Because from where I'm sitting, it looks exactly like that." Bryn pushed back from the table. "You kept information from me about a psychopath who's been messing with my head. Who's clearly been tracking my movements."

Warden leaned forward. "The decision was mine, Bryn. I stand by it."

"Of course you do." Bryn laughed, a hollow sound devoid of humor. "Because you always know best, right? The omniscient Warden, chess master extraordinaire, moving his pieces around the board."

Gunnar reached out, his hand hovering near Bryn's arm but not quite touching. "You had a lot going on —"

"So what?" Bryn snapped, jerking away from Gunnar's attempted touch. "That's my problem to deal with. My trauma, my choice."

"Your trauma affects the team," Warden countered. "It affects our operations."

"So I'm a liability now?"

"That's not what he meant," Emmett interjected, looking distressed.

Giles moved away from the window. "Perhaps we should focus on what Templeton's letters tell us, while keeping the Thanacrine case separate. They appear to be unrelated matters."

"Oh, now you want my input?" Bryn stood up, swaying as his headache intensified with the movement. "Sorry, I'm apparently too unstable to be trusted with information about my own life."

Gunnar stood as well, his expression pained. "Bryn..."

"Don't." Bryn held up a hand. "Just...don't." He took a deep breath, forcing himself to regain control. When he spoke again, his voice was steadier. "Templeton is fixated on me. His references to the Walmart case and Russo are him showing off. He's letting me know he can keep tabs on my work."

"I agree," Warden said, surprising everyone. "Templeton's obsession has always been with you, not our cases. He's using the information to establish a connection. To unsettle you."

Bryn paced to the window, needing distance from the table, from Gunnar, from the letters. "He's playing a game. Letting me know he's watching. That wherever I go, whatever I do, he's aware of it." He pressed his fingertips to his temples, trying to alleviate the pressure there.

"His mention of lupine gene expression and Russo is likely incidental. Information he's gathered to demonstrate his reach," Giles observed. "I doubt he has any actual interest in the Thanacrine case."

Bryn turned back to face the room. "Which means, and I can't believe I'm saying this, that Giles is right.

We need to handle these as separate situations. The Thanacrine case is our priority as a team. Templeton…is my problem."

"No," Warden said. "Templeton is GCR's problem. He's targeting one of our own."

"And I can handle it," Bryn insisted.

"Not alone," Gunnar countered, crossing his arms. "Not a fucking chance."

A heavy silence fell over the room. Bryn could feel Gunnar's eyes on him, but he couldn't bring himself to meet his gaze. The betrayal was too fresh.

"I want access to everything we have on Templeton," Bryn said, addressing Warden. "Everything. No more filtered information. I'm a big boy. I can handle it."

Warden studied him for a long moment before nodding. "Agreed. Emmett, make sure Bryn has full access to the Templeton files."

"Yes, sir," Emmett replied.

"Fine. Now, what about the Thanacrine case? Where are we with Agent Mercer?"

"Not much progress," Emmett admitted. "She's not in any of the standard federal databases. I've got facial recognition running, but so far, nothing."

"Keep digging," Warden instructed. "And I want a complete analysis of the Thanacrine samples we were able to secure. We need to understand exactly how it works."

"I'll coordinate with the lab," Giles offered. "They've already started preliminary tests."

Bryn nodded, his mind working on two tracks despite the pain in his head. "And we need to track Templeton's movements. The letters came from Dallas and Tulsa. He's heading north, possibly toward us. The first one wasn't mailed, so that doesn't help us."

"I'll check transportation records, surveillance footage from both cities," Emmett said. "But it could be that he has other people mailing the letters for him. He could be anywhere."

"He has to have accomplices to know so much about what Bryn is working on," Gunnar said. "We need to think about who that might be."

"That's enough to be getting on with." Warden stood, signaling the end of the meeting. "Bryn, get some rest. You look like hell."

"Thanks for the concern," Bryn replied, but the bite in his words was undermined by the way he swayed on his feet.

"I mean it," Warden said, his tone softening. "We need you at full strength. Especially now."

As the others filed out of the room, Gunnar lingered. Bryn busied himself gathering the letters, avoiding eye contact.

"Bryn," Gunnar began, his voice low. "I'm sorry."

"Are you? Or are you just sorry I found out?"

The hurt that flashed across Gunnar's face was almost enough to make Bryn regret his words. Almost.

"I thought we were protecting you," Gunnar said.

"That wasn't Warden's call to make no matter what he says. It wasn't yours either." Bryn folded the letters then slipped them back into their envelopes. "You know better than anyone what it was like to have Templeton in my head, to see the things he's done. To feel his…hunger." His voice wavered. "You should have told me."

"I know." Gunnar ran a hand through his hair, a rare gesture of frustration. "It was wrong. I made a mistake."

Bryn stood silent for a long moment, torn between his anger and the obvious regret in Gunnar's expression. "I need some time," he said. "And some space."

Gunnar nodded, his face composed now. "Of course. Whatever you need."

"Thanks," Bryn said, hating the formal distance that had sprung up between them. As Gunnar turned to leave, Bryn called after him. "Gunnar?" Gunnar paused at the door, looking back over his shoulder. "I'll get over it. Let me be angry for a while, okay?"

A faint smile crossed Gunnar's face. "Okay."

Left alone in the conference room, Bryn sank back into his chair. He stared at the envelopes, at Templeton's elegant handwriting. He was certain Templeton never did anything without purpose, never wrote a word that wasn't calculated for maximum effect.

What do you really want? Bryn wondered. He was as certain as he could be that the casual mentions of the Thanacrine case and Russo were window dressing. His real target was Bryn himself. Always had been, since that first encounter.

See you soon, the first letter had promised.

Bryn shivered. He had no doubt Templeton would keep that promise. The only question was when and how.

Meanwhile, the Thanacrine case needed his attention too. Agent Mercer, the enhanced sanguines and lupines, the pharmaceutical connection…it was all building toward something big. Something dangerous. Bryn wasn't sure he was ready for either challenge. He gathered up the letters and stood, steadying himself against the table. One problem at a time. First rest, then

Templeton's files. Then he'd figure out how to cope with the dual threats of a psychopath's obsession and a mob-funded, possibly government sanctioned, genetics conspiracy.

Just another day at GCR. He rolled his neck, which cracked like an old man's. *There aren't enough Twinkies in the world to deal with this level of suckage.*

Chapter Eleven

Bryn squinted at the screen of his cell, which was beeping at him. *Warden. Of course.* He debated throwing the annoying object out of the room but thought better of it and answered the call. "I'm asleep," he mumbled.

"Conference room. Twenty minutes." Warden's order was perfunctory. "We have a lead on Mercer."

"We do?"

"Twenty minutes," Warden repeated, and the line went dead.

"Charming as ever," Bryn said. He tossed the phone aside and forced himself to sit up. Gunnar's side of the bed was cold and empty, which gave Bryn a pang of regret. His head felt marginally better after a solid eight hours of unconsciousness but the suggestion of yesterday's pain still lingered at his temples. He ran a hand through his unruly hair and contemplated the effort required to make himself presentable.

Sounds of movement from the kitchen told him that Gunnar was already up and about. Of course he was — the wolf had endless energy, a trait that both impressed and annoyed Bryn depending on the time of day. Right now, with his head still fuzzy from sleep, it fell firmly into the annoying category. Deciding that coffee was his priority, he shuffled out of his bedroom in his shorts and T-shirt, heading toward the enticing aroma wafting from the kitchen. The GCR apartment had its perks, and Gunnar's coffee-making skills ranked high among them.

"Morning," Gunnar said without turning around. "Warden called?"

"How'd you guess?" Bryn asked, making a beeline for the coffee pot.

"Because he called me five minutes ago," Gunnar replied, sliding a mug across the counter toward him. "Conference room. Twenty-five minutes. Lead on Mercer."

"Man of few words, our Warden," Bryn commented, gratefully accepting the coffee. "He only gave me twenty minutes." He took a gulp, closing his eyes in appreciation. "This almost makes being conscious worthwhile."

"You're welcome," Gunnar said, though there was still a slight stiffness to his frame.

"I missed you last night," Bryn admitted. "A lot. I'm going to shower." He downed his coffee. "Save me some of whatever you're cooking. It smells good."

"Breakfast burritos," Gunnar replied. "And I made enough for both of us. I know better than to come between you and food after a reading hangover."

"Your survival instincts are impressive." And with that the tension between them dissolved.

Twenty minutes later, showered, dressed, and fortified with caffeine and one of Gunnar's burritos, Bryn and Gunnar got to the conference room at the same time as Emmett.

"Morning," Emmett chirped, falling into step beside them. "You look better, Bryn."

"Amazing what actual sleep can do," Bryn replied.

"Are you two friends again, because I can't bear it when the team isn't...teamy. You know what I mean." Emmett ducked his head.

Bryn sighed. "Yeah. I was an asshole, as usual. I still think I shouldn't have been kept in the dark but I understand the motivation came from a good place. What's this about Mercer?"

"Facial recognition picked her up at a hotel in Philadelphia last night," Emmett said. "She checked in under the name Claire Hammond."

Gunnar grunted. "Hammond, Hammer... coincidence?"

"There's more," Emmett continued as they went into the conference room. "Warden got the local FBI team to send in an agent to observe. Hammond met with someone from Helix Solutions."

"So, she *is* working for Russo," Bryn said, exchanging a glance with Gunnar.

"That's the thing," Emmett replied, a hint of excitement in his voice. "She didn't meet Russo himself, or any of his known associates. She had a late dinner with a Dr. Peregrine Frost, a geneticist specializing in lupine DNA. He only joined Helix three months ago."

"And the plot thickens," Bryn commented.

"Oh, you don't know the half of it," Emmett said with a grin. "Warden's got a plan."

Bryn groaned. *That* was rarely a good sign. He took a seat and Gunnar settled beside him. Giles raised his coffee mug in greeting. Bryn gave him the finger.

"Now that we're all here," Warden began without preamble, "let's get started." He nodded to Emmett, who connected his tablet to the room's display system.

"We've located *Agent* Mercer, or as she's calling herself now, Claire Hammond. She checked in to the Hyatt in central Philadelphia last night and met with this man, Dr. Peregrine Frost."

The display lit up with a photograph of a middle-aged man with salt-and-pepper hair and wire-rimmed glasses. He had the distracted look of someone more comfortable with test tubes than people.

"Frost is a geneticist who worked at Cornell University," Warden explained. "His specialty is lupine physiology and DNA research. Three months ago, Helix offered him triple his university salary to head up a new research division."

"Thanacrine," Bryn said.

"Almost certainly," Warden agreed. "What's interesting is that Hammond, or Mercer, doesn't seem to want Russo knowing she's talking to Frost."

"How do you know that?"

"We don't for certain, but it's odd that he met her alone. Russo doesn't tend to let his senior people wander around without a minder."

"So, she's *not* working for Russo?" Gunnar asked. "Then who?"

"That's what we need to find out," Warden said. "Tomorrow is Saturday. Frost has a lunch reservation at a steakhouse called Double Eagle on Pine Street, for noon. Mercer's booking at the hotel runs 'til Sunday."

"You think they're meeting up again?" Bryn asked.

"Unknown, but it gives us an opportunity. Local FBI is mobilizing to intercept Mercer at the hotel while we focus on Frost." Warden's gaze swept the room. "Bryn, Gunnar, you'll approach Frost at the restaurant. I want to know what Mercer wants from him and she may well be his strongest memory. Bryn needs to get a read."

Emmett cleared his throat. "Intel suggests Frost is obsessive about his work but socially awkward. Likes his whiskey neat and talks too much after his second drink. He goes to this same steakhouse every week and always orders the same thing."

"Perfect," Gunnar said. "We can buy him a few, loosen him up. What's our cover?"

"You're grad students interested in his work as part of your PhD thesis," Warden replied. "We'll set up some background today in case you need it and make sure Frost gets a call to set up the lunch meeting so you won't be going in cold."

"And what about Mercer?" Gunnar asked.

"Not our concern for now," Warden said. "Agent Bell is coordinating with his colleagues in Philly. They'll move on Mercer while you're with Frost."

"What's Giles doing?" Bryn asked.

"He'll be here with me, doing some research. Now get moving, your flight is at six."

That was vague but Warden didn't elaborate. Bryn shrugged. *Nothing new there.*

* * * *

That evening, Bryn discovered the GCR had a private jet at its disposal. He hadn't expected an operation of the GCR's size to command such resources, but it spoke volumes about the organization's, and Warden's, influence. He felt disappointed that the flight would be too short to fully appreciate the experience, but the prospect of spending uninterrupted time with Gunnar at a high-end hotel that night more than made up for it. The boutique establishment they arrived at was all understated elegance. At check-in, the receptionist maintained professional composure and processed their information without remarking on Bryn's dark glasses.

"Where did Emmett find this place?" Bryn asked Gunnar. "He had no time to set this up."

"Have you seen that man's contact book? The admin army is all-powerful." Gunnar carried their bags as they made their way to the top floor via the elevator. "This is us." The room was along a short hall.

The door to their room closed with a soft click. Bryn took in the luxury around them. There was a warm glow from recessed lighting, a plush carpet beneath his feet, and the crisp linens on the king-sized bed were already turned down.

"Wow," he said, running his fingers along the polished wood of the dresser. "Emmett really outdid himself, and he booked us a double rather than a twin."

Gunnar moved to the window, drawing back heavy curtains to reveal a panoramic view of the city lights. "I told him we'd only need one bed. He blushed. And he likes taking care of the team," he said. "Especially after close calls."

"Like the bomb that wasn't," Bryn murmured. He crossed to the wet bar, examining the selection of crystal decanters. "Drink? I think we've earned one."

"I'll take a soda if there's one in the mini-fridge. Please."

"Yeah, I guess alcohol isn't a great idea."

Feeling fancy, Bryn poured two glasses of soda rather than handing Gunnar a can. Their fingers brushed and he caught the briefest glimpse of Gunnar's intent. His breath caught.

"To cheating death," Bryn said, raising his glass.

"To quick reflexes," Gunnar countered, his eyes not leaving Bryn's face.

They drank in silence. Bryn set his glass down, heart hammering. "I don't know how to do this," he admitted.

Gunnar's expression softened. "Do what?"

"You know I touched you, right?"

"Nearly dying has a way of clarifying things," Gunnar replied. "Look at this view." The city stretched out below them, a tapestry of lights and shadows. "I'm tired of holding back. I want you."

The directness took Bryn's breath away. "Then take me. You know I want it too. More than anything."

"Even after I let you down by not telling you about Templeton's letter?"

"I shouldn't have blamed you. It was a knee-jerk reaction. It was Warden's decision and he's our boss. Plus you have a protective streak the length of the Mississippi."

Gunnar's hand came up to cup Bryn's face, thumb tracing the line of his jaw. "We still don't have to do anything you're not ready for."

"I'm ready," Bryn insisted, leaning into the touch. "I'm just…nervous. Which is ridiculous. I can look into a serial killer's head, but this…"

"This is different," Gunnar finished for him. "This matters more."

"Yeah," Bryn agreed. "It does."

When Gunnar kissed him, it was gentle, questioning, giving him every opportunity to pull away. Instead, Bryn pulled Gunnar closer and kissed him harder.

"Okay?" Gunnar asked when they broke apart, his forehead resting against Bryn's.

"Very okay," Bryn confirmed. "Though I reserve the right to panic later."

That earned him a smile, the kind that transformed Gunnar's serious face. "Noted."

They moved toward the bed by unspoken agreement, shedding layers of clothing along the way. Bryn fumbled with the buttons of his shirt, his coordination gone.

"Here," Gunnar said, moving Bryn's hands aside. "Let me."

There was something intense about being undressed, about Gunnar's careful attention as he revealed each inch of skin. Bryn fought the urge to make a joke to deflect from his own vulnerability.

"You're thinking too much," Gunnar observed, pressing a kiss to Bryn's collarbone.

"Occupational hazard," Bryn replied, his breath catching as Gunnar's lips moved lower. "I can't seem to turn my brain off."

"Let me help," Gunnar murmured, and proceeded to do exactly that with a series of mind-blowing kisses.

There was an ease between them, as if their bodies had been learning each other's rhythms long before this moment. Gunnar was patient, attentive, reading every reaction with the same focus he brought to a case.

He lowered Bryn to the bed before pulling off his shorts, leaving him naked and panting.

"Is this good with you?" Gunnar asked.

"More than," Bryn assured him. "It would be better if you were naked too."

"That I can manage. Don't go anywhere." Gunnar tore off his remaining clothes then got onto the bed next to Bryn.

My god, he's gorgeous. Bryn hoped he wasn't drooling. *But that is never going to fit.* He eyed Gunnar's sizeable, erect dick.

Gunnar chuckled, apparently reading his mind. "That can wait, sweetheart. I have other plans for you tonight." He ducked his head, taking Bryn's eager cock into his mouth.

"Fuck!" Bryn lost all sense of time, space and reality as Gunnar sucked and licked, lightly at first but getting harder. Faster.

There was nothing Bryn could do to hold off his orgasm, which thundered through him like a freight train. He might have yelled. Screamed, even. Whatever he did, he was sure it wasn't cool. He shuddered.

"I'm dead, aren't I? Am I in hell?"

"I think that's the first time I've ever seen you lose control," Gunnar said, grinning. "I like it. Gonna put that expression on your face whenever I can."

"I...that was...*way* too fast. I'm sorry."

"Why? Shows I was doing something right."

Bryn rolled onto his side. He reached for Gunnar's cock, encircling it with his fist. "Your skin is so hot."

"Bryn. Quit talking."

Bryn jacked Gunnar's cock until beads of liquid formed at the tip. He lapped them up. "You taste good."

"You're killing me..."

The stretch in Bryn's jaw muscles as he opened for Gunnar's cock was significant. He couldn't take it all so focused on the head while he squeezed the base. It was quite different from practicing with a cucumber. The random thought made him giggle and splutter.

"You okay down there?" Gunnar gave his hair a tug.

"Sorry...cucumber. And you can pull my hair a bit harder..."

"I... Nope. Got nothing."

Bryn got back to work and Gunnar was reduced to making incoherent sounds. When he came, Bryn swallowed, relishing the taste. Afterward, he flopped onto his back but Gunnar drew him close, tucking him against his side.

"Spectacular."

"Yeah."

Later, as they lay tangled together in the wreckage of the bedding, Bryn traced the line of an old scar that curved along Gunnar's ribs.

"I had no idea it would be like that," he admitted.

"Like what?" Gunnar asked, his fingers combing through Bryn's disheveled hair.

"Like..." Bryn searched for words. "Like it meant something."

Gunnar's arms tightened around him. "That happens with the right person."

"Is that what we are?" Bryn asked, looking up to meet Gunnar's eyes. "The right people for each other?"

"Who else would have you?" Gunnar asked.

"Nice. But...yeah, you have a point."

They fell into a comfortable silence, the sounds of the city a distant hum. Bryn found himself cataloging sensations—the steady rise and fall of Gunnar's chest beneath his cheek, the warmth of skin against skin, the strange feeling of being completely at ease with another person. If he concentrated he would see what Gunnar intended but with him, Bryn seemed to be able to exert some control, though it wasn't a conscious act.

"What happens tomorrow?" he asked.

"We go back to work," Gunnar answered. "We find Mercer and Frost. We do our jobs."

"And this?" Bryn gestured between them.

"This continues," Gunnar said. "If that's what you want."

"It is," Bryn said. "Though I should warn you, I'm gonna mess up. The whole…caring about someone this much thing. It's new territory for me."

"We'll figure it out together," Gunnar promised. "One day at a time."

"Very smart, oh wise wolf," Bryn quipped.

"There he is," Gunnar murmured, sounding pleased. "I was wondering when the real Bryn would resurface."

"Sorry to disappoint with all the earnest confessions," Bryn said, though he didn't feel sorry at all.

"When the snark disappears, I worry."

"Sap," Bryn accused, but there was no heat in it.

"Only with you," Gunnar replied, and somehow that felt like the most significant confession of the night.

"What do you think Emmett will say?" Bryn asked, changing the subject before he got too emotional.

"He'll be happy for us," Gunnar said without hesitation. "Probably confused about why it took so long."

"Warden will figure it out immediately."

"Yeah," Gunnar conceded. "He saw this."

"What do you mean?"

"Full disclosure. Him putting us together wasn't an accident. He dreamed it."

"He what now?"

"He has foretelling dreams."

"He's an augur? Is this another secret that was kept from me?"

"No and no. He's...different, but not on your level and not an augur. He doesn't control it and it's sporadic. I didn't think it was my place to tell you but now...after this..."

"I'm gonna smack him so hard," Bryn said.

"Yeah. That would be fun, but career limiting."

"Like he's gonna fire my ass."

"True. There are worse things, though..."

Bryn decided not to think about that to protect his mental wellbeing. "You think he's seen himself with Emmett?"

"Maybe. Who knows?"

"I won't say anything. He'd tell us if he saw anything related to a job."

"He would."

"I guess he must have been one of the first to be affected."

"Yeah, and none of the protocols were in place back then. Must have been scary, if he even realized what was happening."

"Don't make me feel sorry for him. He's mean to me."

"He keeps your ass in line, that's not the same as being mean."

Bryn grunted. "Maybe. I should shower." He made no move to leave the warmth of Gunnar's embrace. "Unless there's anything else you want to tell me?"

"There isn't and you should," Gunnar agreed, equally immobile.

Bryn knew it was the truth. "In a minute," he said, already drifting.

"In a minute," Gunnar echoed.

Chapter Twelve

The following morning, Philadelphia greeted them with overcast skies and a frigid wind that cut through Bryn's jacket. After their night together, a milestone that had left Bryn both exhilarated and a bit self-conscious in the light of day, the cold helped clear his head. Every now and again he caught Gunnar's eye and basked in the warmth he saw there.

The steakhouse occupied the ground floor of a renovated bank building, its brass fixtures and dark wood interior visible through large windows that must have been a later addition. Bryn and Gunnar sat outside a café where they'd had brunch and were now sipping coffee and watching the street under the protection of overhead patio heaters. Sitting shoulder to shoulder was nice and Bryn found himself leaning toward Gunnar. Their working partnership somehow felt stronger. Bryn wrapped his gloved fingers around his mug, grateful for both the heat and the mission that kept him from overthinking.

"Here he comes," Gunnar said. "Brown leather messenger bag, gray coat."

Bryn spotted him. "I see him."

"Give him time to get settled," Gunnar suggested, checking his watch.

"He's being seated," Bryn said. "Table by the window."

A few minutes later, they crossed the street and entered the restaurant. The warm air inside carried the rich scent of food and there was a constant hum of chatter and laughter. Gunnar waved away the young woman who offered to seat them, explaining they were meeting a colleague.

"Dr. Frost?" Bryn approached their target. "James Barrett, University of Pennsylvania. My lab partner and I are PhD students in the biomed faculty. I hope you don't mind us butting in on you, but our department chair mentioned you worked in town and we couldn't miss the opportunity to come say hi. You should have had a call?" He stripped off his gloved and offered a hand.

Frost shook it. "I did and it's my pleasure to meet you both. I'll be happy to share what I can, though that might not be much. Non-disclosure agreements, you know?"

"Let us buy you a drink. We're so interested in your research on genome sequencing."

"A drink sounds good. I haven't ordered yet so please join me."

Gunnar requested whiskey for Frost and sodas for him and Bryn. As soon as he started drinking, Frost relaxed and seemed happy to talk about his research to a couple of fans.

"The implications for accelerated healing are fascinating," Frost said, halfway through his second whiskey. "The lupine genome contains markers that could revolutionize regenerative medicine."

"I imagine that's what attracted Helix to your work," Bryn prompted.

Frost nodded eagerly. "Exactly! Though, between us, I'm finding the corporate environment... restrictive."

"How so?" Gunnar asked.

"Too many security protocols. Need-to-know basis for everything." Frost lowered his voice. "There's something strange about the samples they've provided. The DNA patterns show anomalies I've never seen in standard lupine subjects."

Bryn felt Gunnar tense beside him. "That's interesting. What kind of anomalies?"

Frost hesitated, then downed the rest of his whiskey. Gunnar called for another. Bryn kept his expression neutral as Frost leaned in.

"The samples show evidence of genetic manipulation beyond anything in scientific literature," Frost confided. "It's as if someone's already been doing what I was brought in to theorize."

"And does Mr. Russo discuss these anomalies with you?" Gunnar asked, the name drop pre-planned and calculated.

Frost's expression changed. "I never mentioned anyone called Russo. I've said too much. Who are you people?"

"Dr. Frost, we need to talk somewhere private," Bryn said, dropping the pretense. "You may be in danger."

Frost grabbed his messenger bag before bolting for the door. Gunnar threw cash on the table then he and Bryn followed.

Outside, Frost darted into the flow of pedestrians. Gunnar signaled to Bryn. "I'll go left and cut him off at the corner." He set off at a loping run.

Bryn wove through oblivious people enjoying their weekend, keeping Frost in view. He caught sight of him ducking into an alley and followed, finding himself in a narrow passage between buildings. Frost stood halfway down, frantically typing on his phone.

"Dr. Frost," Bryn called, approaching slowly with his hands visible. "We're from the GCR. We can protect you."

Frost looked up, panic in his eyes. "You don't understand. If they find out I told you what I did..."

A squeal of tires at the far end of the alley cut him off. A black SUV skidded to a stop, and three men in tactical gear jumped out.

"Get down!" Bryn shouted to Frost, who was doing a great impression of a rabbit frozen in headlights. Bryn shoved him to the ground but was too slow following suit. The first attacker fired a dart that caught Bryn in the shoulder. He yanked it out, but the cold spread of chemicals raced through his system. "Gunnar..." His legs buckled.

"Bryn!" Gunnar's voice echoed down the alley as he appeared at the far end, behind the attackers.

Through blurring vision, Bryn saw Gunnar charging toward him. The second assailant turned, raised his weapon and fired, the sound muted to Bryn's drugged senses. Gunnar staggered but kept coming. He slammed into the man who had the dart gun then drew his weapon but before he could get a shot off, the third attacker swung a baton that connected with Gunnar's skull, sending him crashing to the ground.

"No!" Bryn tried to shout, but his tongue felt thick and useless. As darkness closed in, he saw Frost being shoved into the SUV. Then rough hands dragged him toward the same vehicle. His last view was of Gunnar's motionless form sprawled on the ground.

* * * *

Bryn regained consciousness in slow, painful waves. First came the throbbing in his head, then the rawness in his parched throat, and finally the biting grip of metal against his wrists. He opened his eyes to a room with bare concrete walls. Industrial lighting buzzed overhead. *Fuck that's bright.* He scrunched his nose, confirming that his dark glasses were gone. His gloveless hands were cuffed to a metal chair bolted to the floor. The restraints were tight enough to restrict his movements but positioned to avoid cutting off his circulation. Across from him sat a metal table.

He tested his restraints. There was no give. When he moved, there was a burning at the base of his spine. *They took out the tracker. How long have I been unconscious? Gunnar.* The memory of his partner crumpling to the ground sent a jolt of anguish through him. Was he alive? Had the GCR picked him up?

The door swung open and he had to put thoughts of Gunnar aside. A man came into the room, followed by two guards who positioned themselves on either side of the entrance. The man was impeccably dressed in a charcoal suit, white shirt and lilac floral tie that seemed at odds with their surroundings. His silvering hair was cropped short, and a thin scar dissected one eyebrow.

His pale gray eyes were distinctive. Bryn recognized him from his FBI file.

"Mr. Ashton," the man said, his voice soft. "It's good to finally meet you. I'm Salvatore Russo."

"The Hammer," Bryn replied, his voice grating. He coughed.

"A name that wasn't of my choosing." Russo leaned against the edge of the table. "I've been looking forward to this meeting."

"I can't say the same." Bryn shifted in his chair. "You could have sent a dinner invite."

"Where's the fun in that? I prefer my guests off balance."

"Why am I here?"

"Direct. I appreciate that." Russo smiled. It wasn't a pleasant expression. "You've been quite the thorn in my side, Mr. Ashton. Particularly in the matter of my former accountant."

Bryn shrugged. "He broke the law."

"But wouldn't have been convicted without your particular skills."

Bryn remained silent. There was no point denying it.

"It cost me three offshore accounts and a shell corporation in the Caymans," Russo continued, his voice hardening. "Not to mention the inconvenience of relocating several operations. All because of your...unique talent."

"What have you done with Dr. Frost?" Bryn asked, changing the subject.

"Dr. Frost is continuing his important work," Russo answered. "Though he may regret his loose tongue for some time to come."

"It wasn't his fault."

"He was naïve. He won't be again."

"Where are we?"

"Somewhere temporary. By this time tomorrow, we'll be on our way to more secure facilities outside US jurisdiction." Russo leaned forward. "Somewhere your talents can be put to better use than harassing legitimate businessmen."

"Is that what you call yourself? A businessman?"

"Among other things." Russo's smile didn't reach his eyes. "You and I are not so different. We both see what others cannot."

Bryn glanced at his restraints. "If we're not so different, why am I the one in cuffs?"

Russo straightened. "Precautions. I know what happens when people underestimate you."

"Why didn't you kill me when you had the chance? The shooting outside the hospital — that was you."

"Well, not me personally. I'm not that good a shot. I might have hit you by mistake and if I'd wanted you dead, we wouldn't be having this conversation." Russo locked eyes with Bryn. "I prefer to make use of valuable resources, not waste them."

"I'm not for sale."

"Everyone has a price, Mr. Ashton. Or if not a price, then a pressure point. But we'll get to that. First, I want you to understand exactly what you've stumbled into. Let's take a walk."

He gestured to one of the guards, who released Bryn from the chair but re-cuffed his hands behind his back. He was careful not to make skin-to-skin contact.

Bryn followed Russo from the room because there wasn't much else he could do and he had to admit he was curious. They walked through a maze of corridors and he guessed they were underground. *The basement of a big building maybe. There's no natural light down here. Reminds me of The Facility.*

A gray metal door opened into a lab where several people were working at computers and benches. Dr. Frost was among them. He was haggard, a fresh bruise darkening his left cheek. A flicker of guilt and fear crossed his features when he spotted Bryn. When Russo walked into the lab, everyone froze.

"Carry on, everyone. Frost, show him," Russo commanded. The hum of activity restarted while Peregrine Frost went over to what looked like a large cooler. He entered a code on its digital lock and the lid hissed open, releasing a plume of vapor. Frost removed a transparent cylinder containing what appeared to be tissue samples suspended in a clear solution.

"Thanks to the enhanced version of Thanacrine, the genome integration has progressed," Russo said. "Our latest enhanced subjects can regenerate tissue at remarkable rates and possess strength well beyond normal human or gene-enhanced capacity."

"What do you want these 'super' people for?" Bryn asked. "You've killed so many wolves and vamps already. Your own lab staff in Boston too. Innocent people."

"Collateral damage. Inevitable when we're working on the leading edge of science. The lab staff…well, that was down to you and Boston PD. Couldn't have an augur poking around in their heads after all."

"You're experimenting on real people!"

"To make them better. It's called evolution. We're still crawling out of the primordial swamp. Imagine the advantage we would have in so many situations. We'd be invincible."

"We?"

"The United States, of course."

"So, the funding *is* coming from the government. They couldn't do this legitimately so they're using you in exchange for what? Money? Power?"

"Governments come and go. Politicians think they know everything. They don't."

"And my role in this?" Bryn asked.

"Your ability to read people, their memories, their intentions, whether they're telling the truth, we want to understand it. Map it. Potentially replicate it in our subjects." Russo's eyes gleamed with unsettling enthusiasm. "Imagine it. The perfect interrogators, the perfect spies, the perfect hunters."

"It doesn't work that way," Bryn said. "It's not something you can extract or duplicate. People have already tried."

"Perhaps not directly," Russo conceded. "But with Dr. Frost's expertise in genetic manipulation and neural mapping, we may be able to create something similar. And at minimum, we'll have you."

"I won't cooperate."

"You don't need to. We just need your brain." Russo smiled. "Though your cooperation would make things considerably less…invasive."

"Are you deliberately going for the supervillain vibe, or is that accidental?"

Russo's expression didn't change but he curled his fingers into a fist. "You have tonight to consider adjusting your attitude. Take him away."

The guards dragged Bryn out of the lab. They weren't gentle as they shoved him along more gray corridors then into a small, windowless room.

The cell wasn't much larger than the average closet—a concrete box with a narrow cot bolted to the wall and a stainless-steel toilet in the corner. A single light recessed into the ceiling cast harsh illumination that couldn't be turned off. Russo's goons had removed his handcuffs before shoving him inside, but the heavy metal door had sealed with an ominous thud that made Bryn flinch.

He sat on the edge of the cot, the thin mattress providing little cushion against the metal frame beneath. The room was cold, and they hadn't left him a blanket. Probably deliberate, another discomfort to wear him down before whatever Russo had planned. He'd known worse. Russo could learn a thing or two from Giles Delacourt. Bryn rubbed his wrists where the cuffs had been and ignored the ache in his lower back. His thoughts kept straying to Gunnar. The image of his partner, his lover, falling played on repeat in his head.

"He's alive," Bryn whispered. "He has to be alive." But doubt gnawed at him. He'd seen the way Gunnar had dropped. He'd been shot and taken a blow to the head. His survival would depend on help arriving quickly. *My tracker was still active when he went down. The GCR team will have found him.* The mission had gone sideways so fast. One moment they were getting useful information, the next the world was on fire.

Bryn stood and paced the small cell, five steps in one direction before having to turn. "I should have been faster. Should have sensed the trap." When he'd shaken Frost's hand, there had been no indication that Frost knew he was being played. His intent had involved a juicy steak and a single malt. *Russo was right about that. Frost is naïve. I doubt he had any idea what he was really getting into.*

"If he's gone..." Bryn couldn't contemplate life without Gunnar. He sank back onto the cot, dropping his head into his hands. He could hear the faint hum of the light above, the distant mechanical sounds of ventilation systems, but nothing human. No footsteps of guards patrolling, no noise from other prisoners. The air smelt and tasted metallic. It was as if he'd been sealed away from the world.

Hours passed, marked only by increasing hunger pangs. When exhaustion finally overcame discomfort, he lay on his side, knees drawn up for warmth. He closed his eyes, trying to quiet his mind enough for sleep. His last thought before drifting into a fitful doze was of Russo's words. *"Everyone has a price, Mr. Ashton. Or if not a price, then a pressure point."*

Bryn now understood with terrible clarity what his pressure point was. He hoped Russo didn't know it too. *Please be safe. Please.*

Chapter Thirteen

Bryn awoke at the click of the door lock disengaging. He'd had a restless, exhausting night, his body ached and he really wanted to hit something or someone. Two guards came into his cell. They were different ones from the previous day, both wore dark glasses and tactical gear with no identifying badges. One held a tray that sported a plastic cup of water and a granola bar.

Wannabe special forces. Probably failed the psych eval. "Is that it? I'm a growing boy."

"Eat it, don't eat it. You think I give a fuck?" The guard tossed the bar in Bryn's direction.

Bryn caught it. "Don't like being a jumped-up server then?" He held a hand out for the water. "Gimme." He thought he might get an unwanted bath but the guard handed over the drink rather than throwing it at him. "There's a good boy." *That's it, genius, antagonize the nasty man with the big gun.*

He choked down the pathetic excuse for breakfast, mind racing. Would Russo be moving him today, and where to? How could he find out whether Gunnar was alive? *I need to get out of this place, wherever it is.*

"Let's go," the larger guard said after Bryn had drained the last drop of water. "Hands."

The guard secured the restraints then Bryn was escorted back through the maze of corridors to the same interrogation room where he'd first met Salvatore Russo. The same metal chair bolted to the floor awaited him. The guards secured him to it and took up positions by the door. The room felt colder today, or maybe that was the impact of minimal sleep and lack of food.

He didn't have to wait long. The door opened to admit Dr. Frost, who wheeled in a cart laden with medical equipment. Russo followed close behind.

"Wow. I'm honored to be getting your personal attention, Russo," Bryn said.

"I trust you had time to reflect on our conversation," Russo said, his tone casual, as if they were discussing the weather rather than Bryn's imminent fate.

"Wasn't really in the mood for introspective reflection."

Russo blinked. "A shame. We can all benefit from understanding ourselves."

"I understand myself just fine."

"We'll see."

Frost busied himself arranging instruments on the cart, still avoiding eye contact.

"Is Detective Ericson alive?" Bryn asked.

"Your partner? Why? Is he important to you?"

Bryn schooled his expression. "He's a colleague. You had him shot and beaten, so yes, I'm fucking interested."

"He's probably dead. One less annoyance for me to consider. Prepare him for transport, Frost. Our flight leaves in three hours."

"Transport where?" Bryn demanded, though his guts were churning.

"Outside the reach of US jurisdiction or your agency's interference. That's all you need to know." Russo moved toward the door. "The doctor will handle the preparation process. I suggest you use these last few hours of relative comfort to reconcile yourself to your new reality. We'll talk again at our destination. We won't be traveling together." With that, he was gone, leaving Bryn with Frost and one of the guards.

He said 'probably dead' so he doesn't know for certain. I'd know if Gunnar was gone, I'm sure I would.

"I need to begin pre-transport protocols," Frost announced.

The guard maintained his position by the door, hand resting on his holstered weapon.

"What does that mean?" Bryn asked. "I've had all my shots."

"Keep your mouth shut, or I'll shut it for you," the guard snapped.

"Charming."

"No one said I couldn't damage you, smart ass."

"Did they say you could? I doubt you take a piss without a direct order." Bryn grinned.

The guard took a step toward him but Frost began taking Bryn's vitals, recording each measurement on a tablet. "Subject shows elevated stress markers but is within acceptable parameters for air travel," Frost stated.

Of course I'm fucking stressed. Like he'd be chilled in this situation. "You don't have to do this."

Frost paused for a second or two but then prepared a series of syringes. "This first compound is a stabilizer," he explained as he swabbed Bryn's arm with antiseptic. "It prevents rejection of the subsequent medications and reduces the risk of adverse reactions during altitude changes." The needle slid into Bryn's vein. The liquid burned as it entered his bloodstream. "Next, a mild anxiolytic to prevent panic responses during transit. I can't risk full sedation due to potential respiratory complications at altitude." He administered another injection, this one causing a cool sensation that spread from Bryn's arm throughout his body.

"Anxiolytic…are you giving me Xanax?"

Frost didn't respond but fitted a monitoring device to Bryn's ankle. "This will track your vital signs throughout the journey." The band locked in place with a click and a green light began pulsing.

Bryn noticed that Frost wasn't wearing gloves. Unusual for a scientist handling medical equipment. His bare fingers made contact with Bryn's wrist as he checked his pulse. He broke contact before the guard could notice. "The final injection will make you compliant for transport while maintaining consciousness," he said, preparing another syringe. "You'll remain aware but relaxed and cooperative."

"Screw you."

"He's ready," Frost told the guard. "Alert me immediately if his monitoring device flashes red. Fifteen minutes then you can take him back to his…room."

"You mean cell, you fucking traitor." Bryn rattled his restraints.

The guard nodded, and Frost left with his equipment without looking back. The door closed behind him and, though Bryn wanted to scream after him, instead he focused on himself. He felt strange, like he was wide awake and hyper alert.

Bryn's thoughts kept circling back to Frost's touch. The brief contact had been deliberate and enough for Bryn to read his memory and intent. His strongest memory was of coming into the room hours earlier, during the night when it was empty, standing on the same chair Bryn now sat in. He had removed a vent cover, placed a cell phone inside then replaced the cover. A maintenance badge clipped to his coat told Bryn how he'd gained access. He'd been terrified of being caught. His head had been full of panic and remorse.

Bryn had only had a moment to glimpse his intent, which was, as far as he could tell, to attempt to override the security system, though Frost wasn't certain he could do it. It wasn't random information, it was a plan and the doctor had wanted Bryn to see it. Frost had taken his job for the money but he hadn't known what he was really getting into. Now he was in too deep, complicit in things he couldn't stomach. He wanted out.

Braver than he looks. Bryn glanced at the guard, still standing motionless by the door, then at his ankle monitor flashing green. Whatever Frost had injected him with wasn't what Russo had ordered. It wasn't a compliance drug, it was something to keep him awake, alert, and functioning through fatigue.

How long has it been since Frost left? Five minutes? Ten? Bryn had no way to track time in the windowless room with its unchanging light. But the hidden cell, that was his lifeline. He tilted his head back, marking the ventilation grate in the ceiling. He thought he could see the end of the device, resting against the metal slats.

A wave of light headedness washed over him, followed by an odd surge of energy. His heartbeat accelerated and the monitor light flashed faster. The guard glanced over, frowning.

"Hey," Bryn said. "I don't know what he gave me but I think I'm going to be sick."

The guard's expression hardened. "Not my problem."

"Do you want to clean it up?" Bryn asked, letting his head loll forward. "Or explain to Russo why his valuable test subject choked on his own vomit?"

"Fine. If you're gonna puke, do it here." The guard kicked a metal trash can toward Bryn.

"Need to lean forward," Bryn mumbled, making retching sounds. "Can't…with these restraints."

The guard cursed under his breath. "If this is some kind of trick…" He drew his weapon and aimed it at Bryn's head. "One wrong move and you're dead. Russo can find another test subject." With his free hand, he reached for a set of handcuffs on his belt. "I'm going to undo your restraints, then cuff your hands in front. Try anything, and I shoot you in the head. Understand?"

Bryn nodded, continuing to make gagging sounds.

The guard kept his weapon trained on Bryn as he unlocked the chair restraints. As soon as Bryn's right hand was free, he snapped a handcuff around it, then secured the other wrist before removing the remaining chair restraint. The ankle monitor pulsed yellow.

"There," the guard said, stepping back. "Now puke if you're gonna puke."

Bryn lurched forward, making violent retching sounds over the trash can. Nothing came up but he made it convincing, his body heaving.

"Gross," the guard said, his weapon still aimed but his attention momentarily diverted.

It was enough. Bryn launched himself sideways from the chair, crashing into the guard's legs. Both of them went down hard, the guard's head cracking against the concrete floor. His weapon skittered away.

Before the guard could recover, Bryn brought his cuffed hands down on the man's throat with all his strength. He choked, eyes bulging, hands clawing at Bryn's face. Bryn struck again, this time against the temple. The guard went limp. *Thanks, Gunnar, that worked. I'll never complain about your self-defense tips again.*

Breathing hard, Bryn scrambled to his feet and retrieved the gun. He checked the guard's pulse. He was unconscious, not dead. Bryn searched him and found the key to his handcuffs. He took off the cuffs then rubbed his wrists. *Gunnar's going to need to get some fur-lined ones if he wants to get kinky. Now for the phone.* Bryn clambered onto the chair and reached for the vent cover. It was screwed in place, but loose, and he managed to pry the cover down on one side. There, wedged in the duct, was the phone and a key card. Bryn snatched them and jumped down from the chair.

He stripped the guard of his uniform shirt and cap, putting them on over his own clothes. They were a bit big, but he hoped they'd get him where he needed to be. Best of all, he took the man's shades. His eyes would be a complete giveaway without them. Gloves he would have to manage without.

He considered restraining the unconscious guard but decided against it. It would take time he didn't have. Taking a deep breath, he swiped the key card to exit the interrogation room. *Here goes nothing.* The corridor was empty. He moved with purpose, trying to look like he belonged, and headed for the nearest stairwell. He hoped he was going in the right direction because his recall from earlier was vague at best.

Voices approached from around the corner. Bryn squared his shoulders, tilted his hat down and continued walking, adopting the confident stride of a typical self-important security guard. Two men in lab coats passed him, indifferent. He kept walking, heart pounding. He wondered how long it would be before the energy from Frost's drugs wore off.

A door ahead had a stairwell sign but when Bryn tried the handle it was locked. He swiped the stolen key card but nothing happened. *Don't panic, don't panic.* He tried the card again. This time, the lock clicked open. He slipped through, closing the door behind him.

The stairwell was dim and it was a relief from the bright light in the corridor. Bryn leaned against the wall, gathering his thoughts. He assumed he was underground so had to go up. He started climbing, taking the steps two at a time. One flight, then another. He had reached a landing marked G, presumably for ground level, when an alarm began to blare throughout the building.

"Security breach, security breach," announced a mechanical voice over a PA system. "All personnel initiate evacuation procedures."

The key card didn't work on the door out of the stairwell. *Come on, Frost…override the lockdown system.* Bryn counted to ten then tried again. To his relief, the door opened onto a carpeted hallway. This level looked like ordinary office space. Cubicles, meeting rooms, even potted plants. People rushed about, responding to the alarm. Bryn moved with the crowd and kept his head down. He needed an exit, now.

He followed the biggest procession of people down a side corridor to a security checkpoint near what appeared to be a staff exit. Two guards were checking badges as employees left. Bryn slowed, heart pounding. He had a key card but no badge.

He scanned the area for alternatives and spotted a service door marked Maintenance just before the checkpoint. Bryn veered toward it, swiping the key card. Beyond was a narrow utility corridor housing pipes and electrical conduits. He followed it, the alarm still blaring behind him. The corridor turned, then ended at another door. He went through it into a loading dock with trucks parked in several bays. A guard stood by the external door, checking credentials as people left. Bryn joined a group of workers moving some equipment.

"Need some help?" he asked, grabbing one end of a heavy crate. The worker on the other end nodded, not questioning the presence of a security guard offering his help. Together, they carried the crate to a truck parked near the exit. "Thanks," the worker said, wiping his brow. "You security guys don't usually get your hands dirty."

"Emergency situation," Bryn replied with a shrug. "Everybody helps."

The worker nodded toward the guard at the exit. "Johnson's checking everyone out. Better go do your security thing."

Bryn nodded and walked purposefully toward the exit as if reporting for duty. "Hey, how are you doing?"

"Don't recognize you."

"New transfer from Boston," Bryn replied.

Johnson frowned. "ID badge?"

"Left it in the locker room when the alarm went off," Bryn said, injecting annoyance into his voice. "Look, I'm supposed to secure the perimeter. You want to explain to the boss why I'm standing here instead of doing my job? It's my first day, man, don't drop me in the shit."

Johnson hesitated, then nodded toward the exit. "Go on. But get that badge situation sorted out."

"I owe you." Bryn stepped out into the open air, fighting the urge to run. He was in a parking lot, delivery trucks on one side, and cars on the other. Beyond stretched a perimeter fence topped with razor wire. The other side of it was where he needed to be. *Easier said than done. No way am I get over that without shredding myself.* He walked toward the employee lot, scanning for options. He either needed a vehicle or a way through the wire.

A short distance away, a maintenance shed stood near the fence, partially obscured by overgrown bushes. Bryn made his way toward it. He tried the door. It was locked and needed an old-fashioned key. Bryn looked around and spotted a window, small but possibly big enough for him to squeeze through. Using his elbow, he smashed the glass. The alarm sounding from the building masked most of the noise. He cleared the worst of the jagged shards and hauled himself through the narrow opening, cutting his arm in the process. The pain registered but it was muted by Frost's drugs. Inside, the shed was cluttered with gardening tools, machine parts, and miscellaneous equipment. *Something here has to be useful.*

A pair of bolt cutters caught his eye. "Jackpot." Bryn grabbed them and moved back to the window, scanning the area. The guard was focused on the building entrance, not the perimeter fence.

He slipped out of the window and pushed his way through the bushes to the fence. As fast as he could, he cut a line up the chain-link fence, just enough to create an opening he could squeeze through. He pushed through the opening, tearing his shirt and scraping his shoulder. He was beyond caring. Once through, he darted across an access road and into a stand of trees beyond.

Only when he was concealed in the underbrush did he pause to catch his breath. *Where the fuck am I?* The building he'd left had been a squat three story. Nothing special unless you noticed the beefed-up security. Through the trees, he could see a commercial area. It was a strip mall with shops, restaurants, and people going about their normal lives. *If this is still Philly, it's not downtown.*

Bryn checked the cell Frost had left him. Two signal bars now, which should be enough to make a call. With shaking fingers, Bryn dialed the GCR's emergency number while blood ran in a sluggish rivulet down his arm and across the back of his hand.

A familiar voice answered after a single ring. "Operations."

"Emmett," Bryn said, "it's me."

"Bryn? Where the hell are you? Everyone's been looking..."

"I escaped the building Russo had me in but I don't know where I am," Bryn interrupted, keeping his voice low. "There's a strip mall, I'm in the woods behind it. Can you trace the phone?"

"Are you hurt?"

"Nothing serious. But I need a ride. They'll be looking for me and I'm not far enough away."

"On it," Emmett said. "Stay put and I'll get someone to you. The driver will use the word 'starling'. If he doesn't, run like hell."

"Oh, that's reassuring…"

"Good to hear your voice."

"Gunnar…is he?"

"The worst patient in the history of hospitals? Yep. Gotta go."

The call ended. *He's hurt but alive!* Bryn laughed, his relief tinged with hysteria. He slumped against a tree, breathing hard. Whatever Frost had given him was wearing off. His body ached and his head was fuzzy but none of it mattered because Gunnar was still breathing and from the sounds of it, well enough to be a pain in the ass. He forced himself to move, edging through the trees parallel to the commercial area, finding a position where he could observe the strip mall without being seen.

Every car that pulled into the lot made his heart race. Every distant siren sent a surge of adrenaline through his system. His hands wouldn't stop shaking. Eighteen minutes after the call to Emmett, the longest eighteen minutes in Bryn's life, a black sedan pulled into the far corner of the parking lot. Bryn watched as it idled there, positioned for a quick exit. A lone figure sat behind the wheel.

Bryn gathered his remaining strength. He scanned the area for any sign of Russo's men. The parking lot seemed clear. He stepped out of the trees and walked toward the sedan, fighting the urge to run.

The driver's window lowered as he approached. A face he recognized from Gunnar's security team looked out at him.

"Starling," the man said.

Bryn nodded then slid into the passenger seat.

"I'm Solomon. Ed Solomon. You look like hell," the driver said, pulling away from the curb.

"I feel worse," Bryn managed. "Thanks for coming."

"Are you kidding? Law enforcement's been tearing Philly apart looking for you."

"I'm still in Philly?"

"Yeah. We're heading straight back to Boston. Do you need medical attention first, 'cause you're bleeding on the upholstery?"

"No. Don't stop. I'm sure Warden will stump up for a valet."

"I won't. Recline your seat and get some rest if you want to. Ride's gonna take us about six hours."

Bryn closed his eyes, finally allowing himself to relax. There would be debriefings, medical examinations, questions about Russo. He didn't care about any of it now he knew Gunnar was alive.

Chapter Fourteen

Ed Solomon was a smooth driver and the car glided through the night. Bryn's adrenaline and Frost's drugs had worn off and shattered, Bryn drifted in and out of consciousness. Each time he awoke it was with a jolt to scan their surroundings before he remembered he was safe. Solomon left him alone, speaking only to offer water or to check if he needed anything in his moments of lucidity.

When they crossed into Boston city limits, it was getting dark.

"Almost there," Solomon said, breaking the silence. "Warden will be waiting for you."

"How bad is Gunnar?" Bryn asked.

"I'm no expert but he took a bullet to the hip. Would've shattered a normal human's pelvis, but with his lupine physiology, it's just a nasty wound. The baton strike to his head didn't help matters."

"He has a hard head."

"He's healing. He's also being an asshole about resting." Solomon shook his head. "He keeps trying to leave the hospital, insisting he has to find you. Warden told him he would be tied down or sedated to keep him from getting hurt more. Gunnar said no to the tying down, because you were the only one he wanted to do that with."

"You're kidding."

"He's been out of it. Still fought to help you, stubborn bastard."

Bryn found himself smiling. "Typical Gunnar."

"You said it, not me."

They continued toward GCR headquarters in silence, Bryn's thoughts drifting between relief at being rescued, lingering concern about Gunnar and worry about what lay ahead. Solomon pulled up in Marlborough Street at the front of the building.

"The front door? I'm honored."

"Can you walk?" Solomon asked.

Bryn nodded and pushed the car door open. "I've been kidnapped, drugged, and escaped a supervillain's lair. I think I can manage." His legs felt like rubber, and exhaustion weighed on him, but he managed to stand. Warden emerged with Emmett at his side and the two of them came down the path. Solomon hovered nearby but didn't offer assistance.

"Bryn," Emmett said, stepping forward. "Thank God."

"Thank you, Solomon," Warden said. "You've had a long drive. Go get some food and rest. Emmett has had one of the staff rooms made up for you. I'll get the car moved."

"Yes, sir." Solomon disappeared into the property.

"I know I'm irreplaceable, but this welcome committee seems excessive," Bryn managed.

Warden grunted. "Inside. The medic needs to check you over."

"I want to see Gunnar," Bryn said, heading in without rejecting Emmett's hand on his elbow.

"Trust me, you'll see him sooner than you expect," Warden replied. "Medical first."

Bryn wanted to protest but the entrance hall tilted and he knew arguing would be futile. He allowed Emmett to guide him to the room that served as a medical facility. A white-coated doctor and a nurse were waiting for him. They helped him onto the single bed, and he submitted to their ministrations with uncharacteristic docility. Warden and Emmett hovered nearby.

"The tracker," he murmured as the doctor examined the wound on his lower back. "They cut it out."

"Clean removal, at least," she replied. "Professional work." She applied a dressing to his back. "We'll need to insert a new one, but that can wait until you've recovered. No surgery for you today." She continued her examination. "You're dehydrated, your blood sugar is low and you're exhausted. I'm going to start an IV, and you need rest."

"I don't have time for that!"

"Yes, you do," Warden said. "We'll meet in an hour. That's enough time to get some fluids in you."

"I'll go up to your apartment and get you some fresh clothes," Emmett offered.

"Something that doesn't look like he robbed a mall cop," Warden suggested.

"I'll have you know this is high-end security chic," Bryn retorted, pulling off the ripped, bloodstained uniform shirt he'd stolen. "Very in this season."

"If he resists you, Doctor, you have my permission to sedate him," Warden said. "Any backchat—stick him."

"Hey!"

Warden and Emmett left and Bryn contemplated escape if only to piss off Warden. *Nah. Too much effort.*

The medical team finished their work, leaving Bryn with an IV in his arm and strict instructions to remain on the bed. Emmett came back with clean clothes, Bryn's usual black jeans and a long-sleeved black T-shirt, and left them within reach. "I'll be back in forty-five minutes," he said. "Try not to pull out that IV."

"No promises," Bryn called after him.

When Emmett returned, Bryn was sitting upright, the IV still in place.

"Your color has improved," Emmett said. "Less ghost and more chalk."

"Thanks...I think. I need a shower in the worst way."

The doctor returned and disconnected the line, applied a bandage to his arm, and gave him a pointed look. "Forty-eight hours of rest after your meeting," she said. "Non-negotiable."

"Sure, Doc. I'll pencil that in right after my vacation to Hawaii," Bryn replied. She glared at him, and he held up his hands in surrender. "Kidding. Rest. Got it."

"You'll have to shower after the meeting," Emmett said. "Just put the clean clothes on."

"Gross, but okay." Bryn changed then followed Emmett to Warden's office. Warden was at his desk and Giles was sitting in one of three chairs.

"Where's Gunnar?" Bryn asked, pausing in the doorway.

Before anyone could answer, a commotion erupted in the hallway behind him.

"I said I'm fine, damn it. Get that wheelchair away from me before I show you exactly where you can park it."

The familiar voice was a massive relief. Bryn turned to see Gunnar limping down the corridor, one hand braced against the wall for support. His face was pale and there were dark circles under his eyes. A vivid bruise extended from his temple to his jaw. Their eyes met and everything else fell away.

"Bryn." Gunnar's voice shook.

"You complete and utter fucking idiot," Bryn replied, but there was no heat in his words. "You were shot in the hip. What are you doing out of bed?"

"Coming to find you," Gunnar said, as if it were the most obvious explanation in the world.

Bryn crossed the distance between them in four quick strides, stopping short of throwing his arms around his partner. "You look like hell," he said, drinking in the sight of Gunnar alive and breathing.

"Speak for yourself," Gunnar replied, his eyes never leaving Bryn's face, a small smile playing at the corner of his mouth. "Nice of you to finally show up."

"Yeah, well, evil lairs are so hard to escape these days. No consideration for the guests at all."

Warden appeared in the doorway. "If you two are quite finished, perhaps we could get on? I'm sure we'd all like to sleep tonight at some point."

"Sorry, sir," Gunnar said, though he didn't sound particularly apologetic. He started to limp into Warden's office, but Bryn stepped closer, offering his shoulder for support. After a moment's hesitation, Gunnar accepted, leaning into him as they made their way inside.

"You shouldn't be here," Bryn murmured. "You should be resting."

"Pot, kettle," Gunnar replied. "Besides, did you really think I'd stay in bed once I heard you were back?"

"I heard they were about to tie you down…which is thought-provoking."

"Jesus, Bryn…"

Bryn chuckled. They both took seats in front of Warden's desk, Gunnar wincing as he lowered himself into the chair.

"You two shouldn't be allowed out without adult supervision," Giles said.

Bryn made a winding motion with one hand and raised the middle finger of the other. Gunnar growled.

"So good to have the whole crew back together. Things were way too quiet around here." Giles brushed non-existent lint from a sleeve.

"Isn't it?" Emmett settled into a seat to the side of Warden's desk. "I don't like it when you guys are out doing dangerous stuff."

"It's kinda the job, Emmett," Gunnar said.

"I know, but I want everyone to be safe."

Bryn didn't miss Warden's appreciative expression as he glanced over at Emmett.

"This operation has been compromised at every turn, and we need to understand why." Warden didn't bother with niceties. "Emmett…"

Emmett activated the room's display screen. Images of the building Bryn had escaped from appeared, now surrounded by emergency vehicles and personnel in tactical gear.

"Three hours after you were picked up, Bryn, a joint FBI-GCR team raided the building where you were held. Above ground it seems to have been housing a legitimate business, though we'll be taking a close look at the books. Below ground, most equipment had been abandoned, systems destroyed and any research materials removed." Warden scowled. "We did, however, find Dr. Frost."

"Dead?" Bryn asked, though he already knew the answer.

"Yes, I'm afraid so. Single gunshot wound to the back of the head, execution style. His body was left in a dumpster."

"A message," Bryn said. "Russo wanted us, and his co-conspirators, to know what happens to traitors."

"Indeed," Warden agreed.

"Frost saved my life. He deliberately made skin-to-skin contact and somehow made sure that his memories and intent were what I needed to see. He hid a cell and a key card. Dealt with the security system. Gave me stimulants instead of sedatives."

"Did you learn anything from him, or anyone else for that matter, while you were there?"

"Russo's operation is what we thought. He's creating enhanced super-soldiers from gene-affected subjects and I think he's close. I saw tissue samples he was keen to show off and Frost seemed to think his expertise was only to rubber stamp research that had already been done. Russo gave me a whole speech about creating the perfect hunters, interrogators, and spies. He was particularly interested in my abilities," Bryn added. "He wants to replicate them in his subjects."

"That's not how it works," Giles said.

"I know that, you know that, but Russo doesn't," Bryn said.

"It explains why they took you alive," Gunnar said, his voice tight. "They wanted to study you."

"Russo said they just needed my brain. Whether I cooperated or not was up to me." Bryn suppressed a shudder. "He also mentioned they were moving 'outside US jurisdiction' for the next phase. Had a flight scheduled for about three hours after I escaped."

"Interesting," Warden said. "Perhaps his government paymasters, whoever they are, don't have the grip they probably think they do. Emmett, instruct the tech team to track all private flights that departed the Philadelphia area in that timeframe."

"On it."

"I'd put money on South America," Gunnar said.

"Surprisingly, I agree," Giles said. "I'd guess Colombia. Much looser regulations on genetic research there."

"Emmett..."

"I'll ask Agent Bell if the FBI has any intel. On Russo's connections with Colombia."

"Good. What about funding?" Warden continued. "Did Russo indicate who's backing his operation?"

"He implied government support, but was evasive about specifics. Said 'governments come and go' and that politicians 'think they know everything.' Very James Bond villain, if you ask me."

"It sounds more and more like a rogue faction within one of our agencies," mused Giles. "It wouldn't be the first time an administration hasn't known what was going on right under its nose."

"Sir," Bryn said, addressing Warden, "there has to be a leak. You said it yourself that the operation was compromised from the start. Russo knew we'd be in Philly. He knew we'd be meeting Frost, and where."

Warden nodded. "I've come to the same conclusion. Which is why, effective immediately, we're implementing need-to-know protocols across all operations related to Helix, Russo, or Thanacrine."

"What about the FBI?" Gunnar asked. "We're supposed to be working together on this."

"I've already expressed my concerns to Boston's director," Warden replied. "He agrees that tighter controls are necessary, though I detect reluctance on his part to acknowledge the possibility of a breach at his end."

"So he thinks it's our leak, not his," Gunnar said.

"Essentially. Though he's diplomatic enough not to say so directly."

"If Russo's headed to Colombia, we need to move quickly," Bryn said.

"Leave that with me."

"So what now?" Bryn pressed.

"You and Detective Ericson will be placed on medical leave for a minimum of seventy-two hours," Warden said. "Our analysts will continue processing any evidence from the Philadelphia facility and tracking Russo's movements."

"We can't just sit around while..." Gunnar began.

"You can, and you will," Warden interrupted. "You were shot in the hip and suffered a head injury from that baton strike. Your healing is impressive, but not instantaneous. Bryn was drugged, abducted and has undergone significant physical and psychological trauma. Neither of you is fit for duty."

"With all due respect, sir," Bryn started, "I'm the one who spent quality time with Russo. I know how he thinks and what he looks like, which is a bit different from the ancient picture in his file."

"Which is precisely why we need you recovered," Warden cut in. "Your insights will be invaluable, but not if you collapse."

Bryn wanted to protest but found he lacked the energy. Bone-deep exhaustion permeated his body.

"Seventy-two hours," Warden said. "Both of you." He looked pointedly at Bryn and Gunnar. "Consider it an order." He stood, signaling the end of the meeting. "Emmett will work in my office in the meantime so you won't be disturbed."

"I will?" Emmett was wide-eyed.

"Yes, you will."

"And I will resist the urge to seek out your scintillating company," Giles said.

"One benefit of house arrest," Bryn said. He found himself struggling to stand. He swayed on his feet. Gunnar reached out, steadying him despite his own injuries.

"I've got you."

"Some big bad wolf you are," Bryn said. "Can barely stand yourself." They made their way into the corridor.

"Still strong enough to keep you upright. Besides, we make a matching set. Both of us too stubborn to admit when we're done in."

Bryn eyed the stairs. "It's at times like this I wish we had an elevator."

Gunnar pulled Bryn into a careful embrace. "Take your time."

Bryn buried his face in Gunnar's neck, inhaling the familiar scent of him, absorbing the solid reality of his body.

"I thought I'd lost you," Gunnar murmured against Bryn's hair. "When those bastards took you... I haven't felt that kind of fear since you handed yourself over to a murderer."

Bryn snorted with laughter. "When I saw you go down in that alley my heart stopped. I kept seeing it...over and over...but I decided you couldn't be dead. I would have felt it."

Gunnar's arms tightened around him. "I'm right here. We both are."

Taking it one slow step at a time, they made their way to their apartment.

Once inside, with the door locked behind them, they both seemed to deflate.

"Shower or bed?" Gunnar asked.

"Shower, then bed," Bryn decided. "I smell like a post-hibernation bear."

"That's very specific. Shower it is."

"I need to apologize to Ed Solomon. He had to spend six hours in a car with me."

"Ed's a big boy, he can handle it."

They helped each other undress. There was nothing sexual in the cautious touches, just intimacy and care as they cataloged the physical evidence of what they'd endured. Bryn's fingers traced the bandage covering Gunnar's hip, while Gunnar's eyes lingered on the marks left by the restraints on Bryn's wrists.

Under the hot spray of the shower, Bryn let the tears come. Silent, cathartic tears that mingled with the water cascading down his face. Gunnar held him through it, saying nothing.

Clean and wrapped in soft towels, they made their way to the bedroom. Gunnar lowered himself onto the bed, grimacing as his injured hip protested the movement. Bryn slid in beside him, careful not to jostle him.

"We should talk about what happened," Gunnar said, eyelids drooping.

"Tomorrow," Bryn replied, curling into Gunnar's side, his head resting on his chest. "Right now, I only need to know you're here."

"I'm here," Gunnar murmured, his arm coming around Bryn's shoulders. "Not going anywhere."

"Promise?"

"Wolf's honor," Gunnar said, pressing a kiss to the top of Bryn's head. "Sleep now."

Bryn surrendered to exhaustion, the steady beat of Gunnar's heart the most reassuring sound in the world.

Chapter Fifteen

Bryn wasn't sure of the time when he came around the next day but light seeped around the bedroom blinds. He extricated himself from Gunnar's embrace then padded to the bathroom. His reflection had improved. *Less like death warmed over, more like I'm recovering from a bad dose of flu. Progress.* When he pulled it off, the bandage from his lower back where the tracker had been removed was clean, and the abrasions on his wrists had faded to dull red marks. The cut on his arm was healing and the grazes scabbed over. *Not so horrific.*

When he went back into the bedroom, Gunnar was awake, propped on one elbow. "Morning," Gunnar said, voice rough with sleep. "How long was I out?"

"What time did we get to bed? It's eleven in the morning now." Bryn sat on the edge of the bed. "How's the hip?"

Gunnar shifted. "No idea and better. Healing fast." He grimaced. "Head's still sore."

"You took a baton to the skull. Even *your* head needs time to recover from that."

"Your bedside manner could use some work."

"I never claimed to be Florence Nightingale. You hungry? I can make us something."

"You? Cook?" Gunnar pulled a face. "Now I know my head got hit hard."

"I can toast bread without burning down the kitchen," Bryn said. "Usually."

"Let's not test that theory. We've had enough excitement for one week." Gunnar swung his legs over the side of the bed. "I'll do it."

"You're supposed to be resting."

"So are you. We can rest while making pancakes. Doctor's orders said nothing about avoiding the kitchen."

"Fine, but if you collapse face-first into the batter, I'm taking pictures before I call for help."

"Of course you are."

In shorts and T-shirts, they made their way to the kitchen and while Gunnar gathered ingredients, Bryn made a pot of coffee then perched on a stool at the counter, content to watch his partner work.

"You're staring," Gunnar said without turning around.

"Just making sure you don't fall over."

"Bullshit. You're staring at my ass."

"Maybe. When I was in that cell, I kept thinking about stupid things, like how I couldn't remember if I'd asked Emmett to order more coffee before we left for Philly."

Gunnar paused in whisking the batter. "You did. Three times. Your coffee obsession is well known around here."

"And now I'm...memorizing you. In case I need the memories some other time."

Gunnar set down the bowl and crossed to Bryn to give him a hug. "It's over and we got through it."

Bryn hugged him back. "I know."

"And," Gunnar continued, "Emmett had everything restocked, including the coffee, so we're good on that front for at least a week."

"Excellent, because house arrest without coffee would be against the Geneva Convention, pretty sure."

"No more brooding." Gunnar went back to the pancake making.

"It's my trademark. I need to brood. Angst is my religion."

"Save it for Giles, he enjoys it."

"I don't want to make his life pleasurable. I want him to be miserable."

"Bryn, from what I've seen, Giles Delacourt has the emotional range of an iceberg. You're more likely to get a rise out of Warden."

"Stop spoiling my happy thoughts and give me pancakes. I want chocolate chips in mine."

After breakfast, they got dressed then Gunnar stretched out on the couch with a book while Bryn curled in an armchair with his tablet watching cat videos on TikTok. Every few minutes Bryn would glance at Gunnar to find him already looking, and they would exchange grins.

Lunch came and went and by afternoon, the quiet domesticity had already begun to wear thin.

"I'm going stir-crazy," Bryn announced, setting aside his tablet. "How long has it been?"

"Including last night, approximately eighteen hours since we were placed on leave," Gunnar replied without looking up from his book. "Only fifty-four to go."

"Kill me now."

"You constantly complain about not getting enough time off and now you have it…"

"It's not the same."

"How so?"

"This isn't my choice."

"And you don't like being told to do anything, even if that anything is nothing, if that makes sense?" Gunnar chuckled.

"We could sneak downstairs to check if there are any developments. Emmett would cave if we asked him."

"And have Warden extend our leave by another week? No thanks. You know Emmett would tell him."

"Since when are you the voice of reason?"

"Since I nearly lost you. Again." Gunnar set his book aside. "Come here."

Bryn approached warily. "Why?"

"Because I'm asking." When Bryn was within reach, Gunnar pulled him down onto the couch, arranging them so Bryn's back was against his chest. "Now stop fidgeting and tell me what's really bothering you."

Bryn was silent for a moment. "Russo's still out there," he said. "Planning who knows what. And we're stuck here, useless."

"Not useless. Recovering. There's a difference."

"Semantics."

"No, necessity." Gunnar's arms tightened around Bryn. "I saw the medical report, Bryn. You had traces of a cocktail of drugs in your system. Sex on the beach, screwdriver, mojito, the works."

"Frost saved my life."

"Yeah, and could have killed you in the process." Gunnar sighed, his breath warm against Bryn's ear. "I need you to take care of yourself for a bit. For me, if not for you."

Bryn twisted to look at him. "That's fighting dirty."

"I'll use whatever works." Gunnar brushed a strand of hair from Bryn's face. "Two more days. Then we go back and raise hell until they let us help find Russo."

"Fine," Bryn conceded. "But I don't have to be happy about it."

"How about I kiss you and *make* you happy?"

"That could work."

They spent the rest of the day resting, snuggling and watching bad TV. There was a lot of kissing. Gunnar's lupine physiology worked wonders and by evening, he was walking without a limp. The bruising on his face had faded from angry purple to yellowish green, giving him a less alarming appearance, and his headache had gone. Bryn didn't have the same advantage of accelerated healing, but he felt better for the stress-free day.

Gunnar made tacos for dinner and even let Bryn loose on a side salad. They ate at the dining table by the window. Though there was no view of the street, the sounds of the city filtered up to them on the wind.

"Normal life," Bryn murmured, more to himself than to Gunnar.

"What?"

"People out there going about their lives, no idea what's happening right under their noses."

"That's why we do this. So they can have those lives."

"It wasn't so long ago that I thought I'd have that. School, a career…normal."

"Normal? Boring as hell, probably."

"Says the wolf to the augur."

Gunnar laughed. "Fair point. Would you choose that now, though, if you could have a do-over?"

"I…guess not. Sometimes I wish I wasn't the way I am, but we can do a lot of good."

"Yeah, we can."

After clearing away the dishes, they headed to the couch with a vague plan for watching a movie. Bryn flicked through the channels until he found one with explosions but then muted the sound.

"You know, I've been thinking," he said, his fingers already toying with the button of Gunnar's jeans. "Now you're fixed, I want to take my time and explore every inch of you."

"Oh, you do, do you? And what makes you think I'm going to let you have your wicked way with me?"

Bryn grinned, leaning in to press a kiss to Gunnar's stubbled jaw, his fingers finally popping the button open.

"Because I know you want this as much as I do." He inched down the zipper then took his time lowering Gunnar's jeans to reveal his toned thighs and the outline of his hard cock straining against his boxers. Bryn trailed his fingers up Gunnar's legs, feeling the muscles tense under his touch. "Yum."

"Such a tease," Gunnar said, but his hips bucked, urging Bryn on. Bryn smiled, shifting his attention to Gunnar's shirt, pushing it up to reveal his taut stomach and the light dusting of hair that led downward. He pressed a kiss to Gunnar's navel, his tongue dipping in to taste him. Gunnar's muscles quivered and he gave a low groan. "You know cruelty to lupines is a crime, right?"

Bryn took his own sweet time mapping every scar and every freckle. He kissed and licked his way down Gunnar's happy trail then rolled Gunnar's balls through the fabric of his shorts. Gunnar growled and his hips bucked.

"Bryn," Gunnar warned. "You're killing me here."

Bryn's answer was to hook his fingers into the waistband of Gunnar's underwear and pull them down. Gunnar lifted his hips, allowing Bryn to slide them off, leaving him exposed and erect.

"Fuck, Gunnar," Bryn murmured, his eyes roaming over Gunnar's body. "You're a work of art."

"Get on with it! Less looking more touching." Gunnar sounded amused.

Bryn started at Gunnar's feet, planting kisses up his legs, enjoying the way his body tensed and released with each touch. He spent extra time on Gunnar's calves, kissing and sucking, before moving to his thighs, massaging the muscles there. When he reached Gunnar's hips, he paused. "Ready for this?" He flicked out his tongue to taste the pre-cum glistening at the tip of Gunnar's cock.

"Fuck." Gunnar fisted Bryn's hair, urging him on.

"Patience." Bryn tongued Gunnar's cock while he rolled his balls, feeling them draw up tight. He took one into his mouth, sucking while he stroked Gunnar's shaft.

"Damn it!"

Bryn released Gunnar's ball then trailed his tongue up his shaft before taking the head into his mouth. Gunnar swore and twitched, pulling Bryn's hair harder.

"I'm close…" Gunnar warned, his voice strained.

Bryn increased his pace, his mouth and hand working together to bring Gunnar over the edge. With a cry, Gunnar convulsed, his release spilling onto Bryn's tongue. Bryn continued to lick and suck, drawing out Gunnar's pleasure until he went limp, his breath coming in ragged gasps.

Bryn looked up at Gunnar, a self-satisfied smile on his face, his lips wet with Gunnar's release. "Well, that was fun," Bryn said, his voice filled with mischief. He licked his lips.

"Smug much?" Gunnar said, but there was no malice in his words. He was relaxed and sated. Bryn clambered up Gunnar's body to kiss him, sharing the taste of him.

"Not denying it. Need a nap now."

"Bed then."

"Definitely."

Gunnar lifted Bryn to one side so he could adjust his clothing and kick off the pants that had puddled around one ankle then took Bryn's hand and led him to the bedroom.

"You have a wicked glint in your eye," Bryn said as he allowed himself to be led.

"I have wicked plans for you."

"No nap?"

"No. I'm done waiting."

Once in the bedroom, Gunnar got onto the bed, lifting Bryn over him so that he could straddle Gunnar's hips.

"So this is how it's going to be, is it? You lazing around while I do all the work?" Bryn leaned down to capture Gunnar's lips in a deep, demanding kiss.

"Not quite." Gunnar's reconnoitered Bryn's body, exploring every curve and line. "Take your clothes off."

Bryn scrambled to obey and while he stripped off, Gunnar did the same, though he was already halfway there. As soon as he was naked, Bryn resumed his position and ground against Gunnar. "You're hard again already."

"Wolf, remember?"

"Gene affects have some definite advantages."

Gunnar moved his hands to Bryn's ass, squeezing and kneading, urging Bryn to grind harder against him. Bryn complied, panting as he moved against Gunnar, their cocks rubbing together, the friction building his need. Gunnar nipped at Bryn's neck, marking him.

"Not your chew toy," Bryn gasped, but his head fell back, exposing more of his neck to Gunnar's teeth. Gunnar took advantage, gripping Bryn's hips, urging him on as he sucked and bit.

"Want my marks on you. Want everyone to know you're mine."

Bryn dug his nails into Gunnar's skin, leaving red marks in their wake. "Not just you. Nobody else gets to play with my wolf." He sucked on a nipple. "Like that?"

Gunnar fisted Bryn's hair. "Yeah, 's good."

Bryn roamed Gunnar's chest, tweaking and rolling his nipples. Gunnar's growls grew louder. "Need a condom."

"No we don't. We're both safe. We've had every test known to man and wolf."

"True. If you're good with it?"

"I am."

"Will you be able to…you know, get a read from me?"

"Thankfully not something that Giles tested," Bryn said with a shudder. "So I don't know. Maybe. I'm not reading you now and we're already touching. Does it bother you?"

"You read me all the time. If it happens, it happens. Can't promise that my intent won't be worthy of Pornhub, though."

Bryn gaped. "Really? You went there?"

Gunnar groped in the bedside cabinet. "Lube. In here somewhere. Fuck." He pulled the drawer too far and it landed on the floor, spilling the contents everywhere. "Double fuck."

Bryn leaned over the side of the bed. "Got it!" He handed the lube over and Gunnar poured some onto his fingers. He reached between them, searching for Bryn's entrance. Bryn tensed as Gunnar circled his hole with a finger, then pressed inside.

"Relax," Gunnar murmured, his voice soothing, reassuring. "I've got you."

Bryn took a deep breath and his body eased. Gunnar moved his finger, stretching Bryn's channel.

"You good?"

"More than."

Gunnar added another finger, his eyes locked onto Bryn's.

"Gunnar," Bryn pleaded, his body begging for more. "I'm ready."

Gunnar continued with slow, careful movements. "You're ready when I say you are."

"When's that going to be? Next week?"

What felt like an hour later but was more like a couple of minutes, Gunnar withdrew his fingers and Bryn positioned himself over Gunnar's straining cock. Gunnar gripped Bryn's hips, his fingers digging into the skin, but his touch was gentle, guiding rather than forcing.

Bryn lowered himself onto Gunnar's cock, his body stretching to accommodate Gunnar's size. Gunnar's eyes were locked onto his, his expression filled with concern.

"Burns."

"You can stop any time."

"Not a fucking chance."

When he was fully seated, Bryn took a moment to adjust, his body trembling with the intensity of the sensation. Gunnar held him, waiting for Bryn to take the next step.

"That's it. Take your time."

Bryn began to move, his hips lifting and lowering, finding a rhythm. Gunnar gripped his hips tighter, his body meeting Bryn's thrust for thrust, their bodies syncing. The pleasure built fast. Too fast. Bryn's muscles tensed as he neared his climax. Gunnar's body tightened beneath him, his breaths coming in short, sharp gasps, his eyes locked onto Bryn's.

Bryn moved faster. He grabbed his cock and with a final, desperate cry, he came, his cum painting the hairs on Gunnar's belly. Gunnar held him down, pushing deep inside him and followed suit, shaking with the force of his orgasm.

Bryn collapsed onto Gunnar's chest, his body slick with sweat, his ass clenching as it tried to keep a hold of Gunnar's dick. Momentum ensured that Gunnar slipped free and he pulled Bryn close. It took a while for Bryn's breathing to return to a normal rate.

"That was...fucking great," Bryn murmured, his voice a bit hoarse.

"Yeah, it was."

"We can do it again, right?"

"Oh yeah. We're gonna need a lot of practice."

"Maybe after a nap."

"Deal."

Bryn was happy that Gunnar didn't want to analyze what they'd done. Making love to Gunnar has been perfect. It didn't need post-coital dissection. "I didn't read you."

"No?"

"Nope. Nothing."

"Maybe endorphins get in the way."

"It *was* a pretty mind-blowing orgasm."

"You're blushing."

"Gunnar!"

"What?"

"Nap time. No more talking."

Chapter Sixteen

Despite Bryn's hope of more sexy time with Gunnar, he slept like a log right through the night. Gunnar, usually an early riser, was still asleep when Bryn awoke. *Guess the healing process is doing its thing.* Bryn slipped out of bed to make coffee, discovering an ache in a new location. *Maybe round two wouldn't have been such a great idea.* He gave his ass a rub. *Augurs don't have the same express healing that wolves do.*

He was pouring his second cup when Gunnar emerged from the bedroom, hair tousled and wearing only sweatpants.

"There's a sight worth waking up for," Bryn drawled, leaning back against the counter.

"The coffee or me?" Gunnar asked, stealing Bryn's mug and taking a sip.

"Definitely the coffee." Bryn reclaimed his cup. "Get your own."

Gunnar moved with unexpected speed, pinning Bryn against the counter. "Make me."

"Your hip…"

"Is fine." To prove his point, Gunnar lifted Bryn onto the counter. "See? Good as new."

"Show-off." Bryn rested his hands on Gunnar's shoulders, thumbs brushing along his collarbone.

"I think you enjoy being manhandled."

"I tolerate it." *I fucking love it but I'm not confessing that yet.*

They were interrupted by someone knocking on the apartment door.

"Expecting someone?" Gunnar asked, stepping back.

"At eight in the morning when we're supposed to be on leave? Not likely." Bryn hopped down from the counter. "Perhaps it's Emmett and he doesn't want to use his key." The knocking continued, getting louder. "Whoever it is, is annoying. So it's probably Giles."

"I'll get it," Gunnar said. "You're not dressed for company."

Bryn glanced down at his shorts. "Fair enough."

Gunnar peered through the peephole, then groaned. "You were right, it's Giles."

"You have got to be kidding me." Bryn retreated to the bedroom. "Tell him to go away."

"I can hear you, Bryn," came Giles' muffled voice through the door. "And I wouldn't be here if it wasn't important."

"It's always important with you," Bryn called back, pulling on a pair of jeans. "That's the problem."

Gunnar opened the door. "You'd better have a damn good reason for being here, Giles. We're both on recuperation leave, remember."

Bryn emerged from the bedroom, now dressed but scowling. "Whatever you're selling, we're not buying. I'm enjoying bed rest." He caught Gunnar's eye.

Giles stared at him. "Oh God, you two are going to be even more unbearable now, aren't you?"

"You shouldn't be here." Bryn tossed Gunnar a T-shirt.

"Yes, I'm well aware."

"You're going behind Warden's back?" Bryn asked. "Now I'm interested."

"I thought that might pique your curiosity. I have a situation that requires your particular talents, Bryn. Specifically, your ability to discern the truth."

"And this can't wait until we're officially back on duty because…?"

"Because we need to confirm who stole a historically significant artifact from the Boston Museum of Antiquities, and I want to be certain before we make an arrest."

"What kind of artifact?" Gunnar asked.

"An ornate dagger. A fifteenth century Ottoman ceremonial knife with ivory and silver inlay to be exact." He handed a folder to Bryn.

Bryn flipped it open. A photograph showed an intricately designed knife with a curved blade and a hilt encrusted with silver work and ivory panels. "Pretty."

"And worth two million dollars on the black market. It was stolen three days ago."

"Inside job?" Bryn asked, studying the photo as they all moved to the kitchen.

"Almost certainly."

"So you want me to read the suspects." Bryn closed the folder. "Why can't the cops interrogate them?"

"Gosh, why didn't I think of that?" Giles oozed sarcasm from every pore.

"You want my help or not?"

"Yes. Still not going to tolerate dumb questions because it's against my religion."

"What's that? Devil worship?"

"Funny. We have three suspects, all museum staff with clean records and seemingly airtight alibis. Traditional interrogation methods have yielded nothing." Giles poured himself a coffee. "I need someone who can cut through the lies with absolute certainty."

"What's your real interest in this case, Giles? Museum heists aren't our department." Gunnar crossed his arms, making his muscles bulge and Bryn lick his lips.

Giles hesitated. "The museum's director is an old school friend. She called me personally about this matter."

"Ah," Gunnar said, "the truth emerges. This is a favor for a friend, not official business."

"The artifact's recovery is absolutely official GCR business," Giles replied. "My personal connection to the case is incidental."

"Right," Bryn snorted. "Incidental."

"And what's it got to do with gene-affected people?" Gunnar added.

"One of the suspects is sanguine," Giles said.

Bryn exchanged a look with Gunnar, who shrugged. "Your call."

"If I agree to this," Bryn said, turning back to Giles, "what's in it for us?"

"Besides the satisfaction of helping solve a crime?"

"Yes, besides that heart-warming garbage," Bryn said with an exaggerated eye roll. "And besides helping your old school chum save face."

"I happen to know that Warden is planning to keep you both on desk duty for at least a week after your medical leave ends. Help me with this, and I'll make sure you're back in the field."

Bryn drummed his fingers on the folder. "Warden is a sneaky son of a bitch… One condition."

"I'm listening."

"If I do this, you owe me a favor. No questions asked. To be determined at a later date."

Giles hesitated. "Within reason."

"Within reason," Bryn agreed. "So, where are these suspects being held?"

"Basement meeting rooms."

"You brought them here? Are you crazy?"

"Warden's gone to New York for the day and he's taken Emmett with him."

"Hope Emmett remembered the lube. Okay, give us half an hour."

Giles narrowed his eyes. "Why not now?"

"Because I haven't had breakfast and you do *not* want me doing this on an empty stomach."

After Giles left, Gunnar turned to Bryn. "You sure about this? Helping Giles with his little favor?"

"No, but I'm climbing the walls here. At least it's something to do without leaving the building." Bryn tossed the folder onto the counter. "Besides, aren't you curious about a dagger heist? Especially one that has Giles running personal errands for his buddy?"

"It might be a little interesting," Gunnar admitted, pulling Bryn close. "And watching Giles squirm when you called him out was a highlight of my morning, that's for sure." He grinned. "But if at any point you feel…"

"I'll tap out, I promise." Bryn gave Gunnar a quick kiss.

Thirty minutes later, they were heading down the stairs to the basement level of GCR headquarters.

"I hate having to wear these things," Bryn said. "One day I'm gonna fall on my ass because I can't see where I'm going."

"They make you look mysterious," Gunnar replied.

"They make me look like I'm trying too hard to be cool."

"That too."

"You aren't supposed to agree."

Giles was waiting for them outside one of the meeting rooms. "Glad you could tear yourselves away from the frosted flakes. The suspects are prepped and waiting."

"You do remember this is us doing you a massive favor, right?" Bryn said. "How about some gratitude?"

"How about less attitude? There are three suspects. Marcus Fanshaw, curator of the Middle Eastern collection; Anton Cormino, head of museum security — he's the sanguine; and Tom Redman, the evening shift guard who was on duty when the theft occurred."

"And you said all three have alibis?" Gunnar said.

"Fanshaw claims he was in his office cataloging new acquisitions all evening; Cormino was at a security conference across town and has plenty of witnesses, but could have stepped out without being noticed; Redman maintains he never left his post except for scheduled breaks, during which the exhibition hall was covered by cameras. The footage is his alibi."

"Any physical evidence pointing to one over the others?" Bryn asked.

"Nothing conclusive. The security cameras were bypassed. Not disabled, but looped. The display case shows signs of having been opened with a key rather than forced."

"Who had access to the keys?"

"All three of them, plus the museum director and the head conservator."

"And where were they at the time of the theft?" Gunnar asked.

"At a major donors' dinner," Giles replied without missing a beat. "With over a hundred witnesses."

"Just checking," Gunnar said with a shrug.

"Okay. Do these people know what I am?" Bryn asked.

"They do," Giles confirmed. "They've agreed to the interviews. They weren't in any position to decline."

"Okay, so who's first?"

"Fanshaw. I thought we'd start at the top."

As the three of them entered the small meeting room, Fanshaw's expression was a mixture of annoyance and concern.

"I don't know what good this is going to do. I've told you everything I know already."

"As I explained," Giles said, "the quickest way to get through this is for you to talk to our augur. This is Bryn Ashton and his partner, Detective Ericson."

Bryn approached the table Fanshaw was seated at. "Pleasure to meet you, despite the circumstances." He took a seat. "I need skin-to-skin contact, okay?"

Fanshaw nodded and Bryn grasped his wrist.

"As I already told the police, I was in my office all evening, as the security logs show."

"Truth."

"And you didn't leave your office at all during that time?" Gunnar asked.

"Only to use the restroom, which is just down the hall. Five minutes, maximum."

"Truth again."

"The missing dagger—had you worked with it before? Studied it?"

"Of course. I arranged for it to be included in our exhibition. Ottoman ceremonial daggers are a special interest of mine, especially those from the court of Mehmed II."

"And its value?"

"Historically invaluable, monetarily around two million dollars." Fanshaw sat up straighter. "It's one of the finest examples of fifteenth century Ottoman craftsmanship in existence. It was a coup to have it on loan."

"Truth."

After twenty more minutes of questioning, Gunnar was satisfied that Forsyth hadn't been involved in the theft. Giles escorted him out of the building and when he returned, he brought Anthony Cormino in with him.

Cormino was younger and had the pale skin of a vamp. He was also more defensive. "Mr. Delacourt, I hope we can clear this matter up quickly. My security team's reputation is at stake."

Giles made introductions and Gunnar started over with his questions while Bryn held Cormino's wrist.

"Walk us through your movements on the night of the theft," Gunnar said.

"I was at a security conference across town at the Westin hotel from around six until midnight. Security was tight and there will be multiple witnesses to my presence, including the police chief."

"Truth."

"Who do you think took the dagger?"

"I'm not paid to speculate. But if you're asking for my professional assessment, it had to be someone with intimate knowledge of our security protocols."

"Someone like you?"

"Or Mr. Fanshaw. Or Redman. Or a dozen other personnel." He frowned. "But I didn't take it. I've dedicated my career to protecting artifacts like this."

"Truth." The strength of Cormino's belief in what he was saying came through loud and clear to Bryn.

After a few more questions, it was time to move on. Giles did his escort duties and when he returned, they relocated to the next room along the corridor, where Redman had been waiting.

The man was nervous, fidgeting with his hands, eyes darting around the room. Bryn didn't let that influence him. Anyone would be nervous in the same situation.

"Mr. Redman," Gunnar said. "I have a few questions about the night the dagger went missing. While we talk, the augur will be touching you. It won't hurt."

Bryn sat down. "I'm Bryn. There's no need to be anxious."

Redman was sweating. "I've answered a ton of questions already. I didn't see anything unusual."

Bryn laid his fingers across the pulse point in Redman's wrist.

"You were on duty at the security station outside the exhibition hall, correct?" Gunnar asked.

"Yes, from six in the evening until four in the morning."

"Truth."

"And you never left your post except for scheduled breaks?"

"That's right. I took fifteen minutes at nine like always. I bought a candy bar from the vending machine in the employee break room and used the washroom. At midnight I took a walk around the other halls then sat in the cafeteria to drink my coffee. Liquids aren't allowed at my station."

Bryn caught Gunnar's eye and gave the slightest shake of his head. Redman was lying.

"Mr. Redman, I'm going to be direct with you. You're not telling us the whole truth about that night," Gunnar said.

Redman paled. "I don't know what you mean."

"I think you do. You were told what an augur can do. Something happened during your shift that you haven't shared with us."

Sweat beaded on Redman's forehead. "I told you everything important."

"Lie."

"You can't know that."

"But I do." Bryn removed his dark glasses, revealing his intense, glowing green eyes. "Tell us what really happened that night."

Redman's shoulders slumped. "I didn't believe you were real. Thought it was a trick."

"You need to tell us the truth."

"They threatened my daughter," Redman whispered.

"Truth."

"They had pictures of her. They knew where she goes to school, her schedule." Redman's voice cracked. "They said if I didn't help them, they'd hurt her."

"Who threatened you?" Giles asked, stepping forward.

"I don't know. I never saw a person. I got calls from blocked numbers, photos of my daughter sent to my personal phone. I have the messages. I can show you."

"What did they ask you to do?" Bryn asked.

"To leave my post for thirty minutes instead of fifteen during my early break and to leave a service door unlocked on the east side of the building." Reeves wiped at his eyes. "That's all. I swear."

"Truth."

"Did you see who took the dagger?" Gunnar asked.

"No. When I came back to my post, everything looked normal. I didn't know what they took until the next morning when I was doing my last checks before the shift change."

After another hour of questioning, they had extracted everything Redman knew, which wasn't much. The threats had started a week before the theft, the communications were anonymous, and he hadn't seen the thief. It wasn't a huge amount of help.

Outside the interview room, Giles pursed his lips. "Well, that's something at least. Not what I was hoping for, but progress."

"He's telling the truth," Bryn said, putting his dark glasses back on. "You heard him. He was put in an impossible situation."

"Nevertheless, he compromised security and facilitated the theft of a valuable artifact. The timeline works. The thief had time to get the cabinet key from the office, take the dagger and return the key in half an hour."

"And there's no camera footage?"

"No. That service door has a blind spot and the cameras in the exhibition hall were looped remotely. They show an empty hall at the time the theft must have taken place."

"What will happen to Redman?" Gunnar asked.

"That's not up to me. I'll get the cops to come pick him up."

"At least now you know which museum employee was involved," Bryn said.

"Indeed. Thank you both for your assistance."

"Don't forget the favor you owe me," Bryn added. "I plan to collect at the most inconvenient moment possible."

Giles gave a pained sigh, which put a smile on Bryn's face as he and Gunnar headed back to the apartment. "Not quite the art heist thriller I was expecting," Bryn commented.

"No. I still wonder about Giles' interest in this. There's something else going on here, I can smell it."

"You do have a powerful snoot."

"Hmm, I'm going to choose to take that as a compliment rather than a dig at the size of my nose. You okay? Three reads in a row can take a lot out of you."

"I'm fine. Slight headache is all. Redman was the only real challenge. Fear and deception are hard to untangle sometimes." Bryn sighed. "But I'm glad we did this. At least now the cops can focus on finding who was really behind the theft."

"It was also good to get back to something different rather than focusing on one case. I like variety," Gunnar admitted.

"Yeah. Does that make us weird?"

"Probably, but now we can go back to our recovery time. I believe we should plan to do nothing productive for the rest of the day."

"Sounds like an excellent plan. Come to think of it, I *am* a little tired. We should get horizontal. You know, for recovery purposes."

"Oh, is that what it's called?" Gunnar grinned.

"It is now."

Chapter Seventeen

"If I have to read one more file, I'm going to gouge my eyes out with this pencil," Bryn announced, tossing said pencil across the room where it bounced off the wall. It was the day after he'd read the museum staff. He shifted positions on his beanbag, which made a soft whooshing sound as he sank deeper into it, stretching his arms overhead with a dramatic groan. "I swear they multiply overnight." He reached to grab another folder from the stacks he'd arranged in a semicircle around him. "Remind me again why we came back to work early?"

Gunnar didn't look up from his computer, but the corner of his mouth twitched. "Because you were, and I quote, 'climbing the walls' in the apartment. Warden got worried about the potential renovation bill."

"Right." Bryn changed his position again, which required a series of wiggles and an undignified flailing of limbs. His laptop was balanced on his knees, the screen filled with dense text that made his eyes hurt.

"But now I'm climbing the walls while doing paperwork, which is worse."

"It was a compromise, and Warden didn't give us much choice now, did he? I'm sure Giles would find you something more interesting to do if you asked him."

"I'd rather eat glass," Bryn replied, letting his head fall back against the beanbag. "He'd just lecture me about 'proper recuperation' and 'resetting my energy levels' again." He mimicked Giles' clipped British accent.

"Which you ignored," Gunnar pointed out, gesturing to the bandage still visible beneath the sleeve of Bryn's faded Iron Maiden T-shirt. "That cut hasn't fully healed yet."

"It's a scratch," Bryn protested. "I can't help it if I don't have lupine super-healing. Watching daytime TV was making me lose brain cells by the minute and sadly we can't spend every minute getting down and dirty in bed. At least here I can be...productive and uncomfortable." As if to demonstrate his point, he shifted yet again, causing several files to slide off his lap and scatter across the floor. "Dammit."

"That thing was a terrible idea," Gunnar remarked, watching with obvious amusement as Bryn struggled to collect the fallen papers without getting up.

"It's ergonomic," Bryn said, stretching as far as he could to reach a wayward piece of paper. "Almost...got it..."

"Very dignified," Gunnar commented.

Bryn shot him a look. "We can't all be perfect specimens of professionalism and I'm not the one using my trash can as a basketball hoop." He finally gave up and rolled off the beanbag onto his hands and knees to gather the scattered reports. "Though I have to say, the view from your desk must be spectacular right now."

"Improving by the second."

Bryn wiggled his ass then glanced at the clock on the wall. "Where's Emmett? He's thirty minutes late, which is approximately twenty-nine minutes and fifty-nine seconds longer than he's ever been late before."

"Maybe he realized that trying to organize the two of us is a lost cause and ran away."

Bryn was about to retort when the door to their shared office opened. Emmett appeared, looking disheveled. His normally immaculate shirt was rumpled, and his bow tie was askew. He stopped short in the doorway, taking in the sight of Bryn on his hands and knees surrounded by a sea of papers.

"What...happened here?" Emmett asked. "What have you two done to my filing system?"

"Well, well, well," Bryn drawled, crawling back to his beanbag where he leaned back and laced his fingers behind his head. "Look what the cat dragged in."

Emmett flushed. "Good morning to you too."

"Good morning? It's past nine-thirty. Where have you been?" Bryn narrowed his eyes in gleeful suspicion. "Wait a minute. Is that the same bow tie you wore yesterday?"

"You didn't see me yesterday, so how would you know? But no, it's not," Emmett said too quickly, setting down a container on his desk. "I brought cookies."

"Homemade cookies?" Gunnar asked, looking up from his work with interest. He sniffed. "They smell good. There's something else...oh." He grinned. "Someone's been having a fun time."

"I like...baking."

"You're deflecting, Emmett," Bryn accused. "And since when do you bake?" With a heroic effort, Bryn scrambled to his feet. He sauntered over to Emmett's desk then levered the lid off the cookie tub.

"I've always baked, but I don't get a lot of time," Emmett replied. "And I thought you might appreciate something sweet."

Gunnar came to stand next to Bryn and reached for a cookie. "They're soft."

"Because he just made them," Bryn said, grabbing one for himself and taking a large bite. "The question is, whose kitchen did he use?"

Emmett busied himself with organizing papers on his desk, his flush deepening.

"Oh my god," Bryn said around a mouthful of cookie, crumbs tumbling down his shirt. "These are great. You were at Warden's place, weren't you? You went there after you got back from New York. You and Warden are…"

"We have a meeting in the conference room in fifteen minutes," Emmett interrupted, avoiding eye contact. "I'm going to set up the presentation materials." He fled the office with remarkable speed.

Gunnar shook his head. "You're relentless."

"It's part of my charm," Bryn replied. "Something happened there and I need details."

"Don't embarrass him, he can't defend himself like you can." Gunnar stretched and his plaid shirt rode up, revealing a strip of tanned skin that drew Bryn's attention. "See something you like?"

"Maybe." Bryn moved closer, slipping his fingers through Gunnar's belt loops. "Have I mentioned how glad I am that we don't have to hide this anymore?"

"Only about a dozen times." Gunnar's hands settled on Bryn's hips. "But I don't mind hearing it again."

"Get a room," came Giles' voice from the doorway. "You two make maple syrup seem sour." His gaze swept the office, lingering with distinct disapproval on the beanbag and the surrounding chaos. "What in God's name have you been doing in here?"

"Paperwork," Bryn said. "Isn't that obvious?"

"Did Emmett tell you to get your butts to the conference room?" Giles asked. "Or did you traumatize him with this mess?"

"He's fine and of course he did. He also brought us cookies." Bryn said. "What did you bring?"

"Some much needed sartorial style and a bad attitude." Giles turned on his heel and left.

"There's nothing wrong with my style," Bryn muttered as he and Gunnar followed Giles down the stairs.

"You can't go wrong with black." Gunnar grinned.

"Whereas plaid…"

"Makes me look like a lumberjack. I know. But as you seem to enjoy climbing me like a tree…"

"Oh my God…" Bryn had to adjust his jeans. "You had to say that now, didn't you?"

Emmett had already set up at the head of the table, and Warden stood nearby, reviewing something on a tablet. Bryn caught Emmett stealing a glance at Warden when he thought no one was looking. *Don't say anything, Bryn. Be good.*

"Good, you're here," Warden said as they took their seats. "We have several matters to discuss."

Once everyone was settled, Warden launched into the briefing. "First, an update on our recent operations. Agent Mercer."

Bryn perked up. "With everything that went down in Philly, I'd forgotten she was picked up at the same time. What's the latest?" Bryn asked.

"She's being held by the FBI here in Boston," Warden said. "They've been questioning her for days, but they're not getting much. We don't yet know whether she works for Russo, for some government department or is a plant. She's very tight lipped."

"I could read her," Bryn offered. "Cut through all the bullshit and find out what she is. If she refuses to answer questions, I can still get memory and intent."

The room fell silent as Warden considered this. "With a potential leak, we need to be cautious about working with the Feds."

"Bell will let me read him if he's honest," Bryn pointed out. "We have jurisdiction in gene-related matters, and if she is working for The Hammer, we need to know."

"He has a point," Giles said. "And we need answers faster than the FBI's getting them."

Warden drummed his fingers on the table. "Fine. I'll arrange it. But this is a fact-finding mission only, Bryn. You go in, you read her, you leave. No improvisation."

"When have I ever gone off script?" Bryn asked, all wide-eyed innocence. Everyone in the room stared at him. "Okay, fair point. But I'll behave, promise."

"Gunnar," Warden continued. "Keep him on track."

Gunnar nodded. "Of course."

"While I get this sorted," Warden said, "you can get back to support requests, Bryn. You can start lining up more cases. The backlog is growing and with Russo out of the country, we may have capacity to pick off a few. Emmett can assist."

"Yes, sir," Emmett said.

Bryn caught the look that passed between them and filed it away for future teasing material.

"Gunnar, I need you to work with the security team. If The Hammer is escalating, we need to anticipate his next move. Giles will work with you."

The meeting continued with updates on other matters, but Bryn's mind was already focused on what lay ahead. Reading Agent Mercer could provide crucial information about The Hammer's plans, assuming she knew anything of value, or expose her government paymasters.

As they filed out of the conference room, Bryn caught up to Emmett. "Ready to hit the files, partner? Unless you'd rather bake some more cookies with the boss?"

Emmett's ears turned pink. "Ten minutes. I'm getting us coffee first."

Back in the apartment, Bryn set his laptop up next to Emmett's computer then dragged Gunnar's chair over so they could sit together. Emmett appeared with two extra-large takeout cups from the staff restaurant about ten minutes later.

"One of these is for you...if you promise not to tease me about Warden," Emmett said.

"You're threatening to withhold my coffee? That's devious. I like it." Bryn spun in his chair. "Okay, deal. Gimme."

Emmett handed over the cup before taking his seat. "What case do you want to start with?"

"Something that isn't in the files."

"You aren't going to get me into trouble, are you?"

"Of course not. It's a project I'm working on with Giles." He gave Emmett a quick summary of the museum case and the stolen ceremonial dagger. "I want to find out more about the weapon that was stolen."

"Okay, but we also need to line up some more cases, so how about you make a short list from that mess of files on the floor while I do some research."

"Fine," Bryn sighed. "I have coffee, so okay, but I think I've got the worst side of this deal."

They worked for an hour before Bryn got bored. He returned to sit next to Emmett. "So, what have you found so far about our fancy knife?"

"I've only had an hour, Bryn."

"Yeah and I know you. You work faster than me, Gunnar and Giles together."

Emmett, blushed. "Okay, so it's not just a fancy knife," Emmett said. "It's fascinating. The Ottoman dagger, called a khanjar, dates back to the court of Mehmed the second. I've found references to it in several occult texts, which is a bit freaky."

"I wasn't expecting that! What kind of references?"

"According to this," Emmett said, turning his screen so Bryn could see, "it was one of five ceremonial daggers created for a specific ritual. The daggers were supposed to have been consecrated with the blood of five different supernatural creatures."

"Gross," Bryn said. "Any idea what the ritual was for?"

"That's where it gets interesting." Emmett pulled up another document. "Most sources are vague, but they all point to some kind of summoning or binding ritual involving human sacrifice. I found out that three other knives have been stolen too."

"That doesn't sound good. This thief gets around, wonder if he or she has frequent flyer miles."

"All the thefts seem to have followed the same pattern. Inside jobs, minimal security disruption, targeted extraction of only these specific artifacts. I'd say they were stolen to order."

"So someone is collecting ritual daggers. For what?"

"I guess that's what you need to figure out." Emmett handed him a stack of printed materials. "You can start with these. They're translations of Ottoman court records regarding the creation of the daggers."

Bryn groaned but took the papers. "And here I thought I'd escaped the paperwork."

"Gunnar's always saying that good detective work is only ten percent excitement. The rest is grunt work."

"You got that speech too, huh? Fine. But while I read, you can tell me if Warden is as intense in personal situations as he is at work."

"Bryn!"

"What? It's a legitimate question."

Emmett's face had turned an impressive shade of red. "I'm not discussing this with you. I brought you coffee!"

"Your reaction is answer enough," Bryn said with a grin, turning his attention to the papers. "Now let's see what these creepy daggers were really made for."

As they dug deeper into the research, the historical significance of the daggers became clearer. They weren't just a valuable antiquity, at the time they were believed to be powerful magical tools created for a specific purpose.

"Look at this," Emmett said after an hour of silent reading. "According to this account, the daggers were commissioned by a secret sect within the Ottoman court. People who believed they could harness supernatural powers through blood magic."

"That cannot be good," Bryn commented, skimming through his own documents. "Wait, this says something about the daggers being used to 'bind the essence of the five powers'. Is that referring to the supernatural creatures, do you think?"

"I'd say so." Emmett pulled up an image on his computer. "Each dagger has different markings, look. Symbols representing different kinds of supernatural beings."

"And someone is collecting all of them," Bryn mused. "I wonder why Giles is so interested."

"The others were stolen from collections in Paris, Dallas and Shawnee, Oklahoma."

"So including the Boston one, they already have four out of five. I wonder where the last one is."

"I haven't had a chance to research yet."

"Always the overachiever," Bryn teased. "I guess we should get back to other work but if you get a chance, try to track down the fifth one."

"Okay. It shouldn't be too difficult."

"For you, maybe. And seriously, not even a hint about you and Warden?"

Emmett sighed but there was the ghost of a smile on his face. "Focus, Bryn. Work first, gossip later."

"Fine, but I'm holding you to that. I need deets."

"Then I get to ask questions about Gunnar."

Bryn smiled sweetly. "Well, he's about eight inches, thick, and he can go—"

"Oh my God! Stop! You don't have any shame, do you?"

"Not a shred."

* * * *

After more hours of file reading, Bryn was more than ready for an outing, even if was only to the FBI field office in Boston. He and Gunnar were escorted through security and up to a conference room where Special Agent Bell was waiting for them.

"Well, if it isn't my favorite GCR team," Bell said as they entered. "Come to complicate my life again?"

"Good to see you too, Bell," Gunnar replied. "We're here to talk to your special guest."

Bell's expression turned serious. "She's been a tough nut to crack. In fact, she's been a pain in my ass."

"That's why we're here. Bryn can help us get to the truth faster."

"I don't expect she'll cooperate with a truth read."

"She doesn't need to," Gunnar said. "Her memory and intent should give us something."

"Okay, but I'm sitting in."

"Wouldn't have it any other way."

Bryn lifted his glasses so he could glare more effectively at the two of them. "If you two have quite finished with the bromance, can we get on with this?"

Gunnar shot him an amused glance. "Do you have somewhere else to be?"

"The donut shop, preferably."

"Oh, well in that case, I guess we'd better get rolling."

Bell shook his head. "You two are...unique."

He led them to an interview room where Agent Mercer sat waiting at a table. She looked bored but her expression hardened when she saw who had entered.

"I should have known they'd send you eventually," she said. "I'm surprised it took this long."

"Mercer, or is it Hammond?" Gunnar said, taking the seat across from her. "Whoever you are, we have questions."

"I'm sure you do, but I've told the FBI everything I know," she replied.

"Which was squat," Bell snarled.

She smiled. "I won't be answering any questions from the augur either. How dumb do you think I am?"

"Aw shucks," Bryn said. "Shall I answer that one?"

"Best not," Gunnar replied. "Maybe she isn't important enough to know anything and this is all designed to waste our time."

"That must be it."

A muscle twitched in Mercer's jaw.

"Let's find out, shall we?" Bryn removed his dark glasses, revealing his intense green eyes. "I'm going to need to touch you." He stripped off his gloves, slapping them down on the table.

"It's either this or we keep you in custody indefinitely," Bell said. "Those black sites you've heard about...all real. It'd be the work of a minute to disappear you."

Mercer didn't resist when Bryn stood next to her and grasped her wrist. The moment he made contact, the room disappeared. He zeroed in on her strongest memory first and it was raw with grief. "I see a cemetery. There's rain falling and mourners dressed in black. Their faces aren't clear, as if she doesn't really see them. There are crosses and Russian words carved into the headstones. She's standing beside an open grave, watching as a coffin is lowered into the ground. She's cold but doesn't care. A man puts his hand on her shoulder. He says, 'He will pay, Katarina. I promise you this. He will pay for what he did to our boy.' His voice is heavily accented. That's it." Bryn switched his focus to intent. "Oh, oh wow."

The intensity of emotion crashed over Bryn like a physical wave. It was followed by the familiar spike of pain behind his eyes that always came with difficult readings. This one was worse than usual. The combination of overwhelming grief and cold, calculated murder was like acid on his mental defenses. He released Mercer's wrist and staggered back, one hand pressed to his temple as the migraine hit him like a sledgehammer.

"Fuck," he gasped, fumbling for a chair. The room spun, and he could taste copper in his mouth.

"Bryn?" Gunnar was at his side, helping him into a chair. "What did you get?"

"Give me a second," Bryn managed, squeezing his eyes shut against the pain. "That was...extreme."

Mercer—Katarina—watched him with cold satisfaction. "Hurts, does it? Good."

"Well, aren't you fucking a ray of sunshine," Bryn griped, though his usual snark was dampened by the pounding in his skull. He looked up at Bell, blinking to clear his vision. "She's not FBI or government and she's not working for Russo. This is family business for her. Russian, I think."

Bell's eyebrows shot up. "Russians? That's a new wrinkle."

"Her real name is Katarina. A relative, I'd guess her brother, died in one of Russo's operations, and she's out for revenge." Bryn rubbed his temples, trying to ease the pressure. "But here's the kicker. She's not planning to capture Russo. She wants him dead."

"How dead are we talking?"

"Very dead. The kind where she takes her time about it," Bryn said. "She intends to garrote him. She's rehearsed it over and over in her mind, wants him to know he's dying, wants to watch his face as she slices the wire into his windpipe. Her intent is crystal clear. She wants Russo to suffer the same terror as whoever it was that died."

"My brother. Pavel. Russo had him executed. He was shot in the face," Katarina said.

"Well, that changes things significantly," Bell said. "I know this case. Pavel Kozlov was the heir apparent to the Kozlov crime family, based out of Brighton Beach, Brooklyn."

Katarina sneered at him. "You idiots are so dumb, you don't know how little control you have."

"You can hold her longer, Bell, while you investigate the organized crime connection," Gunnar pointed out. "That should buy us some time to figure out how this affects our operations."

"Agreed." Bell looked at Katarina with new interest. "Looks like you just became a much more interesting person, Ms. Kozlova. We're going to have a lot more to talk about. Thanks to our augur friend here, Brighton Beach is about to get very popular with federal agents."

"Come on," Gunnar said to Bryn. "Let's get you back to headquarters. You look like hell."

"Feel like it too," Bryn admitted, getting to his feet. The room only swayed a little this time, which he counted as progress. He took a last glance at Katarina as they left but her face was blank and emotionless. Her eyes cold.

Bell walked them to the elevator. "I have to admit, that was impressive work. Even if it left our boy here looking like he went ten rounds with a heavyweight."

"Occupational hazard," Bryn said, managing a weak grin. "Though usually the headaches aren't quite this spectacular. That woman has some serious emotional baggage. Her intent was utterly focused. She wants an opportunity to get Russo alone, which might explain why she went to see Peregrine Frost, and she wants Russo to know he's dying."

"What a charmer," Bell said. "I'll keep you posted on what we dig up about the Kozlov connection. This could be the break we've been looking for."

"If Kozlov is willing to send his own niece after Russo, this is personal for him. Family revenge is the most dangerous kind," Gunnar said.

"When do Russian mobsters ever play games?" Bell hit the elevator call button.

The elevator arrived with a soft ding, and Bryn collapsed against the back wall after he and Gunnar stepped inside.

"Seriously, though," Bell continued as the doors started to close, "good work, Bryn. Even if you do look like you need a week at a spa."

"Sounds amazing," Bryn mumbled.

"That was one hell of a reading," Gunnar said as the elevator descended.

"Yeah, well, remind me to charge extra next time someone wants me to dive into the mind of a vengeful Russian," Bryn said. "Some memories are not worth the price of admission."

The ride back to GCR headquarters started in comfortable silence, Bryn slumped in the passenger seat with his head back and eyes closed. He sensed Gunnar's concerned glances every few seconds.

"Stop it," Bryn said without opening his eyes.

"Stop what?"

"The mother hen routine. I can hear you fretting from here."

"That reading took a lot out of you. More than usual."

"I'm fine."

"You're not fine. You could barely stand up straight back there."

Bryn cracked one eye open to glare at him. "I walked out of there under my own power, didn't I?"

"Just about, and you're still white as chalk."

"It's winter in Boston. Everyone's pale." Bryn shifted in his seat, wincing at the movement. "Besides, you've seen me after difficult readings before."

"Not like this one. Her emotions were that intense?"

"Grief and rage make for a potent combination," Bryn admitted. "Plus the whole cold, calculated murder thing. It was like reading someone who's simultaneously on fire and made of ice."

"Maybe you should take the rest of the day off."

Bryn's opened his other eye. "Absolutely not."

"Bryn…"

"Don't 'Bryn' me. I said I'm fine."

"And I'm saying you're not." Gunnar's voice had that stubborn edge that Bryn knew meant he was digging his heels in. "When's the last time a reading left you looking like you went three rounds with a prizefighter? Even Bell commented on it. Twice."

"Flattery will get you nowhere, wolf boy."

"I'm serious."

"So am I. I'm devastatingly handsome even when I'm suffering from post-read trauma. It's a gift."

Gunnar made an exasperated sound. "You're impossible."

"And you're being overprotective. Again." Bryn turned to face him, ignoring the way the movement made his head throb. "I appreciate the concern, really, but I don't need to be wrapped in cotton wool every time I do my job."

"Your job doesn't usually involve diving into the minds of homicidal Russian crime family members."

"My job involves diving into the minds of all sorts of unpleasant people. It's literally what I do."

"This was different and you know it."

Bryn was quiet for a moment, considering. "Yeah, okay, it was different. Her intent was...vivid. But that doesn't mean I'm about to keel over."

"The headache?"

"Will pass. It always does."

Gunnar pulled up to a red light and turned to look at him. "Promise me you'll rest when we get back. No more file reading, no more research projects with Emmett."

"I can't promise that. We still have work to do."

Gunnar growled.

"What? The world doesn't stop turning because my head hurts."

"Your head doesn't just hurt. You look like someone took a sledgehammer to your skull."

"You really need to work on your pillow talk," Bryn said. "Although I have to admit, the whole protective alpha wolf thing does have its appeal."

Gunnar's ears flushed a becoming shade of pink. "This isn't about...that's not what this is."

"Isn't it?" Bryn leaned back in his seat with a satisfied smirk. "Face it, wolfie, you like taking care of me."

"That's not why I'm..." Gunnar stopped, seeming to realize he was being baited. "You're changing the subject."

"I'm pointing out that your protective instincts are showing. Which is sweet, by the way, even if it is completely unnecessary."

The light turned green and Gunnar accelerated, his jaw set in that way that meant he was trying not to say something he'd probably regret.

"Look," Bryn said. "I get it. Seeing me in pain bothers you. But it comes with the territory, and I need you to trust that I know my own limits."

"Do you, though?"

"Excuse me?"

"Know your limits, because from where I'm sitting, you have a tendency to push through things that would sideline most people."

"That's not always a bad thing."

"It is when it puts you at risk."

"Everything we do puts us at risk. That's the job."

"This is different."

"How?"

"Because…" Gunnar struggled for the words. "Because I can't protect you from what happens inside your own head."

And there it was. The real issue, laid bare between them. Bryn studied Gunnar's profile, noting the tension in his shoulders, the way his knuckles were white where he gripped the steering wheel.

"Hey," he said. "Look at me." Gunnar glanced over, and Bryn was struck by the genuine worry in his eyes. "I'm okay," Bryn said. "Really. Yes, that reading was rough. Yes, my head feels like it's been used as a soccer ball. But I'm okay, and I'm going to stay okay."

"You can't promise that."

"No, I can't. But I can promise that I'm not going to take stupid risks to prove a point." Bryn reached over and squeezed Gunnar's arm. "And I can promise that if I ever feel like I'm in over my head, I'll tell you."

Gunnar's expression remained skeptical.

"I will," Bryn insisted. "Cross my heart and hope to die."

"Don't even joke about that."

"Sorry. How about scout's honor instead? But I appreciate that you worry about me. Even if you do go a little overboard sometimes."

"A little?"

"Okay, a lot. Like walk the plank and do a bit of keelhauling a lot. But it comes from a good place, and that means something."

They pulled up in the alley at the back of the GCR building. Someone would be out to take their vehicle to the GCR's garaging so they left it where it was. Gunnar punched in the access code at the security panel on the gate. "Come on, smart ass. Let's get you inside before you collapse on the sidewalk."

"I'm not going to..." Bryn started to protest, then caught the look on Gunnar's face. "Fine. But I'm not going straight to bed like an invalid."

"Okay, but you're taking those pain killers as soon as we get upstairs."

"Deal."

"You know, if the Kozlov family is actively hunting Russo, it means the game has changed," Gunnar said as they headed into the building.

"Yeah, and not for the better. That thought is not helping my headache any, by the way."

Gunnar grunted. "Think I might be getting one too."

Chapter Eighteen

Later that evening, Bryn sat slouched in his beanbag, a cold compress pressed against his forehead, while Gunnar worked at his desk nearby. Gunnar had turned off the overhead lights in favor of a lamp on his desk, which cast long shadows across the cluttered office. Bryn was grateful for the simple consideration.

"You know, staring at me isn't going to make my headache go away any faster," he said without opening his eyes.

"I'm not staring," Gunnar replied. "I'm reviewing case files."

"The same page you've been reviewing for the last twenty minutes? Because you haven't clicked that mouse once."

"It's a very complicated page."

Despite the throbbing in his skull, Bryn smiled. "You're a terrible liar."

"How are you feeling? Really?"

Bryn opened his eyes. Gunnar had abandoned all pretense of working and was watching him with an intense expression that meant he was cataloging every sign of pain or discomfort. "Better than I was two hours ago. Still feels like someone's using my brain as a drum kit, but the meds are dulling the pain. Warden stocks the good stuff."

"Good. Reading that woman did a number on you. I've never seen you react so strongly on connection like you did with her."

"Katarina's emotions were...I don't know. Intense doesn't begin to cover it. The grief was bad enough, but the murder fantasies she's been nurturing? Those packed a punch." Bryn shifted the compress to another spot. "I've never read someone with such a vivid, detailed revenge scenario. I think she must have rehearsed Russo's death a hundred times in her head. Makes her dangerous."

"Makes her predictable. People that focused on revenge tend to make stupid mistakes."

Bryn sat up straighter, wincing at the movement. "Where's Emmett? He said he'd track down that fifth dagger. Or did I miss him going home?"

"He went to grab dinner and check on something. Should be back soon." Gunnar's expression grew concerned again as Bryn rubbed his temples. "Maybe you should call it a night. Go to bed, get some real rest."

"There's too much happening." Bryn reached for his coffee mug, found it empty, and made a face. "Besides, if I go now, I'll lie in bed thinking about everything we don't know."

"I'm sure Warden could provide a sleeping pill."

"No thanks. The last thing I need is more drugs."

Gunnar's phone buzzed before he could respond. He glanced at the screen and frowned. "Bell's calling."

"Put it on speaker."

Gunnar answered the call. "Bell, you're on speaker with Bryn and me."

"Good. I've got updates on the Kozlov situation, and none of its good news." Bell's voice had a rough edge.

"You sound worse than me, Bell," Bryn said. "You need rest."

"Yeah. I remember sleep. Vaguely."

"What do you have for us?" Gunnar asked.

"First, we've confirmed that Katarina isn't working alone. Boston PD spotted at least three known Kozlov associates in the city over the past week. They're keeping a low profile, but they're here rather than on home turf in New York."

"How many people could we be talking about?" Gunnar asked. "There must be more that haven't been spotted."

"Hard to say. Could be anywhere from five to fifteen. The Kozlovs don't typically travel light when it's family business."

Bryn leaned forward. "What kind of resources are they bringing to bear?"

"The kind that makes my job a lot more complicated. We're talking about experienced operators with access to serious firepower. These aren't street thugs, they're seasoned killers."

"Fantastic. Anything else?"

"That isn't enough?"

Bryn exchanged a glance with Gunnar.

"Are we looking at war on the streets here, Bell?" Gunnar asked. "What's your assessment of the threat level?"

"High and getting higher. If the Kozlovs think Russo is planning to eliminate them using high-octane, gene-enhanced fighters, they're not going to wait around for him to make the first move. They'll strike first, hard, and anyone they see as connected to the enhancement program becomes a target. A family vendetta is perfect cover."

"Katarina knows what I am," Bryn said. "Do you think the Kozlovs are aware that Russo has a hard-on for my brain?"

"Nothing would surprise me. I'd recommend increased security measures, at a minimum."

"I'll talk to Warden," Gunnar said. "Anything else?"

"Keep your heads down and watch your backs." The call ended.

Bryn groaned then tossed the now-warm compress at the trash can. "Well, that's just perfect. As if my day wasn't already complete."

"Russo's made a lot of enemies."

"Yeah, but thanks to Katarina those enemies know what we can do and where to find us. I'd say that's a significant disadvantage."

Before Gunnar could respond, the office door opened and Emmett entered, carrying a brown bag that smelled like Chinese takeout and wearing the satisfied expression of someone who'd accomplished something important.

"Please tell me you brought enough food to share," Bryn said. "Because I need to stress-eat."

"I brought enough for four—me, you and two portions for Gunnar," Emmett replied, setting the bag on his desk. "But first, you need to see what I found about the fifth dagger."

"Good news or bad news?"

"Depends on your perspective." Emmett pulled up a file on his computer and turned the screen so they could see. "The fifth dagger is on display at the Peabody Museum at Harvard, in the Medieval Islamic Art collection."

Bryn stared at him. "There were two in the same city, you're kidding me? It's sitting less than an hour away from us?"

"Gets worse," Emmett said. "Remember the letters you've been getting from Dr. Templeton? The postmarks."

"Please tell me you're going somewhere good with this," Gunnar said.

"The postmarks on the letters match cities where other daggers have been stolen. The letter from Dallas was dated two weeks before the theft from the Dallas Museum of Art. The one from Tulsa a month before the Mabee-Gerrer Museum of Art in Shawnee was hit, which isn't that far from Tulsa. The first letter from the Wolf Run didn't have a postmark, but the first theft was from Paris, so that's probably why."

Bryn went very still. "Oh, fuck."

"I would guess that the letters and the thefts are linked."

"We haven't had a letter from Boston."

"But the theft was very recent."

"It has to be Templeton," Bryn said.

"And that's what Giles has been hiding," Gunnar said. "That sneaky son of a bitch already spotted the link but didn't tell us what he was up to. I'll bet good dollars that Warden knows too, hence the 'research' he's had Giles doing for him."

"Giles is going to love this latest development," Bryn said. "But first, I'm going to kill him."

As if summoned by his name, Giles appeared in the doorway. "Love what?" He took in the room. Bryn was hovering near Emmett. Gunnar was pacing. The room smelled of Chinese food.

"Emmett found the last knife," Bryn said through gritted teeth. "Something you want to tell us?"

Giles stepped further into the room. "You worked out the postmark correlation."

"You'd already figured it out, hadn't you?" Emmett asked.

"I thought it was a possibility." Giles' gaze flicked to Bryn. "I think Templeton has been orchestrating the thefts."

"If I wasn't feeling like hammered shit, I'd smack you around the head with Emmett's stapler, Delacourt." Bryn scowled. "You should have told us straight away."

Giles shrugged. "It could have turned out to be nothing. What would have been the point of getting you worked up?"

"Oh I call bullshit, Giles. Since when did you develop sensitivities about my feelings? Did Warden make you take a course?"

Emmett squeaked and pulled at his bow tie. Bryn immediately felt contrite. "Sorry, Emmett. I didn't mean to upset you. Just him." He glared at Giles. "Now look what you made me do."

Giles gave a slow smile.

I really, really want to wipe that smile off his smug face. Bryn kept his mouth shut.

"He's not stealing the knives himself," Gunnar said. "He's got people doing it for him. Probably paying them, or promising them something. As soon as the bodies turn up, we'll find out what they got for their work."

"The FBI aren't getting anywhere tracking him down," Giles continued. "If this is him, and that's still not certain, maybe this will help them get ahead of him."

"I'm not holding my breath," Gunnar said. "He's not stupid."

"No, unfortunately he's not." Giles turned to Bryn. "How are you feeling, by the way?"

"Like I got hit by a truck driven by a vengeful Russian mobster," Bryn replied. "But thanks for asking."

"Good. That means you're not completely addled by pain medication." Giles' tone was brisk. "We need to move on this quickly. If Templeton is collecting ritual daggers, he's not doing it for scholarly purposes."

"What's he going to do when he has all the daggers?" Emmett asked.

"Well, they were designed for human sacrifice," Giles replied. "The ceremony was meant to be as prolonged and painful as possible. I don't think we need Bryn to read his intent."

"Well, that's horrifying," Emmett said.

"If I had to make an educated guess," Giles continued. "I'd say he intends to use the knives on you, Bryn, and he wants your death to be as brutal as possible."

"Thanks for that, Giles. Makes me feel just great. If Templeton wants to slice me up with ancient knives, I'm not really feeling that plan."

"Me either," Gunnar said, a growl rumbling in his throat.

"We have no evidence at the moment, so let's not jump to conclusions," Giles said. "I'm going to have to share this latest development with Warden."

"He's going to be more than pissed," Gunnar said.

"Unsanctioned interviews, working in secret... I don't rate your chances, Giles." Bryn grinned.

"You still think he didn't sanction everything? That's sweet. Of course he knows that you were willing to go behind his back."

"Fuck my life. Someone kill me now."

"So dramatic. We'll need Warden to authorize a team to watch the Museum of Fine Arts. That has to be the next step."

"Fantastic. So let me get this straight," Bryn said. "We've got an impending war between Russian mobsters and Russo's Italian mafia. Russo wants to suck my brain out of my ears and launch an army of gene-enhanced killers on the street, and a sadistic serial killer wants to torture me to death for shits and giggles. On top of that, my boss is probably going to put flogging in the staff handbook as a permissible punishment. This day just keeps getting better."

"Look on the bright side," Giles said. "At least the Russians will want you dead quickly."

"That's not comforting," Bryn replied. "At all."

"So what now?" Gunnar asked.

"For tonight? Nothing," Giles responded. "We need more intelligence before we move and I need to go see Warden." He glanced at the Chinese takeout. "Is there enough food there for one more? I haven't eaten since breakfast."

"There's always enough Chinese food," Emmett said, pulling containers out of the bag. "I got extra of everything."

"Bless you, Emmett," Bryn said, "you're officially my favorite person today. I'm starving." Bryn swayed. "Also, my blood sugar is probably in the basement thanks to the reading hangover."

Gunnar was at his side, steadying him with a hand on his elbow. "Easy."

"I'm fine," Bryn said automatically, then caught the look on Gunnar's face. "I'm fine-ish. Better with food."

They gathered around Emmett's desk, which was transformed into an impromptu dining table. Emmett distributed containers of all their favorites and various entrees.

"So," Bryn said around a mouthful of food, "how do we go about stopping an escaped serial killer from completing a freaky murder ritual? Because that wasn't covered in my 'How Not to Get Slaughtered' training manual."

"Carefully," Giles replied. "Templeton isn't some random madman. He's intelligent, methodical, and he enjoys what he does. He's a master manipulator because he seems to have a network of people willing to carry out his instructions at great personal risk."

"What if we take the last dagger and deny him a full set. Won't he call it a day?" *I can hope.* Bryn grabbed a spring roll.

"I think he'd adapt. He has an end game in mind and won't want to be denied his fun."

"What about the museum?" Emmett asked. "Should we warn them?"

"They need to know someone is coming after it, but we need to let it happen."

"What? Why?" Bryn sputtered.

"Because if he follows the pattern, someone will be fearing for their loved ones if the robbery isn't a success. He needs to think he's succeeded."

"We track the thief to Templeton," Gunnar said.

"That sounds like a horrible idea," Bryn said.

"Gunnar's right," Giles said. "Finding Templeton and taking him down before he gets anywhere near you is our only option. We need to be subtle. Controlled. Not something you three thrive on, admittedly."

"Hey," Emmett protested. "I can do subtle."

"You brought cookies to work because you spent the night at your boss's place," Bryn pointed out. "That's many things, but subtle isn't one of them."

Emmett's cheeks turned red. "I thought we agreed not to discuss that."

"We agreed I wouldn't tease you about it. Stating facts isn't teasing."

"That's absolutely teasing," Gunnar said.

"Is not."

"Is too."

"Children," Giles interrupted. "Perhaps we could save the relationship gossip for a less potentially fatal moment?"

"Point taken," Bryn said. "But for the record, when this is all over, I want details about everyone's love life. It's only fair." He grimaced at Giles. "Except yours. I already feel sick, and don't need to add to it."

Giles smirked. "Trust me, my love life would split your head wide and have your brains leaking from your ears."

"Gross and no, not happening," Emmett said.

"We'll see," Bryn replied.

Giles shook his head. "Finish eating, then get some rest. Tomorrow is going to be a long day."

The last thing Bryn wanted to do was rest. What he wanted was for Gunnar to pin him to the bed and do whatever the hell he wanted to him. That was the therapy he needed. Not that that was something he ever intended to share with Giles fucking Delacourt.

Chapter Nineteen

The following morning, Bryn hovered behind Emmett in the office, peering at his latest whizzy spreadsheet. "I haven't had enough coffee to get my head around this," he complained.

"You're on your third mug," Emmett said.

"Not seeing your point. Tell me again how you've analyzed case priorities." Bryn shifted from foot to foot, enjoying the dull muscle aches that had resulted from Gunnar paying him a lot of close personal attention the previous night.

"I could color-code everything better to make it visually easier for you?" Emmett suggested.

"Yeah, that might be best. I can do colors."

"How's your head?"

"Attached."

"That's good," Emmett replied, all bright-eyed enthusiasm. Today's sweater vest had a pale pink diamond pattern and his bowtie was a darker shade of pink. Bryn had, as usual, selected a wardrobe of all black and the contrast between them was extreme.

Gunnar's expression was one of amused tolerance. His cell rang and he reached for it. "Oh hey, Bell. I'll put you on speaker. Bryn and Emmett are here."

"Morning all. I hope you've had your coffee because I have news."

"Not enough," Bryn complained, "you never call with good news like The Hammer got eaten by a shark or Everard Templeton's parachute failed to open during a charity skydiving event."

Bell snorted with laughter. "Nothing that good, Bryn. We had to release Katarina Kozlova this morning. We couldn't hold her indefinitely without charges, and knowing someone's planning murder isn't the same as being able to prove it in court." Bell's sigh was audible over the connection. "She walked out of here an hour ago with a smug smile on her face."

"Fantastic," Gunnar said, untying then re-tying his messy bun. "So now we've got a revenge-obsessed murderous Russian loose in the city, and no way to track her."

"Gets worse," said Bell. "She made a point of asking the receptionist for directions to the nearest flower shop. Said she needed to pick up something for a memorial service."

"Her brother's memorial?"

"Yes. The Kozlov family is having a big service for their fallen prince. That's why they've been gathering in the city. If Russo is planning a preemptive move, that's where he'll do it."

"With half the Russian mob no doubt in attendance," Gunnar said. "Christ, Bell, this could turn into a bloodbath. If the Kozlovs know what Russo is doing, why would they set themselves up as targets?"

"Russo has been out of the country. I think it's a case of complacency. They don't think he's ready to take them on yet."

"But he is!" Emmett exclaimed.

"Is it wrong that a bit of me says let them get on with slaughtering each other?" Bryn asked, sitting his ass on the edge of Emmett's desk.

"No comment." Bell's tone was wry. "Ask me what else, I dare you."

"Jesus, Bell, isn't that enough for this time of day?" Gunnar was getting growly.

"You'll love this. Fifteen minutes after we released Kozlova, one of The Hammer's lieutenants walked into our office asking for protection."

Gunnar stared at his cell. "What the actual fuck?"

"Yeah, that's what I said. Danilo Malavita. Mid-level guy, been with Russo's organization for about five years. He's scared out of his mind, claiming his boss has lost it and is planning something that will start a war."

"As opposed to their normal criminal agenda, I suppose," Bryn griped. "Because that pushes pacifism down everyone's throats, doesn't it?"

"And he wants to make a deal?" Emmett asked.

"Hi, Emmett, yes, he wants full witness protection in exchange for everything he knows about Russo's current operations. Says he never signed up for what Russo's planning to do."

Gunnar glanced at the clock. "Bryn needs to read him while he answers questions in case he's a plant."

"Indeed. Can you be here by ten?"

"We'll be there."

After Gunnar ended the call, Bryn sat on the edge of Emmett's desk swinging his legs. "Well, things don't stay still for long around here, do they?"

"You up for this? I should have asked before volunteering you," Gunnar said, grabbing his jacket.

"Of course. This'll be interesting."

"I'd take the bike but Warden won't let me at the moment. He likes armor-plated glass between you and the outside world."

"Maybe we should bring Emmett. He gets a gun." Bryn pouted.

Emmett bounced. "Ooh, road trip! But I don't have a gun anymore. I don't like them so Warden said I didn't have to carry one."

"You have him wrapped around your little finger, don't you?" Bryn grinned.

"We'll check in with Warden on the way out," Gunnar cautioned. "I'm sure he'll have an opinion, so behave."

* * * *

Thirty minutes later, Bryn was slumped in the passenger seat of the car, nursing a travel mug of coffee that was strong enough to wake the dead. Gunnar was behind the wheel and Emmett was in the back. Giles hadn't been around when they left and wasn't needed for this job anyway.

"This could be rough on you," Gunnar said, glancing over at Bryn.

"Do I have a choice?" Bryn took another sip of coffee. "If this guy has actionable intelligence about Russo's plans, we need it now and we need to know this isn't a trap."

"I know. But pushing yourself when you're already running on fumes isn't a great idea."

"It's my job," Bryn said. "You don't need to baby me. In training I managed a lot more readings before I passed out. Fun memories. Besides, cooperative subjects are easier to read and I doubt this guy will be as intense as Katarina was. That woman's head was a minefield full of bombs with ultra-sensitive triggers."

"I packed snacks," Emmett contributed.

"And that's why you're the most important member of this team," Bryn said, grateful for the change of topic. He and Emmett spent the rest of the journey discussing the relative merits of Cheetos over Lay's Bugles and whether Hershey's Kisses were worth unwrapping.

They met Bell at the federal building, where he escorted them through security to an interrogation room masquerading as something less intimidating.

"We should have our own office at this place," Bryn commented, "we're here so often."

"We couldn't afford to fund your coffee habit," Bell said.

Danilo Malavita was already seated at a table, flanked by two agents. He was a thin man in his forties, wearing an expensive suit and tie, but his knee was bouncing and there was a visible twitch beneath one eye.

"Mr. Malavita," Bell said as they entered, "these are the specialists I mentioned, from GCR. They're going to help us verify your information."

Malavita fixed on Bryn, and he blanched. "You're the augur. The one who can read minds."

"Truth, memory and intent," Bryn corrected, settling into a chair across from him. He pulled off his gloves but kept his dark glasses on. "I'm not psychic, just gene-altered. I'm guessing you know what that means."

"I heard stories. Russo's been obsessed with finding you for months. He was apoplectic when you got away in Philly. I was in a different city and felt the sonic boom." Malavita's hand shook as he reached for his water glass. "That's part of why I'm here. What he's planning…it's not only criminal, it's insane."

"Why don't you tell us what you know," Gunnar said. "Bryn will verify it."

"And I get witness protection?"

Bell, from his position by the door where he was standing with Emmett, nodded. "That's the deal."

"Okay then. From the raids that have been happening on drug manufacturing sites, I guess you already know that Russo's been working on the development of a synthetic drug. A drug that works on lupines and sanguines. It makes them stronger, faster, more dangerous. Enhancing the enhancements, if you like."

"We know."

"It's been trial and error. A lot of failure. He refined the drug by using it on subjects coming in for regulation testing and now it works. He's got six or seven men ready to go."

"How do you know?" Bell asked.

Bryn reached across the table. "I need to hold your wrist, Mr. Malavita." Malavita held his arm out and Bryn gripped his wrist. "Okay. Carry on."

"I've seen them in action. They're not gene-affected humans anymore, they're monsters. They can do things…" Malavita shuddered. "Russo's planning to use them to eliminate the Kozlov family. All of them. Every last one. It's Russo's idea of a test of their capabilities and obedience before he puts them to work on the streets."

"Truth." Bryn leaned forward, ignoring the spike of pain behind his eyes.

"When?" Bell asked.

"He's been waiting for the right opportunity, and Pavel Kozlov's memorial service is perfect. He'll do it there. The entire family will be in one place."

"And you have a problem with that?" Gunnar's voice carried a note of skepticism.

"I signed up to run numbers and collect debts, not to be part of a genocide," Malavita snapped. "Russo's talking about this like it's some kind of demonstration. Showing the other families what his enhanced soldiers can do. He's going to start a war that will burn down half the city. The Kozlovs are only the beginning."

Bryn removed his glasses then pinched the bridge of his nose. "He believes he's telling the truth."

Malavita stared at him. "Your eyes are...glowing."

"Yeah. I swallowed a uranium pill with my coffee this morning. I'm going to take a look at your memory now." He left his glasses on the table. After a second, the image came through. "He's standing in what looks like an aircraft hangar." Bryn described what he was seeing. "Russo is there, and a group of men. They look gene-enhanced. Mostly wolves I think, maybe one or two vamps. Russo is making a speech. 'When we're finished, every other family in the city will know exactly what happens to those who cross us. When we're done with Boston, we move on to New York, Chicago, Miami. We'll take out the cartels, the Yakuza, anyone that gets in my way.'"

Bryn shifted his focus to Malavita's intent. The man's fear was genuine, as was his horror at what

Russo was planning. But there was something else, a desperate hope that cooperating with the FBI would keep him alive long enough to disappear.

"He's genuine in as much as he wants to save his own skin," Bryn said, releasing Malavita's wrist. He pressed his fingers to his temples as the familiar headache began to build.

"So Russo's planning to hit the memorial service with an enhanced team and he sees it as a show of power," Gunnar said.

"How many enhanced soldiers?" Bell asked.

"There were six I saw but there may be more, of course," Bryn clarified.

"What about Russo himself?" Gunnar asked. "Will he be there?"

Malavita shrugged. "He'll be coordinating from a distance, but close enough to see the results. Fucking power hungry maniac. He had a good thing going, why does he need more?"

Agent Bell cracked his knuckles. "You'll testify to all of this in court?"

"If it means Russo goes down and I get to live through this, yes, providing you protect my identity."

Bell's phone buzzed, and he glanced at the screen. "Excuse me for a moment." He stepped out of the room, returning a few minutes later. "That was our surveillance team. The memorial is at two this afternoon but they've spotted some of Kozlov's people scoping out the area around St. Nicholas Cathedral."

"Then that's our window," Gunnar said. "If Russo's going to move, it'll be then."

"We should get back to headquarters," Bryn said. "Warden needs to know about this."

"You need anything?" Gunnar asked.

"Emmett's snacks and a bottle of water in the car will do." Bryn managed a smile. "Besides, this is the fun part, right?"

The ride back to GCR headquarters was tense. Bryn forced himself to focus on the implications of Malavita's information. "Russo perfected the drug and created super-soldiers," he mused. "How do we fight something like that?"

"Armed," Gunnar replied. "And with a lot of backup."

Emmett leaned between the seats to give Bryn a candy bar and some water. "Here. I think it all sounds very scary."

Bryn unwrapped his treat then took a huge bite. "Me too, Emmett, me too."

When they got back to Marlborough Street, they found Warden in his office, reviewing something with Giles. The moment they walked in, Warden gestured for them to take seats.

"I take it the reading was productive?" he asked.

"Productive is one way of putting it. Russo's planning to massacre the entire Kozlov family at Pavel Kozlov's memorial service this afternoon," Gunnar said without preamble. "Using enhanced wolves and vamps."

Warden frowned. "He made the drug work then. How many?"

"Six to eight confirmed but we can't be certain of final numbers. There may be more. He's going for a scorched earth approach."

"And the FBI's response?"

"Bell's coordinating with his superiors, but he'll be coming through official channels to request our help because of the gene-altered connection."

Giles leaned back in his chair. "This could be exactly what we need. If we can capture some of these enhanced men, we'll be able to analyze the drug."

"At the cost of how many lives?" Bryn asked. "The Kozlov family may be criminals, but they don't deserve to be slaughtered."

"No one's suggesting we let that happen," Warden said. "But Giles has a point. This is an excellent opportunity to get more intelligence. The Feds should be able to close a net around Russo's team now we know what the plan is."

"Using the Kozlovs as bait," Bryn said, not bothering to hide his distaste.

"Using the situation to our advantage," Giles corrected. "The memorial service is happening whether we act or not. At least this way, we have a chance to prevent a massacre and capture some of Russo's people. Maybe Russo himself, if we get lucky."

"What about warning the Kozlovs?" Emmett asked.

"Absolutely not," Giles said. "If they know we're there, they'll either run or try to handle it themselves."

"And if something goes wrong?" Bryn challenged. "If Russo's soldiers are as enhanced as Danilo Malavita thinks they are?"

"Then we adapt." Warden turned back to them. "This is what we do, Bryn. We take calculated risks to protect civilians from threats they can't handle themselves."

Bryn wanted to argue, but the pounding in his head was making it difficult to think. The logical part of his mind knew Warden was right. They couldn't pass up this opportunity. But the part of him that had read Katarina's memories, that had felt her grief and rage, rebelled against using people as pawns.

"Fine," he said. "But I want to be there."

"Absolutely not," Gunnar said. "This will be far too dangerous and besides, you're in no condition to be in the field. You're not hiding that headache very well."

"I'm perfectly able to sit in a surveillance van, nice and safe," Bryn retorted. "Besides, you have someone else who can poke around in people's heads if it's needed?"

"He has a point," Warden said. "But you stay in the van. Gunnar, you're his shadow."

"Wouldn't have it any other way," Gunnar replied.

A slow smile spread across Giles' handsome face. "This should be entertaining."

"Glad you're amused," Bryn said. "What's your role in this circus?"

"Backup. Someone has to keep you from getting yourself killed."

"Your confidence in us is overwhelming," Gunnar said.

"I prefer realistic," Giles replied. "You two have form."

"Emmett, I'll need you to monitor communications and liaise with the FBI, please," Warden said.

"I can do that," Emmett said, though he was pale and there were worry lines around his eyes.

"Good." Warden nodded. "We have four hours to coordinate with Bell's team and get everyone in position. Giles, Emmett, you're with me. Bryn, go upstairs and rest. That's an order."

"But..."

"That's an order," Warden repeated. "Gunnar, make sure he actually rests instead of pacing around the apartment planning ways to improvise."

"I don't improvise," Bryn protested. "I adapt creatively to changing circumstances."

"Same thing," Gunnar and Giles said in unison.

"Traitors," Bryn said, but he was already heading for the door. "Fine. But I want details once you and the Feds have concocted a cunning plan.

"You'll get one," Warden promised. "And Bryn? Good work on the reading."

As they climbed the stairs to their apartment, Gunnar nudged Bryn. "Have you been watching *Blackadder* reruns on BritBox again?"

"We're in the stickiest situation since Sticky the Stick Insect got stuck on a sticky bun."

"That's what I thought."

"I can keep going…"

"Let's not go there."

"Spoilsport. You know," Bryn said as he wandered into their bedroom, pulling off his top, "when I imagined my career, I never pictured myself in a surveillance van watching enhanced humans try to massacre Russian mobsters."

"Not what they cover in the training manual at the police department either," Gunnar agreed.

"Think we can pull this off?"

Gunnar was quiet for a moment. "Ask me in six hours."

"That's not reassuring."

"Would you prefer I lie to you?"

"Sometimes, yes." Bryn gave him a quick kiss. "But not today. Today I need you to be honest with me about everything."

"Including the fact that I'm terrified of letting you anywhere near this operation?"

"Especially that. See you in a few hours, wolf boy."

"Try to get some actual rest, smart-ass."

"I'll do my best."

Bryn dropped his pants then climbed into bed. Sleep was all the cunning plan he could handle at that moment.

Chapter Twenty

The surveillance van was cramped, hot, and smelled like stale coffee, sweat and boredom. Bryn shifted in his seat next to an FBI agent, who'd introduced herself as Beth, and was watching a bank of monitors showing feeds from in and around the Cathedral of the Holy Cross.

New England's largest Catholic cathedral dominated the corner of Washington and Malden in the South End of Boston, its towering Gothic Revival spires dramatic against the gray sky. The massive stone structure, with its pointed arches and intricate rose windows, seemed rock solid to Bryn. He didn't like that the building might witness violence. *Though it's probably seen its fair share in almost one hundred and fifty years. Emmett would know.*

"Movement on the east side," an FBI agent's voice crackled through the van's radio from her position across the street. "Three vehicles, tinted windows."

Bryn leaned forward, studying the screen. The images were grainy but he could make out a male driver in the lead van. "That has to be Russo's men. They aren't even trying to be subtle, are they?"

"No, they aren't," Beth agreed.

"Hold positions," came the response from Special Agent Bell. "All units, confirm readiness."

The teams sounded off in rapid succession and Bryn clenched a fist, his stomach knotting. Things were getting real. Gunnar, crouched beside him in the van, checked his weapon for the third time in five minutes. He was positioned between Bryn and the door. It was a tight space for his big frame. "I don't like this. We're too exposed." He wrinkled his nose. "Also, it stinks in here."

Beth chuckled.

"We're a hundred yards away from the action," Bryn reminded him. "I'm as safe as I'm going to get. This van is supposed to blend in, isn't it?"

"Famous last words. Any seasoned criminal can spot a surveillance van from a mile off. There are too many civilians around. Bell will have to let Russo's boys go into the cathedral before he moves in or innocent people could get hurt."

"It's a catch-22, isn't it," Bryn commented. "Clear the bystanders and Bell shows his hand. Let Russo move his men in and he risks a bloodbath in the cathedral."

"The Kozlovs aren't defenseless," Gunnar said. "They won't be dropping their weaponry in the collection plate."

"And somehow, that's not reassuring."

On the monitors, the cathedral's internal CCTV showed that the memorial service was underway. The Kozlov family and their associates had gathered in impressive numbers — at least sixty people were seated in wooden pews beneath the vaulted roof. Stained glass windows cast colored light across the assembled, black-clad group. The altar was adorned with flowers and photographs of Pavel Kozlov.

"It looks so peaceful and I'm starting to feel like a voyeur. Where's Russo?" Bryn asked, scanning the feeds. "Malavita said he'd be close enough to watch."

"The observation team tracked him going into the building across the street," Beth said. "Third floor, northeast corner. We've got eyes on the windows up there but there aren't any cameras. There's a spotter on another building watching him the old-fashioned way, with binoculars."

"No drones?" Gunnar asked.

"It would have to hover outside the window and besides, you think we have that kind of budget?"

"I'll bet Russo's enjoying this," Bryn said in disgust. "This is entertainment for him. He must know we're here by now but he won't care. People are objects to him. Pieces on a chess board ready to be sacrificed."

"Targets are moving. All units, prepare for..." Bell's communication cut off in a burst of static as men poured from the three vans.

"Jesus," Beth breathed. "Look at them move."

"If we didn't know better, they could be military special forces," Bryn said. Russo's men were dressed in black tactical gear and carried automatic weapons. They ran at high speed, fluid and smooth.

"He really has created super-soldiers," Gunnar said. "Apex predators. I should be out there."

"Or you could avoid getting unalived by staying in here with me and Beth."

The first soldier hit the cathedral's heavy wooden doors like a battering ram, splintering the wood with a single strike. The others poured through the breach and the memorial service erupted into chaos. Bryn watched the feeds in horrified fascination.

"All teams move in," Bell's voice crackled through the radio.

One of the enhanced soldiers grabbed a man twice his size and threw him across the cathedral's center aisle like a rag doll, his body crashing into the wooden pews. Another moved in a blur between the massive stone columns, taking down three armed Kozlov men before they could get off a shot.

"This is going to be a massacre," Bryn said.

"Fire at will," Bell's voice was tight with tension. "I repeat, fire at will."

"This plan is going to hell!" Bryn snapped, watching as another enhanced soldier tore through a group of people trying to flee toward the side chapels.

There was a sudden screech of tearing metal and the van's rear doors were ripped clean off their hinges. Bryn had just enough time to see a figure in tactical gear, moving with inhuman speed, before Gunnar threw himself forward with a guttural growl.

"Bryn, get down!"

The enhanced soldier was larger than the ones they'd seen in the cathedral. He reached for Bryn but Gunnar intercepted him mid-lunge. The two of them crashed into the van's equipment banks in a tangle of limbs. Beth was thrown from her seat, hit her head and slumped to the floor unconscious. Bryn scrambled to get out of Gunnar's way but in the tight confines of the van he couldn't avoid the kick that connected with the back of his knee, and he went down.

It wasn't a fair fight. The enhanced soldier was stronger and faster than Gunnar, and seemed immune to pain. He grabbed Gunnar by the throat and lifted him off the ground with one hand until Gunnar's head and shoulders were bent against the roof of the van.

Bryn didn't think—he moved. He ripped off his gloves and his glasses then lunged forward and grabbed the enhanced soldier's exposed wrist. The soldier dropped Gunnar, apparently distracted by Bryn's eyes.

What Bryn found in the soldier's memory was horrifying. He had ripped apart another man at Russo's command and had enjoyed it.

"Fuck," Bryn spat out, but his actions had achieved his goal and given Gunnar time to regroup.

"Get out of my fucking head!" the soldier snarled. A backhanded blow caught Bryn across the chest, sending him flying out of the van. He hit the pavement hard, pain exploding through his ribs. Winded, he struggled to breathe.

His dramatic exit gave Gunnar the opening he needed. With a growl, he pounced and grappled with the soldier. They crashed around the interior of the van, destroying equipment and generating sparks from damaged electronics.

Bryn's chest felt like it was on fire. He could taste blood in his mouth, and when he attempted to stand, the world spun. Through the van's shattered doorway, he could only watch as the fight raged on. Gunnar had managed to wound the soldier. Blood streamed from several gashes, but the man's enhanced healing was already beginning to close the wounds. Worse, he was starting to adapt to Gunnar's fighting style. With a violent blow, he knocked Gunnar to the floor. The soldier turned toward Bryn with predatory focus.

"Russo wants you alive, but he didn't say you had to be undamaged."

Bryn spotted movement in the back of the van behind Gunnar. Beth rolled onto her side then fired several shots at Gunnar's attacker. Bryn lay flat as bullets flew. Behind him the sound of gunfire from in and around the cathedral intensified, punctuated by screams and the crash of falling debris.

"We need to get to Russo," Bryn yelled. "If he's directing this, maybe we can force him to call them off."

With a roar of fury, Gunnar launched himself at the soldier, using all his lupine strength to tackle him. As they rolled in a tangle of limbs, Gunnar yelled, "Go! Get out of here!"

Bryn didn't argue. He hauled himself up then limped across the street, moving through the chaos as more and more emergency vehicles screamed toward the cathedral. He made his way to the building that had been pointed out as Russo's observation post, a red brick office complex from the early 1900s. Inside, the reception area had been abandoned. Ignoring the elevator, Bryn made his way up the narrow stairs, his breathing getting more labored with each step. He wrapped his arms around his torso in an attempt to squeeze away some of the pain.

"Third floor," he muttered to himself, "northeast corner." He reached the right floor and moved down the hallway. Through a partially open door, he could hear Russo's voice. He sounded excited and pleased.

"Magnificent," he was saying. "Look at them work. Each one worth a dozen normal men."

"How did the FBI get here so fast?" another voice replied. "They're making headway."

"Doesn't matter," Russo said. "My men won't stop until I tell them to."

Bryn took a deep breath, ignoring the pain from what were probably cracked ribs, and pushed through the door. The room beyond contained equipment not dissimilar to that in the observation van, with monitors showing feeds from inside the cathedral. Russo stood by the window that looked across at the cathedral. He was wearing an earpiece and watching the chaos with obvious pleasure.

"You!" he snarled when he saw Bryn. "The augur. Perfect timing—you can watch your friends die."

"Call them off," Bryn said, realizing he had no idea what to do next. He had no weapon and was in no condition to fight Russo or his companion, who didn't seem to be gene-enhanced.

Russo laughed. "Call them off? Why would I do that? They're doing exactly as I ordered."

"Stop and I'll go with you. Give you what you want." It was a desperate move.

"You're more trouble than you're worth. I appreciate you saving me the time to track you down. I suppose it was you who discovered what I was going to do? You're the reason the Feds are here making my life difficult. You'll have to pay for that."

Bryn glanced around for something he could use as a weapon but there was nothing to hand and Russo's very large friend was moving toward him. *Fuck, I should have thought this through. No more improvising, Bryn, you idiot.*

"Kill him," Russo commanded. "He's more trouble than he's worth. But make it slow."

The hulking man lunged. Bryn jerked sideways but not fast enough to avoid being struck on the shoulder by the edge of a thick forearm, spinning him into a metal cabinet. Pain flared white-hot in his ribs, and he slumped to the floor with a hiss.

"Rude," he wheezed. "I think that dislodged a kidney."

The man advanced, looming over him like an angry silverback with a grudge. Bryn braced for impact but then the door he had entered through burst inward with a shriek of torn hinges. Gunnar stormed through, his shirt torn and face bloodied.

"Did someone order a rescue with extra violence?" He growled, already moving.

"You're late," Bryn croaked.

"I was kinda busy if you recall, and when I told you to get away, I didn't mean for you to run straight to the enemy," Gunnar shot back.

Gunnar and Bryn's attacker collided like wrecking balls. The force of impact as they hit the wall cracked plaster. Bryn dragged himself upright with a groan. "Can you make this quick?"

"Really?" Gunnar shot him an exasperated look between punches.

This wasn't a gene-enhanced soldier, it was just a man, albeit a huge one. Gunnar made short work of him with a knee to the groin followed by a hammer punch to the back of the neck. The guy went down like a felled tree.

Across the room, Russo paled. He spun toward the door only to find someone already standing in his path. Giles. The man didn't walk into a room, he *arrived*, all cool detachment and immaculate attire. His calm, dispassionate confidence made Russo flinch.

"You're...also late," Bryn said, squinting at Giles through a haze of pain.

Giles glanced at him. "You're bleeding on the floor."

Russo reached for a weapon. Giles was faster. There was a blur of movement and Giles had disarmed Russo and taken a firm hold of his collar. With the barest effort, he dragged Russo across the office.

"Wait!" Russo shouted.

"Oh, hush," Giles said and, with less ceremony than if he had been taking out the trash, he hurled Russo at the nearest window.

The strength behind that throw must have been significant because the glass shattered in an explosion of sound and glittering light. A few seconds passed before a sickening crunch sounded from the street below.

Gunnar, his boot pressed into his opponent's back, stared. "Did he just...?"

"He did. Three floors down. Ouch. That must have bruised."

"You don't think holding him for questioning might have been a good idea?" Gunnar asked Giles.

Giles brushed a few bits of glass from his sleeve. "He was boring me."

Bryn huffed, holding his ribs. "Well, at least that's one of today's nightmares over."

"You're welcome," Giles said, eyes flicking to the man on the floor. "Why is this one still breathing?"

Gunnar poked the man with the toe of his boot. "We can interrogate him instead. When he regains consciousness."

Giles shrugged. "Okay, but the window is available...just saying."

Bryn limped over to the gaping hole to take a look. Down below, Russo's lifeless body had attracted a ring of agents and emergency personnel. A red puddle stained the street.

"Gross. Think Bell will want a statement?" Bryn asked.

"He'll get a shrug," Gunnar replied, crouching beside him. "Can you walk the stairs?"

"That's optimistic." Bryn winced. "I can sort of *lean*. It's adjacent to standing."

Giles picked his way over shattered glass. "You two are incredibly high maintenance."

"Oh, please," Bryn shot back. "You haven't even broken a sweat."

Gunnar chuckled and put an arm around Bryn's shoulders. "We done here?"

"For now," Giles said, already moving toward the stairwell. "We can send the Feds up here to retrieve that pile of meat."

Bryn and Gunnar followed him into the hallway, bruised and bloodied, but standing. Behind them, a shattered window marked the end of Russo's reign and the beginning of a huge pile of paperwork.

Chapter Twenty-One

The road nearest the cathedral had been blocked off and was now a chaotic scene lit by flashing lights. Bryn sat on the edge of a gurney inside an ambulance, wincing as a paramedic taped his ribs while Gunnar paced nearby.

"Hold still," the paramedic said. "You have extensive bruising and I'm making an educated guess that you have some cracked ribs. If you had a run in with one of those monsters, you're lucky that's all you've got."

"Lucky is my middle name," Bryn said, then caught Gunnar's glare. "What? It could have been worse."

"It shouldn't have happened at all," Gunnar said. "You're turning my hair gray."

Before Bryn could respond, Agent Bell appeared in the doorway, looking like he'd been through a blender. His suit was torn and there was dried blood on his shirt. A black eye was blooming and his lower lip was swollen. One arm was in a sling.

"What happened to the arm?" Gunnar asked.

"Someone tried to rip it off," Bell said. "I was lucky. The agent that intervened has a skull fracture."

"What about Beth?" Bryn was worried. She'd taken a hard hit.

"She has a headache and a sprained wrist, but she'll be fine. She asked after you two, actually. Wants to thank you for drawing that enhanced bastard away from her." Bell pinched the bridge of his nose. "Doc wanted to sign her off but she said she types with one finger anyway."

Bryn nodded. "Good. That's good. I thought everyone typed with one finger. Except Emmett, of course."

"What was the body count in the cathedral?" Gunnar asked.

Bell's expression darkened. "Fifteen casualties, but it could have been much worse. I have a lot of walking wounded. We managed to take down four of the super-soldiers, though it took everything we had. Two escaped in the confusion after Russo...fell...out of that window and stopped giving orders."

"Escaped how?" Gunnar's voice carried a dangerous edge.

"They just...ran," Bell admitted. "Faster than we could chase them. We had perimeters set up three blocks out and they still got through." He shook his head. "We've never dealt with anything like this before but we'll track them down. They don't exactly blend in."

"What about the Kozlovs?" Bryn asked, though he wasn't sure he wanted to know.

"That's...complicated." Bell glanced around, then lowered his voice. "Katarina Kozlova saved half the people in that cathedral. She's a damn good shot. When Russo's men came through the doors, she was first to react, almost like she was expecting something. She bought time for her family to escape and for our people to get into position. She didn't make it, but she passed knowing Russo was dead. I told her."

"The rest of her family?"

"Kozlov senior had a massive heart attack. He's dead. Three other family members are in critical condition, but they might survive. The organization will be in a mess, but not extinct. They won't be causing problems anytime soon."

The paramedic finished prodding Bryn and stepped back. "You're done. Take it easy for the next few weeks, and if you experience any difficulty breathing or sharp pains, get to an ER. You're not showing any sign of a punctured lung so x-rays aren't necessary. Cracked ribs don't always show up anyway."

"Thanks," Bryn said, awkwardly pulling his shirt back on.

Bell's phone buzzed. He glanced at it and sighed. "That's my boss. I need to get back and start writing reports that no one will believe." He paused. "We'll be dismantling what's left of Russo's operation over the next few weeks. Those two guys that got away are a priority, but we also need to shut down the remaining drug labs and round up his lieutenants, if they haven't already hopped flights to Bogota."

"What about the Thanacrine formula?" Gunnar asked.

"We should be able to recover new samples from the bodies here. Our scientists are already working on analysis from the raided labs, trying to figure out how to counteract it. If we can develop an antidote or neutralizer..." Bell shrugged. "It would level the playing field. Best case scenario is that the drug has died with Russo."

"Let's hope that's the case," Gunnar said.

Bell nodded. "Before I go, I want to say that was good work today. All of you. If you hadn't confirmed the truth about Russo's plan from our informant, we'd be looking at a body count in the dozens."

After Bell left, Giles appeared. "Ready to go home?" he asked.

"Where did you disappear to?" Gunnar asked.

"Went to call Warden. I gave him a quick update."

"I'm more than ready to leave," Bryn said, sliding off the gurney. "Let's go before Bell decides there's someone left alive he wants me to read."

The ride back to GCR headquarters was quiet. Bryn dozed fitfully against the passenger window while Gunnar drove. Giles occupied the back seat.

"You know Warden's going to have words," Giles said, breaking the silence.

"I know," Bryn replied without opening his eyes.

"Strong words."

"I know."

"Loud words."

"I get it, Giles." Bryn rubbed his neck, trying to ease an ache.

Gunnar pulled up outside the front of the converted brownstone saying that it was easier to get to the front door rather than dealing with the back entrance. By the time they made it to the door, Emmett was already there, bouncing on his toes.

"Are you okay? Is everyone okay? I heard there were casualties and gunfire and..."

"We're fine, Emmett," Gunnar said. "Bruised but fine."

"That's good. I was worried. Warden wants to see all of you in his office. I'll find someone to move the car."

"Yeah, I should have gone around back," Gunnar said, "but it's farther to walk and Bryn has cracked ribs."

"Oh, ouch! It's no problem. I was looking out for you."

They made their way inside, Bryn trying not to wince with each step. Warden's office door was open, and he was standing behind his desk, his expression ominous. On his desk, Bryn spotted what looked like an evidence bag containing a white envelope. *Oh no. It can't be. After this shit show of a day, I do not need this.*

"Before we discuss your unauthorized heroics," Warden said, "the FBI found this in the cathedral, tucked behind one of the prayer candles near the altar." He held up the evidence bag. "It's addressed to you, Bryn. From Dr. Templeton."

Fuck my life. "He was there?"

"Him or his messenger. We don't know when the letter was placed there but it probably happened after everything was over and Russo's men were gone. Bell's people are reviewing all the CCTV footage, but with everything that happened..." Warden shook his head. "He could have walked in and out in the chaos wearing a clown suit and we'd never have noticed him."

"What does it say?" Gunnar asked.

"I haven't opened it yet." Warden set the bag down. "We can deal with this tomorrow if you're not up to it, Bryn."

Bryn stared at the letter, feeling a familiar chill. It was possible that Everard Templeton had been watching him. Had probably been observing the mayhem unfold.

"I need to see it now."

Warden nodded. "Very well."

"You do it."

Warden slipped on a pair of latex gloves then opened the evidence bag. The letter was written on the same expensive cream paper as the previous ones, in the same precise handwriting.

Warden read aloud, "'My dear Bryn, what a fascinating afternoon this has been. It has been some time since I witnessed such beautiful anarchy. You continue to surprise me with your courage, though I worry you're becoming reckless. A mind like yours should be preserved, not risked in such crude, violent circumstances. Mr. Russo's creations lacked artistry. True power lies not in brute strength but in understanding the human psyche. I look forward to our eventual meeting. Until then, do try to be more careful. Yours sincerely, Everard.'"

The office fell silent.

"He was watching," Bryn said. "The whole time, he was watching."

"We'll increase security," Warden said.

"He's getting bolder."

"All the more reason to keep you safe," Gunnar stated.

"What he said," Giles agreed.

"I won't be a prisoner because of him," Bryn said. "I don't think any security, short of a locked cell, will deal with him. There are enough restrictions on my life already."

"We can talk about appropriate measures," Warden said. "Now sit, all of you." He gestured to the chairs in front of his desk.

"Special Agent Bell called twenty minutes ago and gave me a preliminary report," Warden began. "His story was similar to what you had already detailed, Giles." His gaze fixed on Bryn. "Though Giles glossed over your little solo mission to confront Russo."

"I was trying to…"

"You were trying to get yourself killed," Warden cut him off. "Again. What possessed you to charge into that building without backup?"

"He was directing the operation. I thought if I could get to him…"

"You thought?" Warden's voice rose. "You thought you could take on Russo and whoever was with him with cracked ribs and no backup?"

"I had backup," Bryn protested. "Gunnar showed up."

"Eventually. I was a little busy, if you recall," Gunnar said. "Do you have any idea what I felt when I fought my way out of that van and realized you'd disappeared?"

"You did tell me to run. You didn't specify where to. Besides, it worked out." Bryn sulked.

"By sheer luck!" Warden slammed his hand on the desk. "You could have been killed, Bryn. Or worse, you could have been captured again. Do you understand what Russo would have done to you?"

Bryn shifted in his chair. "Yeah, well I think I annoyed him too much because he just wanted to kill me. I know the risks of this job."

"No, you don't," Warden said. "Because if you understood the risks, you wouldn't keep taking them. This isn't the first time that you've gone off script and put yourself in unnecessary danger."

"I'm not fragile."

"No, you're not. You're essential," Warden said. "Your abilities make you one of the most valuable assets we have. You're also irreplaceable. We can't train another augur, Bryn. There isn't one. If something happens to you, that's it."

The room fell silent. Bryn stared at his gloved hands, feeling the weight of Warden's words. "I'm not an asset," he said. "I'm a person. And sometimes people have to make choices about what's right, even if it's dangerous."

Warden's expression softened. "I know you are. And I know your instincts are good. But your value to this organization means we can't afford to lose you."

"So, what are you saying?"

"I'm saying that from now on, you don't go anywhere near active combat situations."

"You're benching me?"

"I'm protecting you."

"From what? Doing my job?"

"From getting killed because you don't value your own life," Warden said. "Your job doesn't need to involve combat operations."

"My job," Bryn said, his voice rising, "is using my abilities to help people. If that means taking risks, that's what I'll do."

"It means taking calculated risks under controlled conditions," Warden interrupted. "Not charging into buildings full of armed criminals."

Gunnar cleared his throat. "With respect, sir, Bryn's actions today prevented further casualties. If he hadn't distracted Russo…"

"If he hadn't been there, Giles could have handled Russo without risking an augur's life," Warden said.

The argument might have continued, but Emmett spoke up from his corner chair. "Actually," he said, "Bryn's right."

Everyone turned to stare at him.

"I mean," Emmett continued, his cheeks reddening, "not about the part where he ran into danger without backup. That was terrifying and please don't do it again, Bryn. But about using his abilities to help people. That's what makes him good at this job."

"Emmett…" Warden began.

"No, let me finish…sir," Emmett said, surprising everyone with his firmness. "Bryn took risks today, yes. But he also saved lives. The agent in the surveillance van might be dead if he hadn't drawn that enhanced lupine away from her. The FBI might not have been able to coordinate their response without the intelligence from Malavita that he confirmed was true and Salvatore Russo might still be out there planning his next attack if Bryn hadn't forced the confrontation."

"The ends don't justify the means," Warden said.

"Maybe not," Emmett agreed. "But sometimes the means are the only way to achieve the ends. Bryn's not reckless because he doesn't understand the risks. He's willing to take risks because he understands the consequences of not taking them."

The office fell quiet again. Warden studied Emmett for a long moment, then shifted his gaze to Bryn. "Is that how you see it?" he asked.

Bryn considered the question. "I see people in danger, and I see a way to help them. Sometimes that way involves risk. I'm not trying to be a hero, Warden. I'm trying to do the job you had me trained to do."

Warden was quiet for a long moment, then sighed. "You're not wrong. But you're also not invulnerable. Today could have gone very differently."

"But it didn't."

"This time."

Gunnar leaned forward. "If I may…what if we established protocols for situations like this? Clear guidelines for when field operations are acceptable, with mandatory backup and communication requirements?"

Warden considered this. "You'd be responsible for enforcing those protocols."

"Absolutely."

"And you'd be willing to physically restrain him if necessary to keep him from doing something stupid?"

Gunnar glanced at Bryn, who rolled his eyes. "If necessary."

"Hey," Bryn protested. "I'm sitting right here."

"Which is more than we could guarantee if you keep pulling stunts like today's," Giles said.

Warden rubbed his temples. "Fine. We'll draft protocols. But until they're in place, you're on restricted duty. And given Dr. Templeton's interest in you, that restriction is non-negotiable."

"Warden..."

"That's final, Bryn. You scared ten years off my life today. You've got a serial killer writing you love letters, and I'm too old to keep having heart attacks every time you decide to improvise."

Bryn wanted to argue, but exhaustion was catching up with him. His ribs ached, his head was pounding, and the adrenaline crash was making him feel sick. He located Warden's trash can just in case.

"Can I go now?" he asked.

"Yes," Warden said. "But I want a full written report on my desk by tomorrow morning."

"You wouldn't be you if you didn't."

Gunnar helped Bryn out of the room and in the hallway, Emmett caught up with them.

"That was quite a speech," Gunnar said to him.

Emmett blushed. "I just... I worry about Bryn too, you know? But I also understand why he does what he does."

"We all do," Gunnar said. "That's what makes it so terrifying."

As they climbed the stairs to the apartment, Bryn leaned on Gunnar. "So," he said, "what are the odds Warden follows through on those protocols?"

"High," Gunnar said. "He's not bluffing about being worried and on this, I agree with him."

"As long as it doesn't stop me from doing the job."

"It won't," Gunnar assured him. "It'll make sure you survive to keep doing it."

"That's the plan," Bryn said, opening their apartment door. "Now, can we please order pizza and pretend today didn't happen?"

"Only if you promise not to answer the apartment door if anyone suspicious sneaks up here," Emmett said.

"That includes Giles, right?"

"You're very naughty."

"Who's going to get up here with the security in this building, Emmett?"

"I don't know. It could happen."

"Okay, Gunnar can answer the door today," Bryn said. "But I'm not promising anything about tomorrow. I may feel the urge to rush into the hall and let any old psycho in."

Emmett stared at him then broke into a fit of giggles. "I'm being silly, aren't I?"

"You think?"

Gunnar guided Bryn toward the couch. "Rest and pizza is all you need to be thinking about right now."

"And garlic dough balls. Oh my God, what if they don't have any?" Bryn feigned outrage at the possibility.

"One crisis at a time," Gunnar said. "One crisis at a time."

Chapter Twenty-Two

The pizzas had been ordered, delivered, and mostly consumed. The remnants lay in the boxes on the coffee table. Bryn was stretched out on the couch, one arm draped over his eyes, while Emmett sat cross-legged on the floor sorting through requests for help on his tablet that he'd brought through from the office. Gunnar had made tea and produced an unopened box of Twinkies for dessert. Bryn had eaten three, hence his current sugar coma.

They'd been sitting in comfortable silence for about twenty minutes when there was a soft knock at the door.

"I'll get it," Emmett said, bouncing to his feet.

"I thought Gunnar was supposed to be answering the door," Bryn snarked.

"Go ahead, Emmett," Gunnar said, "ignore him."

Emmett returned with Giles and Bryn uncovered his eyes to find out what he wanted. He looked...wrong. His usual perfect posture had given way to a slight slump, and his skin had taken on a grayish pallor that made him look older than his thirty-something years. There was a tension around his eyes that spoke of controlled discomfort.

"Giles?" Bryn said, struggling to sit up despite his protesting ribs. "You look like shit. What are you doing here? I thought you'd gone back to your hotel to brood in private like a proper vampire."

"I had intended to," Giles said, ignoring the jibe and settling into an armchair. "But I find myself in need of...assistance."

"Well, that's refreshingly honest," Bryn said. "You must be feeling bad."

"When did you last eat?" Gunnar asked. "And I don't mean whatever sad excuse for nutrition you've been subsisting on."

Giles was quiet for a moment. "I've had plenty of raw steak, including some after we got back from the cathedral, but..."

"Oh, lovely," Bryn said. "Bloody flesh is so tempting."

"But that's not enough, is it?" Gunnar said, ignoring Bryn's commentary. "Raw meat usually sustains you fine, but not after what you did today."

"No," Giles admitted. "It's not enough. When I move that fast and use my full strength, I need more. My reserves are more depleted than I anticipated."

"I don't understand," Emmett said, looking confused.

"Giles isn't a normal sanguine, Emmett. He's much more vamp than most vamps, if you know what I mean?"

"Not really."

"He's strong, Emmett and very fast. You haven't seen him in action but you have to have noticed he's a bit...fangy."

"Dear Lord help me," Giles declared. "Emmett, what Bryn is so eloquently trying to say, and failing, is that I'm more akin to a true vampire than most sanguines."

"Than any other sanguine," Bryn clarified.

"Yes...but that also means that on occasion, when I've exerted myself, I need to consume blood. Fresh blood, from the vein."

Bryn looked at Giles, then at Gunnar, then back at Giles. He'd been dreading this moment since Giles had arrived in Boston. It had been a year since his training ended, a year since he'd last done this, and he'd been perfectly happy to keep it that way.

"Okay," Bryn said, rolling up his left sleeve with obvious reluctance. "Come here."

"Bryn, no," Giles said. "I won't ask that of you. Not after —"

"You're not asking. I'm offering. Grudgingly. Try to keep up."

"You hate it."

"I hate a lot of things about you," Bryn said flatly. "But you're verging on translucent at this point, and if something happens tomorrow, we need you functional. Not decorative. This isn't the fucking Twilight saga. Don't turn this into a damn drama."

"I don't give a fuck how hungry you are, Giles," Gunnar snapped. "Figure it out. You don't get to touch him. Not after what you put him through."

"A blood bag might suffice," Giles said.

"You need warm blood from a vein, so suck it up, vamp boy," Bryn said from behind Gunnar. "Blood bags would leave you weaker and vulnerable if something went wrong. What happens when you collapse mid-fight because you were too proud to ask for help?"

Gunnar whirled around to face Bryn. "Are you out of your goddamn mind? After everything he did to you? The way he treated you in training?"

"Gunnar..."

"No." Gunnar did his best impression of immovable granite. "I know what his 'training' did to you. This is a safe place. He doesn't get to hurt you again."

Giles flinched, but said nothing.

"Look," Bryn said, his irritation building, "I know this is awkward. I know we all wish we didn't have to do this. But, Gunnar, we need him alive and useful, not stubborn and dead. So let's get it over with."

"Over my dead body," Gunnar said, stepping closer to Giles with predatory intent. "Touch him and I'll tear your throat out with my bare hands."

"Your conditions?" Giles asked Bryn, deliberately avoiding Gunnar's murderous glare.

"Gunnar stays," Bryn said without hesitation. "If something goes wrong, he pulls you off. And next time, figure out your feeding schedule before you get to the point of collapse. I'm not your fucking juice box. Gunnar, take a step back. This is my decision, much as I appreciate your willingness to dismember him. Maybe stick a pin in it and we can revisit that idea later."

Gunnar growled but moved back. "If I so much as sense you're taking more than you need, or causing him unnecessary pain," he said, "I'll make what you did to Russo look like a pleasure flight."

Emmett's eyes were huge. "You mean Giles is going to..." He made fang gestures with two fingers.

Bryn couldn't help but smile. "Yes, Emmett, he is. Maybe you could create a nice chart for him to monitor his energy levels or something?"

"Yeah, I could figure something out. Oh! I could sync it to his phone and watch."

"Great idea!"

Gunnar moved to sit on the couch beside Bryn, his body radiating tension as he positioned himself like a guard dog. His hand settled on Bryn's shoulder, but his eyes never left Giles, tracking every movement.

Giles rose from his chair, his usual grace absent as he approached with obvious reluctance.

"Wrist," Bryn said, extending his left arm. "And Giles? Gunnar's got excellent reflexes and, as you may have noticed, very little patience when it comes to people hurting me. More than they already have."

The pointed comment made Giles wince. "Understood."

"Two minutes," Gunnar said. "Not a second more, and if you traumatize him the way you did during training, I'll hunt you down and feed you your own fangs."

The bite was quick and clinical, nothing like the dramatic neck wounds of vampire movies. Giles pierced the skin below Bryn's wrist, and Bryn felt the familiar but strange sensation of feeding. Not quite pain, not quite pleasure, but something that made his skin prickle and brought back unwelcome memories. Gunnar's grip on his shoulder tightened to the point of pain, and his free hand hovered inches from Giles' throat, ready to make good on his threats. The protective fury radiating from him was palpable, and Emmett had unconsciously scooted further away. Bryn didn't blame him.

The feeding lasted maybe two minutes before Gunnar's patience snapped. "Enough," he snarled, his hand shooting out to grab Giles by the throat. "Get off him. Now."

Giles pulled back immediately, already looking better with color returning to his face and the tension around his eyes easing. Gunnar didn't let go, his fingers tightening on Giles' throat as he leaned in close. "If you ever ask for this again, I'll stake you myself. Find another way to manage your feeding, or find another donor. He's not your fucking personal blood bank."

"Better?" Bryn asked, rolling his sleeve down with a jerk, unbothered by Gunnar's reaction.

"Much. Thank you," Giles managed, once Gunnar finally released him with a shove.

"Don't mention it. Seriously. To anyone. Ever. I don't need to get a reputation as a vamp's snack dispenser."

Gunnar remained tense, his eyes never leaving Giles as the vampire moved back to his chair. "This was a one-time exception, Delacourt. Don't mistake necessity for forgiveness."

Before anyone could respond, there was another knock at the door. This time Gunnar answered it, returning with Warden in tow.

"How are you feeling?" Warden asked, taking in the scene.

"Like I was the one that got thrown out a window," Bryn said. "But alive, so there's that."

"Good. I wanted to speak with all of you before you turned in for the night." Warden settled into the chair Giles had vacated. "I've been on the phone with Washington for the past hour, briefing them on today's events."

"And?" Gunnar prompted. "Are we getting medals or official reprimands?"

"And they're impressed. Disturbed by the implications of Russo's enhancement program, but impressed by how we handled it. There will be an

investigation into the source of some of his funding."
Warden's gaze shifted to Giles. "They were particularly
flattering about your contribution, Giles."

Giles straightened. "I didn't do anything special."

"Apart from saving my life, probably Gunnar's too,
along with a whole load of FBI agents and half the
Kozlov crime family," Bryn contributed.

"Which brings me to my next point," Warden said.
"I'd like you to move here on a permanent transfer
from The Facility."

Bryn gaped at his boss in horror. "A what now?"

"You mean it?" Giles looked surprised.

"Was anything I said unclear? I'm offering you a
permanent position with this team, Giles. You'd be
working with them exclusively."

The room fell silent. Giles stared at Warden, clearly
processing the offer. Bryn scowled like he'd been
offered a root canal without lidocaine.

"You want him to transfer permanently?" Bryn
asked. "Here? With us? Every day?"

"I want him to consider it," Warden said. "Giles
works well with this team. He understands your
abilities and...history. And after today, I think we need
someone with his particular skill set on a permanent
basis."

"What about Giles' current workload at The
Facility?" Emmett asked, shooting nervous glances
between Bryn and Giles.

"The work can be picked up by others. There are no
augurs in need of specialized training at the moment.
Other staff can handle routine processes."

Bryn looked around the room, at Emmett, who was
clearly torn between excitement and worry; at Gunnar,
who looked resigned rather than pleased; at Warden,
whose mind was made up. "Fantastic," he said.

"Because what this team needs is more complicated history and awkward silences."

"Bryn," Gunnar said, "maybe we should…"

"Should what? Pretend this is a great idea? Pretend we're all one big happy family now?"

Giles' remained serene. "If my presence here is going to be a problem…"

"Your presence is always a problem," Bryn snapped. "The question is whether it's a useful problem or just a painful one."

The tension in the room was thick enough to cut with a knife. Gunnar's hand found Bryn's shoulder again, a steadying pressure.

"What about it, Giles?" Warden asked, ignoring the byplay. "Are you interested?"

Giles was quiet, probably assessing the level of Bryn's hostility. "I accept," he said.

Emmett looked relieved. Gunnar nodded once, accepting the inevitable. Bryn wanted to throw something, and would have if his ribs didn't hurt so much.

"Excellent," Warden said, standing. "Welcome to the team. We can pick up the details tomorrow. Emmett, I need you to come with me. There are some admin matters we need to discuss."

Emmett's cheeks flushed. "Yes, sir. Right now?"

"Right now," Warden said, and there was something in his tone that made Emmett straighten.

"Yes, sir."

As they headed for the door, Warden paused. "Get some rest. All of you. Tomorrow we consider our next moves regarding Dr. Templeton."

The door closed behind them, leaving an uncomfortable silence.

"They aren't going to do admin," Bryn said.

"I don't believe they are," Gunnar agreed.

"Well," Giles said after a moment, "this should be interesting."

"That's one word for it," Bryn said. "I can think of several others. Most of them not for use in polite company. Or this company."

"Look, if this is going to be a problem…"

"Everything's a problem, Giles. The question is whether we can work around it or if it's going to blow up in our faces." Bryn stood up, wincing. "I don't think there's anything on my entire body that doesn't hurt. I'm going to bed." He left Gunnar and Giles sitting in the kind of silence that spoke volumes about the complicated dynamics they'd all have to navigate going forward. He paused behind the bedroom door, curious to hear what the two of them would say.

"He'll come around," Gunnar said, though he didn't sound entirely convinced.

"Will he?" Giles replied.

Gunnar considered this. "Maybe. Eventually. Bryn has three years' worth of good reasons to hold a grudge against you, but he's practical above all else. You're useful."

"Useful enough to outweigh the past?"

"That remains to be seen."

"I should head back to the hotel. Give everyone time to process this."

"Probably wise," Gunnar agreed.

Bryn kept still while Gunnar walked Giles to the door. After he'd gone, Gunnar stood in the hallway for a moment, then came to the bedroom.

"I know you were listening."

Bryn shrugged. "Come to tell me I'm being unreasonable?"

"No. Your unreasonableness is justified, but we'll deal with Giles anyway."

"How diplomatic of you."

"I have my moments." Gunnar closed the door behind him. "You okay?"

"Define okay. My ribs hurt, I just fed a vamp I'd rather avoid, and said vamp is now going to be my permanent coworker. So by my standards? Fantastic."

Gunnar sat on the edge of the bed, and Bryn settled beside him.

"For what it's worth," Gunnar said, "I think you handled that better than expected."

"What, the feeding or the potential tantrum?"

"Both. Warden dropped a bombshell without warning you. I was impressed by your restraint in not actually throwing anything."

"I wanted to, and the night is young," Bryn said.

"This complicates things," Gunnar said.

"Everything's already complicated," Bryn pointed out. "At least now we can be miserable together on a more regular basis."

"Very romantic."

"I'm a romantic person."

"You're many things," Gunnar said, settling his arm around Bryn's shoulders. "Romantic isn't one of them."

"Rude. I can do hearts and flowers." Bryn leaned into Gunnar's warmth. "So what now? We all pretend to be supportive teammates while I resist the urge to stake Giles?"

"Pretty much. Though I'd prefer you resist the urge to stake anyone. It'd be messy, and he did save our asses today, much as I hate to admit it."

"Spoilsport."

Gunnar kissed the top of Bryn's head. "I'll make it up to you."

"You'd better. Because if I'm going to survive having Giles around full-time, I'm going to need all the incentive I can get to behave myself."

"I'll see what I can do."

"How about you start by kissing me? That seems like a good option, favorable to all parties involved."

Gunnar cupped the nape of Bryn's neck in the possessive way that made Bryn's insides turn to goo. He let Bryn move at his own pace, being careful not to jostle him and Bryn knelt on the mattress, being equally tentative in the way he moved. He tangled a hand in Gunnar's hair.

"Love your hair," he murmured. "It's so silky."

"And manly. You forgot manly." Gunnar kissed Bryn's jaw, then the corner of his lips.

"Oh, yeah. That." Bryn nipped at Gunnar's lower lip then licked away the sting.

"You getting a taste for blood too?" Gunnar mapped the curve of Bryn's shoulder blade, tracing light circles beneath his shirt. Bryn shut his eyes and pressed a hand to Gunnar's chest, feeling the low rumble of a growl that meant he was making an effort to hold back.

"No. Happy to leave the red stuff to Giles…and also not to talk about him ever again."

Gunnar lowered him to the mattress. "Careful, we both know you're terrible with doctor's orders."

Bryn croaked a laugh and flopped, letting Gunnar settle over him. "Says the worst patient on the planet. Worried I'll break?"

"Worried I won't be able to stop if you do," Gunnar murmured. He pushed his knee between Bryn's, and braced his weight on his elbows. Bryn shuddered at the touch.

Gunnar deepened his kisses and let his touch wander, gentle at first, then more greedy once Bryn begged, "Don't stop." The nagging pain in his ribs was nothing compared to the ache of his need. He hooked his fingers into Gunnar's belt loops and tugged. Gunnar took the hint and shimmied out of his jeans and shorts. The sight of his flushed, rigid cock had Bryn licking his lips. "Want you in me." He craved the completeness of Gunnar filling him but his body had its own agenda, rewarding him with white-hot pain every time he twisted wrong. "Shit." He sucked in his breath. Gunnar went still.

"Are you…"

"I'm good," Bryn said. He was. He wasn't. He was everything at once, raw edges and flayed nerves, the pain making everything more real somehow. "Hold it there for a second."

Gunnar loomed over him, uncertain, eyes bright with want and concern. That combination made Bryn ache in a way that had nothing to do with his ribs. Every second Gunnar didn't move, didn't close the gap, Bryn wanted him more.

"Fuck me, Gunnar. Do it now."

Gunnar's eyes darkened. "I don't want to hurt you."

"You didn't. You won't. I need you."

Gunnar stripped him, careful with the shirt but rougher with the jeans and briefs, pulling them past Bryn's knees and off. Fresh bruises had blossomed, livid on Bryn's pale skin. Gunnar gripped his hips and there would be more marks but Bryn welcomed bruises that came from love not violence. That came from Gunnar.

Gunnar found lube from somewhere then pinned him in place. He slathered his cock in gel before wiping the excess on Bryn's thigh.

"Hey! That's cold."

"No shit, Sherlock. It's all over my dick, remember?"

He pushed into Bryn's channel, slow and steady. The initial pain was a distant echo to the fire in his ribs, but after a second the pleasure blew out everything else.

Gunnar got into a rhythm. He pressed Bryn's knees apart, hips rolling slow and deliberate, tilting Bryn's pelvis just enough. Bryn urged him to go faster, harder, but Gunnar only gave it in increments, dialing up the force a little more with each pass.

"Are you hurting?"

"Shut up." Bryn managed to grate out the words. "Fuck me." He dug his heels into Gunnar's hips, urging him deeper. "Don't you dare stop."

Bryn's cock ached. He reached down to stroke himself, but Gunnar swatted his hand away. "Let me," Gunnar rasped, voice almost gone. Then he fisted Bryn's shaft and Bryn's brain malfunctioned.

Gunnar's rhythm splintered at the end, and he buried his face in the crook of Bryn's shoulder, muffling his groan as he came. Bryn felt the heat bloom inside and he shivered with something that felt like triumph. He finished a moment later, Gunnar's hand locked around him, his grip making everything bigger. He didn't want Gunnar to move. Didn't want the world to come back in.

They stayed there, until after a minute, Gunnar eased himself out, then rolled onto his back. Bryn turned to look at him, really look — the flush in his cheeks, the way strands of his hair stuck to his damp skin. Gunnar caught him staring and gave him a lopsided grin.

"You always have to test limits, don't you?"

Bryn shrugged, or tried to. "How else do I know where they are?" He wasn't sure when he started laughing, but it bubbled up of its own accord, and Gunnar joined in.

"We should sleep. It's been quite a day. I love you."

"Yeah. Love you too." Bryn closed his eyes, feeling the bruises, the ache, the warmth inside and out. He told himself that if he could fall asleep right there, next to Gunnar, then everything would sort itself out by morning. He didn't believe it, but the self-deception made it easier to breathe.

Gunnar didn't say anything else. Bryn didn't need him to. For now, everything worth saying had been said, and anything left was a problem for tomorrow.

Sign up for our newsletter and find out about all our romance book releases, eBook sales and promotions, sneak peeks and FREE romance books!

Want to see more from this author?
Here's a taster for you to enjoy!

The Augur: Seeing Evil
L.M. Somerton

Excerpt

The last thing Bryn Ashton expected on a Sunday was a phone call at six-thirty in the morning from his boss telling him there was a dead body on Boston Common.

"I thought we agreed," Bryn said into his cell, not bothering to hide his irritation, "that unless the world was ending, my Sundays were sacrosanct. Twenty-four hours of blissful ignorance." Next to him, his partner, Gunnar Ericson, stirred with an unintelligible grumble.

"Wassup?"

"No idea." Bryn switched his cell to speaker. "But it's too damned early for this."

"Unfortunately" — Warden's voice came through the speaker with its usual dry precision — "the world has a tendency to ignore your scheduling preferences."

Bryn rolled over in bed, wincing as the movement sent him a sharp reminder about his healing ribs. Three weeks of light duties had done wonders for his recovery and the cracked ribs and general battering he'd sustained during the Boston Cathedral incident were finally healing properly. There was just an occasional twinge.

"What's going on, Warden?" Gunnar dragged himself into a sitting position.

"A child, a nine-year-old boy called Timmy Smit," Warden said, "was found this morning by an early jogger on the Common. Preliminary examination suggests he's been dead for approximately six hours."

"Without wishing to be cold, why does that concern us? It's a Boston PD case, isn't it?" Bryn questioned.

"In normal circumstances it would be."

Oh fuck. "How did the child die?" Bryn asked.

"Throat cut. Clean, precise. No defensive wounds." Warden paused. "There's something else, Bryn. Something left at the scene."

The words hit Bryn like a physical blow. He sat up too, any hope of an energetic lie-in with Gunnar long gone. "What kind of something?"

"A drawing. Child's crayon on construction paper. It's a stick figure with your name written beneath it."

"Son of a bitch. Templeton."

"My thoughts exactly. How quickly can the two of you get to the scene?"

"Half an hour." Bryn was already swinging his legs out of bed. "Has anyone else seen the drawing?"

"Only the first responders. I called in the Feds and Special Agent Bell has the scene locked down tight."

"Okay." *Nothing about this is okay.*

"Giles will meet you at the Common. Gunnar, there will be a car waiting for you outside. I'll call Emmett in so that he can provide support when you get back here."

Bryn ended the call and turned to find Gunnar watching him with dark eyes that missed nothing.

"I can smell your stress," Gunnar said. "This is bad." His voice was still rough from sleep.

"The worst." Bryn stood up slowly, one hand pressed to his ribs as he started pulling on clothes. "Looks like the psycho doctor has decided to resume his hobby. He's back and the sonofabitch is making it personal."

* * * *

Boston Common at seven in the morning was usually a peaceful place, with joggers making their circuits, dog walkers letting their pets exercise their noses and weekend workers taking a short cut. Today, it looked like a crime scene, which was exactly what it was.

Gunnar flashed his credentials to the uniformed officer manning the perimeter and ducked under the yellow tape. He held it up for Bryn to follow.

"I'm not looking forward to this," Bryn muttered.

"It's not something you ever get used to," Gunnar replied. "Seeing the body of someone who dies by violence is not great. When it's a child…"

He didn't have to finish. The body was about fifty yards from the main path, in a small clearing that would have been hidden from casual view.

"Smart positioning," Gunnar observed.

"Well, we know Templeton is far from stupid. If this was him."

Special Agent Bell came across to them from where he'd been standing watching the crime scene techs at work. "I'd say good morning, but it isn't. I thought you were still on light duties, Bryn."

"I am, so don't ask me to pick-up your donut bag because the weight might damage me."

"He's getting back to his usual, charming self, isn't he?" Bell addressed the question to Gunnar, who had a smirk on his face.

"Tell me he's wrong." Gunnar nodded toward the covered form on the ground a few yards away. "What do we have?"

Bell flipped open his notebook. "Timmy Smit, nine years old. Parents reported him missing yesterday afternoon when he didn't get off the school bus. We've got a preliminary timeline suggesting he was grabbed sometime between three and four. Driver doesn't recall him getting on the bus so it's likely he was taken outside his school."

"Cause of death?"

"Single cut across the throat. Clean, precise. No hesitation marks, no defensive wounds. Kid likely didn't see it coming, which is a small mercy."

"Any signs of sexual assault?"

"ME's preliminary says not, but we'll know more after the autopsy." Bell shuddered. "Whatever this bastard's motivation is this time, it doesn't seem to be sexual."

Gunnar frowned. "He got off on his earlier killings, we know that, but it was the act of killing that got him going. This is still a bit off Templeton's MO, though. He was into torture and strangulation. Are you sure this is down to him?"

"As sure as we can be at this point." Bell handed over a clear plastic evidence bag. "Because of this."

Gunnar held up the bag so Bryn could see the drawing it contained. His stomach knotted and he had to fight the urge to throw up. The drawing was how Warden had described it, a stick figure in crayon. What he hadn't mentioned was that the figure had short black hair and bright green eyes. Beneath the drawing, in a child's blocky handwriting, were the words *For Bryn*.

"Jesus Christ."

"He made the kid draw this?" Gunnar's voice sounded far away somehow, even though he was within touching distance.

"We still don't know for certain it was him," Bryn said, though he didn't believe it. "We've made a lot of enemies." A sixth sense told him someone was approaching even though they made no noise. Bryn sighed. "Giles."

Giles was impeccable as always, despite the early hour. He took in the scene without displaying any obvious emotion.

"Good morning, esteemed colleagues," he said, his cultured British accent carrying just a hint of sarcasm. "Not the most enjoyable way to begin the day, is it?"

"Any day with you in it doesn't start well, Giles," Bryn replied, eliciting a slow, lazy smile from the sanguine.

Giles's expression grew serious as he looked at the evidence bag. "It's a shame you can't read anything from inanimate objects."

Bryn shook his head. "Unless you've found a witness who saw the murder, Bell, I'm useless here."

"The jogger who found the body," Bell said. "Name is Carmen King. She's pretty shaken up, but she's coherent. She's waiting in a patrol car. Gomez is with her. We're going to get the cops to give her a ride home but wanted you to get a read first."

"Did she see anything before she found the body? Anyone leaving the area?" Gunnar asked.

"She says she saw a man walking away from this area just after she found the kid. Average height, dark coat, gray hair. Nothing distinctive. But she was distressed by what she'd found and not really paying attention."

"I'll talk to her, she may have seen more than she realizes," Bryn said. "Have you explained to her that I'm an augur?"

"Yeah. She's willing to be read."

"Are you sure you're up for it?" Gunnar asked.

"I'm fine," Bryn said. "I think a dead kid surpasses my personal comfort, don't you?"

"Okay." Bell pointed to a patrol car parked on the road that skirted that part of the common. "Over there."

They walked the short distance, dew on the grass soaking the bottom of Bryn's jeans. He glanced back at Giles who would no doubt be wearing expensive Italian footwear and experienced a fleeting moment of satisfaction.

Carmen King sat in the car, wrapped in a blanket, her face pale and drawn. The door was open and Bell's partner, Agent Gomez, hovered next to it.

"Ms. King?" Gunnar approached her first. "I'm Detective Ericson with the GCR. I know this is difficult, but I need to ask you some questions."

She nodded. "Okay. You're a wolf. My husband is lupine."

"Yeah, that's right. My partner here is an augur. He needs to be touching you to take a peek at your memories."

Bryn stripped off a glove then extended his hand. "It won't hurt. Is it okay if I hold your wrist?"

Maria looked at his outstretched hand, then back at Bryn's face. "If it helps catch whoever did this to that little boy, yes."

The moment Bryn made contact he got a clear view of her strongest memory. He saw the Common through Carmen's eyes, felt her steady rhythm as she jogged her usual route, the morning air crisp in her lungs. Then the moment she veered off the path to investigate what looked like a bundle of clothes. He swallowed as he felt her horror when she realized she had found a child and her panic as she scrambled for her phone and made a desperate 911 call. And then she focused on a figure walking away from the area. Average height, dark coat, but something about the way he moved…

Bryn released her wrists. "Thank you. I got a good read because your memory was so fresh and strong."

"Did you see him?" she asked. "The man who did this?"

"I saw what you saw," Bryn said. "It's a start."

As they walked back toward the crime scene, Gunnar fell into step beside Bryn. "Tell me."

Bryn related what he'd seen in Carmen King' memory. "The way the man moved…there was something deliberate about it. Not hurried, not panicked. Like he was taking his time and wanted to be seen."

"Templeton always was a methodical bastard," Bell said.

Giles had been examining the drawing through the evidence bag. "The child's handwriting shows no signs of distress or coercion."

"What's your point?" Agent Gomez asked.

"My point is that whoever did this took considerable time with the victim. Time to build trust, perhaps even to make the act of drawing seem like a game." Giles's voice had a cold edge. "This wasn't a grab-and-kill. This was psychological manipulation followed by murder."

"Jesus," Bell muttered. "You're saying he befriended the kid first?"

"I'm saying whoever did this is far more sophisticated than your average predator," Giles replied. "The question is whether Dr. Templeton has evolved his methodology or if we're dealing with someone new."

"The drawing is specific. The hair, the eyes, my name…whoever made that child draw it knows what I look like," Bryn said.

"There were a lot of rubberneckers at the cathedral," Gunnar pointed out. "Some random murderer *could* have taken your picture, but I'd say we need to assume the worst. Sometimes the obvious answer is the right one."

Bryn clenched a fist, stretching black leather across his knuckles. "Which means he's been planning this for a while, and that this poor kid is just the opening move."

"Then I suggest we stop discussing it and start hunting," Giles said, "because if this is Templeton and he's playing games, this child won't be his last victim."

The weight of those words settled on Bryn's shoulders. "Thanks, Giles. Way to lighten up an already shitty morning."

Back at GCR headquarters, they convened in the conference room where coffee and pastries were waiting. Bryn grabbed a cherry Danish before anyone else could steal it. He muttered, "Emmett, I love you," as he took the extra-large coffee cup that had a B written on the lid, then sat in his usual spot. Gunnar slid into the chair next to him while Giles settled opposite them.

Warden came into the room a minute later.

"Gentlemen. I trust you're all finding this morning's events as disturbing as I am."

"Nothing says welcome to the new day like a dead child and a personal message from a serial killer." Bryn put his pastry down, his appetite gone.

Warden's expression remained impassive, but Bryn caught the tightening around his eyes that indicated his boss was not happy.

"Agents Bell and Gomez will be working with us on this. They have the federal resources we need and recapturing Templeton is still on their to-do list."

Gunnar gave a slight nod. "They understand how we operate. They'll be useful."

"Has anyone spoken to Timmy's parents?" Bryn asked.

"Yes, they've been informed and interviewed. They're…devastated, as you'd expect." Warden sighed. "I can't even imagine how they're feeling."

Gunnar shook his head. "Me either. Have they noticed anything unusual recently? Anyone watching Timmy, or following him?"

"Not that's mentioned in the notes that were sent over but I want you to talk to them too, once Bryn has rested."

"What about the drawing?" Giles asked. "Any chance of getting prints from it?"

"It's being processed," Warden replied. "But if this is Templeton, he's not going to be that sloppy."

"No," Gunnar agreed. "But he might have made other mistakes. He's emotional now, personal. That changes how people operate."

"We can only hope."

Emmett ran into the room, his face flushed. "Oh good! You're all here. This came in the mail." He held up a white envelope. "It's addressed to you, Bryn."

Oh fuck. Bryn ducked his head. He didn't want to see pity in his colleagues' eyes. "Give it to Warden, Emmett."

"When did this arrive?" Warden asked.

"About twenty minutes ago," Emmett replied, handing over the envelope. "Security had collected the mail and it was in the pile. CCTV footage shows a bike courier delivering it. He had a logo on his cap, so the team is already tracking him down."

Warden opened the envelope. "There's something else in here besides the letter." He shook it and a small object fell out onto the table. It was a child's crayon, worn down to a stub.

Bryn swallowed hard. He felt sick.

"Emmett, fetch me an evidence bag and some latex gloves," Warden said. "If it's the same crayon used for the drawing, it should have Timmy's prints or DNA on it."

"What does the letter say?" Bryn asked, proud that his voice wasn't quavering.

Warden pulled out a single folded sheet of paper. "It's the same handwriting as the previous letters," he said. "*Dearest Bryn, I hope you enjoyed my first gift. Timothy was such a good boy. He drew your picture exactly as I described it. He wanted so much to please me. Children are wonderfully trusting, don't you think? They believe adults when we tell them we're playing a game. I have so many more games to play, and gifts to give you.*

This is just the beginning, Bryn. I'm just getting started and only you will be able to stop me. Your devoted admirer, Everard."

The room was silent as Warden finished reading. Bryn could hardly breathe.

"I guess we know for certain that it's him then," Bryn said.

"Yes." Warden put the letter on the table. "I'm afraid we do."

"He escaped months ago," Gunnar pointed out. "This is a pretty sudden escalation from sending the occasional letter. He's taking risks and that works in our favor."

"Does it?" Bryn asked. "Because right now it feels like he's holding all the cards."

"And what's his next move?" Giles questioned. "He's made contact, delivered his message. What does he do for an encore?"

"I don't want to think about that," Bryn said.

"But we have to," Giles said. "Remember the daggers we believe he's collecting and what you saw in his intent when you touched him, Bryn. His plans for you aren't going to involve afternoon tea and scones, are they? Ritual torture and a prolonged death is what he wants for you."

"Thanks, Giles. Just the reminder I needed." Bryn glared at the sanguine. *I can think of a few ways I'd like to get rid of you that would make Templeton look like Mary fucking Poppins.*

"He's exposed himself to one witness already," Warden said before Bryn could give voice to his thoughts. "Others may have seen him with the child. We use the one advantage we have."

"And what's that?"

"You, Bryn. He's obsessed with you, blames you for taking away his freedom to operate at will. He was convicted because of your testimony. He's on the run because of you. He'll be looking for opportunities to get close to you."

"Then maybe we give him one," Bryn said. "On our terms."

"No," Gunnar said immediately. "You're not using yourself as bait."

"We may not have a choice," Bryn replied. "He's going to keep killing children until we stop him, isn't he?" The investigation was just beginning, but Bryn already knew it was going to be the fight of his life. "Templeton is out there somewhere, planning his next move, and some innocent kid is going about their day, completely oblivious to the snare he could be setting." *And I don't know how many more deaths I can have on my conscience.* Beneath the table, he took Gunnar's hand. Gunnar squeezed his fingers, providing a trace of comfort. *He understands, but is that enough?*

About the Author

LM lives in a small village in the English countryside, surrounded by rolling hills, cows and sheep. She started writing to fill time between jobs and is now firmly and unashamedly addicted.

She loves the English weather, especially the rain, and adores a thunderstorm. She loves good food, warm company and a crackling fire. She's fascinated by the psychology of relationships, especially between men, and her stories contain some subtle leanings towards BDSM.

LM is a past winner of the National Leather Association – International's Pauline Reage Award for best novel and John Preston award for short fiction. She has twice won the Golden Flogger Award for best BDSM novel in the LGBT category. She has received multiple Honorable Mentions in the Rainbow Awards and won the Action and Adventure category of Divine Magazine's Book Awards.

L.M. Somerton loves to hear from readers. You can find her contact information, website details and author profile page at https://www.firstforromance.com

ENTWINED PUBLISHING